FIGHT BY THE TEAM

A Team Fear Novel

CINDY SKAGGS

CONTENTS

Edited by Jessa Slade

Cover design by L.J. Anderson

Manufactured in the United States of America

First Edition August 2016

To Debbie, for helping me through my most terrifying days.

PROLOGUE

No one claimed the body. Yellow crime scene tape snapped in the wind, torn and shredded like forgotten party streamers. Wood boarded the windows, blinding the house. The media disappeared to the next great American tragedy, leaving the ranch house a macabre footnote in history.

Rose camped out for ten days in a crap motel room in the dusty Texas town, waiting to pay respects to PFC Madigan who had given his life as a sacrifice that could by no means pay penance for all he had done or that had been done to him. Ten days with the stench of the cattle awaiting slaughter and an ever-present hot wind. Ten days to consider his complicity in his teammate's death. Ten fucking days too long. The bodies of Madigan's wife and kid were shipped to family back East for proper burial, but they left Madigan to rot in the morgue fridge, destined for a pauper's grave.

Nothing about that shit was right. Rose made the calls,

first to the family who didn't want to take his call. He arranged for a simple pine box and a no-frills grave marker.

PFC Madigan. Twenty-three years old. Husband, father, hero.

The words he couldn't put on the stone were longer than his arm. Warrior, rebel, man of radical action. Experiment. Soulless, hopeless, worthless. Monster. At the bottom of the stone, Madigan's last words were etched: *No fear.* A fitting epitaph, more curse than blessing, the truth of their very existence.

There was no service, no hymns, no priest to give final absolution, but when the sun reached its zenith in the blazing sky, a procession pulled through the metal arch of the country cemetery, kicking up dirt and stirring up ghosts. Eleven vehicles, eleven men, eleven experiments who had gambled their very humanity for mother Army. Four months ago, mother Army had cut them loose. Each now sported a Section Eight discharge, medically unfit for duty; and the attack on their honor and service burned worse than the unforgiving Afghan sun.

Madigan was their first casualty. A new father, Mad Dog had been angry and paranoid, unemployed, and—apparently—bat shit crazy, and only the men arriving at the cemetery understood why.

A motorcycle roared into the lot last. Ryder was the second in command next to Captain Johnson, but the captain was MIA. Dressed in black leather, Ryder dismounted and followed the trail of silent men through the stark field of weathered headstones.

The sun beat down like hellfire on the men of Team Fear. Rose grabbed a twelve-pack of near-beer from the cooler in the back of his pickup and walked to the rectangle of freshly turned earth. The heat index was high enough to make his eyeballs sweat. He swiped it away and tossed a frosty beer to the men as they arrived to circle the grave. They twisted the caps off, the hiss of released pressure sending chills across overheated skin.

"To Mad Dog." They lifted their bottles in silent salute, sharing one last drink with their fallen brother. Across the grave, Gault's eyes tightened. Rose lifted his eyes to the sky to avoid meeting Gault's gaze, to avoid the shame hiding there. They'd failed Mad Dog. They'd failed the team. Rose swallowed the beer, washing away the bitter taste of regret. Sweat dripped down, stinging and making his eyes water. When he finished, he swapped his empty for the last full bottle in the twelve-pack. He twisted the lid before pouring it over the grave.

"Never did get a taste for this crap." Santiago's dark eyes hid behind black shades. "Miss the real thing."

Nods of assent from the men. Craft, a tall, agitated man still dressed in camo—still a warrior—tossed his empty into the box with a clatter. He pulled a fifth of whiskey from a pocket.

"Stand down." Ryder stepped toward the booze like it was the enemy.

"Back off, brother." Craft turned his upper body away and twisted the cap. "It's not for us. For Mad Dog." The earth drank the whiskey, leaving the soil barely damp. "I figure he's gone, he may as well enjoy the real deal."

"Damn straight." Gault gave him a quick fist bump. "You buy the shit we read in the paper? That Mad Dog went all Kandahar on his family?"

Rose pressed his thumbs against his eyes, rubbed deep to

push back the memory. "Saw it myself." The image from the upstairs haunted him. Some things you couldn't unsee. Blood had washed the walls. Maggie's dead eyes stared sightlessly. Rose's sister Camy was the same age, and the comparison did little to help Rose sleep at night. Protection was his default, and he hadn't been able to protect Maggie Madigan whose life had been cut short because some Department of Defense scientist was playing God.

The drug protocol they had volunteered for had turned Madigan rabid, had made it possible for him to kill those he loved. If Madigan flipped his lid, the drugs could alter any of the men standing in the miserable Texas heat, including Rose. "It happened."

"Saw Mad Dog pull the trigger." Ryder squinted against the sun's glare. "We all know why he did it. He couldn't live with what he'd done."

"Fuck this shit." Stills tossed his beer bottle at the empty twelve-pack. It landed against the others with a clatter. "Fuck this morbid shit. I'm remembering Mad Dog plotting to kill Craft after the skunk sprayed him. The man had a plan."

"Only way to get rid of eau de skunk was to bury the body," Fowler added.

Craft choked out a laugh. "I didn't know that."

"Oh, yeah." Santiago's lips twisted into a smile. "Mad Dog was extreme."

The men broke into small groups, telling Mad Dog stories while ants crawled through the dried-up river of whiskey. Rose stood at parade rest next to the grave, listening to the stories and trying to reconcile the man he called brother with the carnage he'd seen in the upstairs bedroom. He wanted the shadow of doubt the others clung to, but he'd seen the evidence. From that moment, he'd wondered who was next. Which one of the men talking trash would lose their sanity and destroy someone they loved? By accident. Rose had to believe Madigan hadn't wanted to kill Maggie and the baby. He sure as shit meant to kill himself.

According to Ryder, Madigan had been rambling. Afraid. Ryder had said Mad Dog was shaking with fear, which made no damn sense. *No fear* wasn't a motto. They were medically enhanced to prevent excitability. The day it happened, something in Madigan's eyes had shifted. He'd been fully aware when he'd pulled the trigger.

Santiago was the first to depart. "Long drive home." He twirled his keys around one finger, the nervous movement belying his easy demeanor. "Any of you assholes need me, call."

"Live by the team, die by the team." Ryder shrugged his shoulders as the weight bearing down on him settled into place. "You need help, we're there. Every last man."

Gault's fierce determination creased grooves in his square face. "We're not losing another teammate."

"Hooah," the soldiers agreed. Numbers were shared before the men retreated to their vehicles. Finally only Rose and Ryder remained at the graveside. "What happened to your car?"

"Sold it." Ryder rubbed a hand over the back of his neck. "Sports car attracted too much attention. I figure we've done enough of that already."

The words lifted the hair on the back of his neck. Ryder had a habit of keeping information to himself. "Something you want to share with the rest of the class?"

Ryder glared at the flat horizon. "Not a thing. Just watch your back."

"Right." They'd been through hell together. Rose knew Ryder's tells. "You're about to do something stupid."

"I'm not about to follow Mad Dog into the great big PX in the sky if that's what you're asking."

"That leaves a host of dumbass moves wide open."

Ryder pulled sunglasses from an interior pocket of his jacket and put them on before turning to shake Rose's hand. "Watch your fives and twenty-fives."

The second reminder to watch his back rubbed him wrong. Rose pulled Ryder in for a shoulder bump. "Stay frosty."

With a last clap on Rose's back, Ryder took the nearest exit, the roar of his motorcycle lasting long after he'd disappeared down the dirt road. The dust settled, the sound faded, yet Rose couldn't leave Mad Dog to the ants and the Texas heat.

A calm akin to that of the Tomb of the Unknown settled over the cemetery. The silence, the stillness, the sacredness were like that tomb, but Madigan's grave was a forgotten, shameful secret. There were no soldiers keeping silent vigil. No public rituals. Rose stood sentry for several quiet minutes, acknowledging what his teammates could not. They were all destined for a plain pine box.

Rose choked down a lungful of oppressive air. He'd fight the slide into inhumanity as long as he had fight left, but when the time came, he'd end himself before he took any innocents with him. That was his sacred vow.

He had family to protect. Iowa was a long-assed drive away, but after nearly two weeks in the miserable Texas heat, Rose needed to check on his mother and sisters. He needed to eliminate the memory of Maggie's dead eyes. Go home, he thought, make sure life went on despite the crap in his head, and then it was time to settle his affairs. Protect what was his. Friends from back home could keep his sisters safe if anything happened to him, if he needed to go underground or worse. He didn't have much time before he was called back to the team.

Determined, he marched back to his truck. Whatever Ryder wasn't telling him was big and it involved the experiments. It involved Team Fear. They were out of the Army and out of the experimental program that had failed. They were no longer soldiers. No longer whole. They were the walking wounded, each and every man. Mad Dog was the tip of spear.

Time could not heal all wounds.

CHAPTER ONE

Present day

Debi tiptoed across the rough carpet with her boots in one hand and car keys in the other, searching for the exit in the dark. A slim line of light signaled the door in the no-tell motel where they were staying. She reached for the doorknob and hit solid mass.

"Where do you think you're going?" The deep male voice zipped out like a Taser, striking her chest and spiking her nerves.

"Crap." She stumbled back, tripped over a dining chair, and landed on her ass. Pain shot up her spine, and then a dull throbbing started where her backside hit the concrete floor. The anemic carpet did nothing to break the fall. "You scared the crap out of me." The man shouldn't move without a whisper of sound. He was built like a Humvee, so he ought to make some freaking noise. She put a hand to her heart to soothe the raging panic that threatened to burst the erratic organ from her chest. "What are you doing, sneaking around this time of night?" She had no idea what time it was.

"Could ask you the same thing."

"I wasn't—" She cut herself short. Honesty, she owed him as much honesty as she could afford. "Of course I was sneaking around." Why else get dressed in the dark? "As much as I enjoy your protection services, a girl needs time alone." The truth was a little more mortifying than that.

Rose flipped a switch and one of the side lamps turned on. The light stinging her eyes, so she blinked away the pain. When her vision cleared, she saw the most ripped human being she ever laid eyes on. Abs and biceps and whatever the hell was not so discreetly hidden in his boxer shorts. All of it hard-packed flesh. Male perfection. That right there was why she needed out. Twenty-four/seven with a man built like Thor made her as anxious as a horse at the starting gate. She had to get away or jump his muscular ass, and as fun as that sounded, adding sex to the wreck of the last week was a seriously bad idea.

They were on the run from a rogue military group who wanted to eliminate Rose and the rest of his former Special Forces team. For all anyone in their cozy little group knew, Debi was collateral damage in a fight that had nothing to do with her, but the psycho from Team Echo had said Debi knew more than she let on, which was scary true. The stress of it had her jonesing for a nicotine fix, and she really didn't want the beautiful man in front of her watching her suck poison into her lungs.

"Help me up." She lifted a hand and Rose yanked. The man didn't know his own strength so he nearly lifted her off her feet. She landed against his chest. Solid contact, and God help her, the man was built. She swallowed and stepped away from his tempting flesh.

The team had three rooms down one side of the dusty motel. Debi's best friend Lauren and her husband Ryder had one room, the soldiers in one, and Debi in the middle with the bodily perfection of Sergeant Rose as a bodyguard. He was the kind of soldier who made you want to enlist in whatever games he wanted to play. He turned to double check the locks, exposing the shadow of a drawing. The tattoo was the last thing she needed to see. Tattoos and muscles were as far from academic as she could get. Rose turned to face her, a look of disapproval flexing in his strong jaw.

It was time to put some serious space between her lusty thoughts and the ginormous tattooed man in front of her. He stood as the perfect foil to her ex. Damnit all to hell. On the run was not the time for fun and games. "I really need to get out on my own." Her voice came out breathy. A pulse jumped in her neck.

"If you need feminine products, I don't mind running to the store, but you're not going out alone."

Heat burned her neck and face. The big guy was offering to buy tampons. Good God. She couldn't meet his gaze. Instead, she turned and yanked the covers over her tangled sheets. As accommodating as he was, good money said he would draw the line at making a cigarette run. The clock showed it was shortly before sunrise. She'd never get to sleep now, not that she'd gotten much since the run-in with the men from Echo. "I don't need any help in that department, thanks."

"We're not sending a woman out alone." Rose walked around and straightened the covers on the other side of the bed. Half-naked man, tangled sheets, and crazy chemistry. A flush simmered under her skin, and it had nothing to do with embarrassment. She needed sex or a smoke, and right now, the cigarette was less dangerous.

"Relax, Rosie." The silly nickname helped put emotional distance between them, because they were squared off on opposite sides of the bed and her imagination had her bridging that gap. "I'm not going to chase down the psychos from Echo on my own. I just..." The quiver in her voice pissed her off. She fluffed a pillow and slammed it against the faux wood headboard. "Need. Out."

He stared at her like he saw straight to her soul. "Explain." He sat on the poorly made bed, his blue and green boxers clashing with the orange bedspread.

She tried to keep her gaze above his shoulders. Tried. Really hard. "I'm not used to so many people in my space." She paced away to keep her wandering eyes from seeing more than she should. Her fantasies were realistic enough without all the details fleshed out. "I have zero time or space to myself. I'm not the kind of girl who stays home all the time. I'm out, doing things. I have a business—" She cut herself off to reorganize her thoughts. "I have business to take care of, and I can't simply walk away from my responsibilities. There's food in the fridge at the ranch that's going to rot, I have a job and a life, and sitting in this tiny room, listening to you guys plot strategy has me one step from turning into a raging witch." Too many unfiltered words spilled from her mouth.

"Cabin fever?"

The laugh bubbled up, half hysterical. They had checked into the motel four days ago, and that was four days too many. "God, yes."

"That's a half truth. You're hiding something. Why don't you tell me the rest?"

The attack by Team Echo was the living embodiment of the anxiety that had defined most of her life. She was quite possibly going crazy. On the run, she hadn't had time to think —thank God—but four days in this ratty motel room freaked her out. Too much time to think. Too much time to add fear to the mix. "I'm terrified," she answered. It was simplistic, but the best way she could possibly explain.

"That's normal."

She snorted, and she was so far gone, she didn't mind him seeing the unladylike reaction. Beat the heck out of him witnessing a panic attack. The last man who saw her freak hadn't bothered with a follow up call. The fear was ugly, no doubt. At the thought, her breath panted out, her heart raced, and, despite the cold leaking inside from the crappy motel door, sweat slicked her skin. She wanted to keep pacing, away from him, but she needed to get a grip before he saw a full-blown attack.

She dropped into the dining chair and let her head hang between her legs. The look she aimed for was mopey. Mopey was one of the Seven Dwarves, right? Mopey sounded better than Fearful. "God, I could use a cigarette right now."

"You smoke?"

"Quit. Two years ago." The day her father had kicked her out of his life.

"Why start back now?"

The list was long. "Psychotic killers, drug dealers, and medically enhanced soldiers." And that was just the beginning.

"You survived all that with flying colors. You don't need a cigarette now."

Oh, she definitely needed one. "Obviously you've never

smoked." She reacted to all tension with a need for a cigarette. They calmed her when little else did.

The bed squeaked and moments later, a hand the size of a platter rubbed between her shoulder blades. "What's going on?"

Her hands shook, so she braced them against her thighs. "Not a thing."

"Looks like a thing." He settled into a rhythm of caressing her back. "Pulse is high, breathing erratic, and you haven't used sarcasm in the last ten minutes."

A laugh tried to bubble through the panic. She took a halting breath.

"Sweetheart, you'll feel better if you tell me what's going on."

"What's going on is some real psychos are chasing us."

"And they're nowhere around. So whatever is trapped inside, let it out. Yell, scream, cry—"

"I don't want to cry."

"But do you need to?"

She needed to do something. Sitting around had only made the panic worse. She focused on his touch until the panic eased.

He kneeled in front of her and braced his hands on her thighs. "Better now?"

It was a testament to how messed up she was that she didn't try to sneak a peek at his assets. Tears threatened. She didn't want to talk about it, so she nodded her head. "I'm fine. You should go back to bed. Get some sleep."

"Is that what the people in your life do?"

Talk about a landmine. Crap, he was hitting every one of

her triggers. "Honest to God, I don't want to talk about what just happened."

"Ok, what happened is off the table." He nodded his head, all agreeable like, which was definitely suspect. "When's the first time you remember having a panic attack?"

See, she knew that agreeable nature was a lie. He wasn't going to let it go. "Most people ask why." And they assumed some defect inside her.

"I'm not most people."

That was the unadulterated truth. "I need some space," she said. She'd studied panic attacks and fear until her mind was numb with it. Most people wanted comfort after an attack, but she'd found little comfort from those closest to her. Distance and denial were the true heroes. Rose stepped away, taking his heat with him. Moments passed before the bed springs moaned and he'd taken his seat back on the bed.

He'd done exactly as she asked, and she felt cold.

A rhythmic squeak filled the silence and she wondered if he was rocking on the bed. Minutes passed before she realized she was the one rocking out on the four-legged chair, arms wrapped around her middle. He didn't say a word and his infinite patience wore her down. "I was still in grade school. I was at my father's condo." The slick marble floors and granite counters were unreal, unlike anything in her mother's house. Debi had raced through the condo in her stocking feet, screeching with delight at the speed, gliding on the polished floor like she was skating. "I fell, split my head open." One minute she was upright, the next her face planted on the marble. "Blood flew everywhere." Her father had gotten her a towel, and then spent more time cleaning the floor than assessing her injury. He hadn't explained that she was going to be okay. The white kitchen towel had soaked with her blood, and the less he talked to her, the less she could breathe. "The attacks are a weakness." The words cut through the silence in her head. *Knock it off. Tears don't change anything. There's nothing to be afraid of.*

But she had been afraid, afraid of her father, afraid of the attacks, afraid of... Everything. It was the last time she'd seen her father before she applied to the university as an undergrad. "I don't like blood."

"You've seen more than your share these past few days."

She nodded as any response caught in her froggy throat.

"Want to know what I think?" he asked.

Her chest ached.

"Sweetheart, you held it together in the townhouse when Echo kidnapped you. It's only now that you've had a chance to think about it that your brain gets in the way. As long as you stay busy, you're fine."

She peeked up through her hair. No judgment marred his strong features, and she saw the truth in his eyes. He didn't judge or hate her. And he made a good point. "So you're saying that staying here is bad for me."

He laughed, the warmth of it dispelling the remnants of fear. "That's a pretty fair rationalization."

"One that works for me." As did sarcasm.

"I have an idea for getting out if you're interested."

"Is that a trick question?"

"Look at me."

The focus in his intense eyes was absolute. Crossing her arms over her chest, she returned his gaze, hoping her thoughts weren't written all over her face. "What do you have in mind?"

"It's mission related, and there are rules."

"Military men and their rules." She'd agree to anything that got her out of this small torture chamber. "Do you have a job for me that doesn't require cooking and cleaning, Rosie?"

He barked out a laugh that softened his lips and brought a full-out smile. Devastating. The little quirk of his lip lit up his eyes and weakened her knees. "Have I done something to make you think I'm a chauvinist asshole?"

The opposite, actually. He'd acted like a gentleman from the moment he'd barreled into her life, literally, when he tackled her into safety after members of Team Echo had tried to infiltrate the ranch. "I know your type. Me man. You woman." She grunted like a caveman. "Where's my dinner?"

The smile on his face grew until he flashed white teeth that glinted against his tan face. "Is it all military men or just me?"

Her pulse jumped in reaction to the smile. "What are you talking about?"

"That you hate?"

"I don't know what you mean. You and the rest of the team are the only military men I know."

"All men, then." He said it as a statement, not a question.

"I don't take orders and I don't sit in the back seat."

"Have I asked you to walk three steps behind me?"

Debi leaned back on her heels. "Not yet, but you have all kinds of rules."

"For your safety."

"And there's that." Debi pointed an accusatory finger at him. "You're overprotective, overbearing, and bossy." The topic was much safer than her attitude toward men, so she grasped it. "Come to think of it, you do ask us to walk behind you." Yeah, she was being whiny, because he took the lead so he'd take the brunt of any attack.

"You want to vent?" He gave her a come hither move with his fingers. "Bring it, sweetheart. Get it all out."

The reasonable tone deflated her. She bent to snatch her keys off the floor and tucked them in the front pocket of her jeans. "I'm good."

"Not even close. You should see your face. Spill it so we can get to work."

He wanted her to keep venting? At this point, her father would be making phone calls and turning his back to her. "You'll think I'm a complete witch."

"I won't think you're a witch, I'll think you're a female, simple as that, but, sweetheart?" His gaze skimmed her from chest to stocking feet. "I'm fully aware you're a woman, so go ahead and vent."

The lower timber of his voice sent shivers along her arms. She flicked the beige curtain aside and saw a dim promise of sunrise lightening the overcast sky. "It's cold out."

"Quit changing the subject. Man up, Debi, and tell me what's in your head."

Her heart skipped a beat. That was the first time he'd used her name. "Did you tell me to man up?"

The mattress squeaked, causing her to turn. Rose leaned against the headboard and rested an arm against a raised leg, a predator at rest, languid grace that could turn lethal. His expression was inscrutable. "We can sit here all day, but that'll keep you off the mission."

"Fine." First he offered to buy her tampons and now he was telling her to vent. Who was this guy? She dropped into the hard chair that had tripped her. She let her head fall back to stare at the yellowed ceiling tiles. "Letting men call the shots doesn't work for me." The brief stint she had spent near her father had been a disaster, and her experience with other men wasn't much better. Her skin prickled at the idea of letting men take control.

"You want to be a part of the mission? I don't have a problem with that. It's all hands on deck as far as I'm concerned, and since it's not safe for you to go home, you should keep busy."

Wow. Her mind blanked at what to her was a unique response. He was willing to let her play with the big boys. "What are you working on?" Other than the vague whispering, she didn't know enough to help.

"We're working to figure out who was behind the experiments. I want to know what the hell they pumped through my veins to make me fearless. To permanently alter me." Anger broke through his normal calm and the look in his eyes went hard at the mention of the experiments. "You want a piece of that?"

"I'm a chemist, or I was." Saying it in past tense hurt. It was the job she had worked her whole life to get. "I know my way around a science lab, and something tells me you can use that. I sure as heck can't sit around waiting for the big heroes of Team Fear to figure out this disaster."

"Is that it?" He settled deeper into the pillow behind his back. A muscular man against the soft, white bed. Damn but her hands flexed to get in on the action. "Get it all out now. It's a one-shot deal."

Well, if he wanted honesty... "I can't sit around and let a he-man rescue me."

"He-man?" A light twinkled in his dark eyes, and she couldn't tell if he was teasing her for her impulsive choice of words.

"All of you are—" She lifted a hand to gesture up and down his body. "Built like tractors, ready to plow down anyone or anything in the way."

"That's the nicest thing you've ever said to me."

The rise of heat was instant. "Don't let it go to your head, Rosie. What's the mission?"

"We need to know what they dosed Ryder with the other night."

Debi nodded. In an attempt to make Ryder go crazy, Echo had given him a medical cocktail that sent him into a murderous rage, something that nearly got them all killed. When they were still in the Army, the men had volunteered for an experimental program to make them fearless. Sounded great on paper, but the reality failed to meet expectations. If the guys from Team Echo were any indication, removing the physiological reaction to fear had untethered some link to their humanity. "Baby Faced Joe said it was the same drug that turned you guys fearless."

"And we trust Team Echo to tell the truth?"

"Good point." Her mind flipped through the scenario and the answers weren't good. Echo could have given Ryder any drug or a catalyst to what already flowed through his veins. "I should have taken a blood sample."

Rose laughed. "Dial back the guilt. You were surrounded by more dead bodies than a morgue, and we bombed the house to cover the evidence. None of us were thinking straight. So now we are. We fix the problem."

"How?"

"Echo laced his bottle of water with an unknown substance. He drank the whole damn thing, but there were two bottles, so there's potentially a full bottle in the fridge in Lauren's office on campus."

"Potentially?"

"Depends if Echo cleaned up the scene before luring Ryder to the townhouse. We killed four of their men, so details may have gotten overlooked. The evidence could be in Lauren's office."

Her heart raced with the thrill of being a part of the investigation and the dread at going back to campus. "You want me to get the evidence from Lauren's office."

"Not you. We."

"But—"

"Take the offer. I can find her office on my own, but you want some fresh air. I can make that work since I want in without attracting unwanted attention."

She snorted in disbelief. "I hate to break it to you, Rosie, but you attract attention." Hell, given the opportunity, he'd probably attract groupies.

"I have a gift for getting in and out of any location undetected, which is why I snuck into Madigan's house while Ryder brazened through the front, so I'm not worried about getting inside Lauren's office."

"Right." No way did a badass like Rose sneak anywhere. "You look nothing like the boys on campus and you are *not* an academic." He was warrior strong, which was part of her problem. The attraction hit on a primal level, but she was salivating to get out of the motel room, even if it meant more time in Rose's presence. "I'll drive."

He stretched and stood to his full height. "Sweetheart, my ass won't fit inside your girly economy car."

Her VW was perfect. For her. But he was right. Not one of his long legs would fit inside her VW, even with the seat pushed all the way back. Debi leaned over to grab her boots and pulled them on her stocking feet. "Alright, Rosebud, but hurry up. We need to get in and out before the first classes start." Before she ran into complications.

CHAPTER TWO

A bird swooped across the quad, black against the canopy of a rare snow. A flash of red menace glistened on its ebony coat as it made a low dive, squawking like a bad omen. Debi tripped over a nonexistent crack in the sidewalk. The bird's laughter trilled across the open space in the middle of campus.

"Steady." Rose grabbed her elbow to keep her from slipping on the wet cement. If he could do the same to stabilize her nerves, she'd be set. Nothing good had ever happened to her on campus. The kidnapping a few days ago capped a very nasty history with the illustrious institution.

A large group of students spewed from the administration building as the first classes of the day let out, because Rose took too long getting ready and informing the team. The whole teamwork thing was outside her norm. Researchers hoarded their findings like ill-gotten booty, but she'd sucked it up and listened to the briefing, complete with contingency plans. She endured another long hour on the road with Rose. The confines of his pickup truck weren't much better than the motel room. In the cab of the truck, she smelled his aftershave, felt his heat, and tolerated his silence. The bite of cold from the rare winter weather was a welcome respite from the ride, even if it meant they had arrived on campus.

The snow didn't stick on the cement, so the sidewalks were like pie wedges cutting through the quad. One path led to admin, another to the science building on the far end, surrounded by a modern art piece the university had overpaid for. If anyone on campus had a budget, it was the science guys. Science was the good old boy program, and her ex was the golden boy who could do no wrong. Oh, he did wrong, but he brought so much money into the coffers through research grants that he wrote his own rules. Even the pristine snow couldn't hide the darkness underneath the polished campus veneer. Maybe she was the only one who sensed it.

The students leaving the administration building crossed through the middle toward them, sticking to the sidewalk as if walking on the snow was out-of-bounds. Debi held her breath as they neared, then released it on a puff of white when no familiar face took shape in the crowd.

Next to her, Rose walked like he was marching into battle, his suspicious eyes scanning the group for danger. Finished with the students, he altered his focus like he expected a sniper in the bell tower. Not that they had a bell tower, but it didn't keep him from scanning the rooflines for a threat. The awareness in his eyes sent a shiver through her that had nothing to do with the cold. She rubbed a hand over her arms. Maybe she should be bundled like the students, but she'd left home with only the clothes on her back, and her silent bodyguard hadn't declared the situation secure enough to return home.

As the students neared, Rose pulled her away from the sidewalk and into the thin layer of white. He placed his body between her and the students who passed by talking about homework, professors, and weekend parties, reminding Debi of her first hopeful year on campus. Her heels sank into the damp earth as she waited for them to pass. When they did, Rose grabbed her arm and led her to the administration building, blocking like he expected trouble. Her breath started coming in quick gasps as her nerves threatened a panic attack. She instinctively moved closer to Rose, who exuded safety in the same way a tank promised protection. A tank might be dangerous, but only if you got in its way.

When her best friend offered to introduce her to tall, blond, and quiet, she should have said no. The man in question was a Nordic type—she didn't have any trouble picturing him as a pillaging Viking—yet for all of his intimidating presence, he was a medic, a man of healing. His face was wide, with a square jaw that looked like it could take a solid hit. In fact, he'd taken a few in the past week. He had a black eye, fading to yellow, and a scratch on his face that was scabbed, and somehow those markings made him more ruggedly handsome.

If the Vikings had a religion, she'd convert, because his body was toned and tight and worthy of praise, but he'd also only said one word to her in the last fifty-seven minutes, which stretched her already taut nerves, but since she was breaking into an office and stealing evidence, Rose was definitely the man she wanted at her side. He didn't speak much, but when he did, his low voice crashed over her like a tidal wave, covering her in his strong masculine energy. In the past few days, she'd pretty much used that energy as a blanket to ward off an attack.

The farther they moved from the science building, the easier she breathed. She trusted the tough soldier beside her to protect her from bullets, but there were worse things that could come at her here. She could have said no when he suggested the mission, but they needed to know what Ryder had been given. Plus, it occurred to her a little too late; she and Lauren needed to know what drug had incapacitated them a few days ago. Rose wouldn't let her go alone, not after what happened at the bank, he had said, as if his rule was law. She'd made a half-hearted attempt at arguing, especially when the morning wore on and they still hadn't left the no-tell motel, but she'd had too many bad things happen in the last week. When she wasn't dealing with a panic attack, she was a relatively sane individual. If Rose wanted to be her bodyguard, he had her blessing.

A few steps up and through a door that Rose held open, Debi entered the administration building. The halls echoed with painful silence, so she couldn't avoid the coffee kiosk in the corner under the stairs. The brunette barista with her hair in a messy bun raced around to intercept Debi before they disappeared into the bowels of the building.

Rose stepped between them.

"Wait, you're Professor Ryder's friend, right? From the other night? I'm Beth, one of her students. Is she okay?"

Debi didn't want to have this conversation. The girl had unknowingly helped the bad guys incapacitate Debi and Lauren. Beth thought she was saving her favorite professor from an abusive husband, but she'd really stepped in the middle of a war. Debi pushed around Rose. "She's fine, no thanks to you."

"Why didn't she come back to class?"

Debi stretched her neck, but the tension knotting her muscles wouldn't ease. "She's finishing her dissertation long distance, and you're lucky we aren't pressing charges. You knocked us out. Let strange men cart us off campus. That's accessory to a felony, sweetheart." It bugged her to use Rose's word, but in Texas, sweetheart could be an insult as well as an endearment. "And you stepped into the middle of something you don't understand." She bit her tongue to keep from spewing more anger at the girl whose face turned whiter with each word. Debi had to remember that a psycho had manipulated the girl.

"I'm so sorry. I didn't mean to—" Beth cut herself off. She twisted her hands together in agitation. "What happened to Joe?"

Baby Face Joe was dead by Ryder's hand, the only way to save Lauren, but it was better for Beth to think Joe had used her than that he was dead. "Find a new boyfriend, one who doesn't use you to get to someone else."

Rose grabbed her arm. *Shut up*, he mouthed. "We need to go."

"Yeah, yeah." It was probably best Debi didn't destroy the poor girl. For all Beth knew, the cute soldier she'd started dating was a real sweet guy with all the best intentions. Debi made it several steps at Rose's side before she stopped. Blaming Beth wasn't fair. She had been a pawn, used by a man much the way Debi had been not that long ago. Manipulated. Duped. She'd been a fool, just like the coffee girl. "Beth, I know Lauren doesn't blame you. She'd want you to forget it and move on."

A tear dripped from her expressive eyes. "Tell her I'm sorry."

Debi released a hard breath. "She knows."

Debi grabbed Rose's hand to pull him down the hall and away from the barista. The heat of his big hand burned, so she dropped it as she led the way down the wide hall toward Lauren's office. "The place seems harmless enough," she said to hide her nerves.

"Not safe. This is where you got kidnapped."

Leave it to him to crash the illusion of safety. "You're a cheery man to have around, Rosie."

"The name is Rose or Sergeant."

"I am aware." But the big, bad soldier was fun to rattle. He was often blunt to a fault, but she was glad he was there, walking with her through the treacherous halls of academia.

"Hold up." Rose broke the silence that so often defined him. He placed an arm between them and scooted her behind. "Let me go first."

"Have at it, Rosie." She was all for letting the soldier take the first hit. He was probably bulletproof. He unlocked the door with the key Lauren had given them. The cramped space was filled with a desk, two office chairs, and a sofa other professors had handed down like old clothes. There were no intruders. No guns. She released a breath. "It's almost a letdown."

"Could be a trap." His deep voice rumbled low, causing a corresponding tremor in her abdomen. "Get what we need and get out."

"What does it take to get you to loosen up?"

"World peace." The unexpected humor brought a laugh from her that broke some of the tension in the room. It was short lived as he turned and closed them inside. He dominated the room, filling the space with his innate intensity. "But how about we start with no one trying to kill me or mine."

And there went the levity. The office looked much the way she'd left it the night she and Lauren were kidnapped. That night, Lauren was the bait and her husband the bear who nearly stepped into the big-assed trap. He'd been dosed with an unknown substance from a bottle of water he had gulped in this very room. He'd woken disoriented and confused.

Rose pulled Ziploc bags from his backpack. The paper teacup that had been laced with some sort of sedative was sitting where she left it a few nights before. She put it in the plastic bag, hoping she could identify the drug she'd been given. Nerves sizzled along her skin. She didn't like knowing someone had drugged her. Experimental drugs were risky, something she knew firsthand.

Rose went to the fridge. "Ryder said he put the unused bottle of water in here." The fridge was filled with close to a case of water Lauren typically kept in her office on campus.

"Bring it all." They could test every bottle if they had too. Debi bent to pick up the empty from the floor where Ryder had dropped it. "It's bone dry. Hard to get a good reading from, but I'll swab it and see what I can find." A part of her thrilled at the possibility of pulling out her lab supplies and getting back to the work she loved. The other part dreaded playing with things she didn't understand. She straightened her shoulders and turned to watch Rose work.

It wasn't exactly a hardship. The man was built, and his backside was a gift from Nordic gods. Firm, round cheeks were encased in denim. Mm-hmm. She turned to Lauren's desk before he busted her checking out his ass.

Rose marked the water bottles from the front row of the fridge and the ones in the door with different symbols. "We'll test this first and work our way to the bottles in the back."

"You volunteering to be my lab assistant, Rosie?"

"Rose," he corrected, pushing for her to call him by his name. "I want to know what they pumped into my veins."

Rose and the rest of the men were angry for what had been done to them. They'd signed on to an elite team in the military, part of a larger experiment to eliminate the physiological response to fear. From a scientific viewpoint, the idea was inspired, but the men hadn't been told of potential side effects, some they were still dealing with months after being kicked out of the Army. Months after stopping the medication. They were dealing with paranoia and anger and a host of side effects they had yet to document.

Rose packed the bottles while Debi flipped through the files, pulling everything related to Lauren's dissertation so Lauren could work from the privacy of their hideout. They couldn't come back to the campus until the bad guys were eliminated, if such a thing were possible. Lauren was a target because of Ryder. She was the weak link he'd die to protect. Debi couldn't come back for reasons she didn't want to ponder. Two of those reasons were walking free on this lousy campus. She wanted off campus without confronting either man, and she'd really like to avoid any more alone time with Rose. He upset her equilibrium. She slammed the file drawer closed. She really hated being in this place. "Ready?" She tried to keep the agitation from her voice. She'd obviously failed by the look Rose gave her.

"Got a hot date, sweetheart?"

"Sure, I've got a hot date with the pool boy at the lovely one-star motel we're staying at."

"Pool's closed, if you hadn't noticed."

"Oh, I noticed."

"Romeo will have to wait. And that one-star motel beats the hell out of getting kidnapped or killed."

"Not by much," she muttered. She woke every morning feeling like bed bugs were crawling on her skin. "Ready to go, Rosie?"

"Quit calling me that ridiculous nickname."

The order twisted her up inside. There was something seriously wrong with her when his hard-ass orders got her all hot and bothered. When in doubt, brazen it out. "Am I getting to you, Rosie?" She hoped so, because so many days in the same tiny motel room with the big guy, and he was definitely under her skin.

She knew more about him than she did her last boyfriend. Some cruel god had bathed his golden skin with pheromones. She could pick out his scent from the half dozen others in their room. He spoke rarely, noticed everything, and kept a notebook with lists of things he knew, didn't know, and needed to find out. Whether he knew it or not, he was a researcher trying to get to the bottom of the poison the Army had injected in their veins.

All that made him interesting, but what made him irresistible was the way he called all women sweetheart. He had a soft spot for women she never would have thought possible in a man so physically powerful. He opened the door for her, anticipated her needs, and even went to the store to get her toiletries when it became obvious she couldn't go home. At night, he stationed himself on guard duty, and while she hated the need for protection, she couldn't ask for a bigger or scarier protector.

At night when she couldn't sleep in the unfamiliar bed with possible bed bugs, she heard him toss and turn, nearly as sleepless. The soft snuffle he made when he dreamed made her want to slip into his bed and burrow close. After the maid came in and mixed up the bed linens, Debi could smell which pillow he'd slept on the night before. She was freaking toast unless she put some distance between the two of them. She took a step back until her thighs hit the desk. She knew one sure way to get him to back off. "Tell you what, Rosie. Give me your first name and I'll lay off."

He filled the distance. "Let it go."

A grin popped out, tightening the muscles in her cheek. She busted out laughing. The big guy was trying to intimidate her, but all he was doing was forcing her claws in deeper. "Dwayne?"

"Drop it."

"Melvin? Primrose?"

A film dropped over his eyes and his features smoothed. Quite a trick to shut off all emotion; one that sent goose bumps washing over her skin in trepidation. He was more like the guys from Echo than any of them wanted to believe.

"Move out." He grabbed the bag of water bottles and the Ziploc with the empties, and stepped into the hall. Even in his pique, he still held the door open and motioned her in front of him. The rest of the trek through the administration building, he treated her to a silence that scraped her nerves. The halls packed with students on the way to or from lunch. This was why she'd wanted to get to campus early. She wanted to avoid the students, the teachers, and the coffee kiosk in the corner under the stairs.

Rose muttered what sounded like a curse under his breath. Tension corded his muscles, sending her heart racing.

"What is it?"

He pulled her out of the flow of traffic. "I think I saw someone I know."

She snapped the hairband on her wrist to halt the fear, but it was too late. Her legs trembled beneath her. Anyone he knew was either fearless, crazy, or dead.

CHAPTER THREE

The sight of a lost soldier set off explosions in Rose's mind. He stationed Debi near the coffee shop with strict orders to stay put. The busy administration building was as safe as they could expect. He double-timed it through the hall after a man who looked suspiciously like their fearless leader. Captain freaking Johnson. The hair was longer and darker. He carried a backpack and fit into the student crowd as much as a man the size of an ox could blend, but he hadn't hidden his precise movements. The economy of movement, the innate awareness had caught Rose's attention as they passed each other.

If Captain Johnson was walking these halls, the university was a hot zone.

The crowd swirled like a rushing river, too fast to notice one woman barely hanging on through churning mass of bodies.

Skin brushed as the crowd flowed around her. Heat rose through her body as Debi cast a furious glance around the area, looking for Rose. Someone grabbed her from behind. Debi twisted to break free, turned, and found herself enveloped in a hug. The other woman held on like Debi would bolt, which she might, but there wasn't the time or space.

"I can't believe you're here," the woman said into her ear.

"Hannah?"

"You sound surprised to see me." Hannah leaned back and tucked a stray hair behind her pierced ears. "Should be the other way around. I'm glad to see you, but surprised. I really thought you'd never step a foot here after..."

After her father had publicly rejected her. Debi swallowed the remnants of her pride. She lifted Lauren's files like a shield. "I had to pick up Lauren's dissertation. She's—"

"I heard she quit."

Bad news traveled fast. "Not exactly. Her husband got military orders, so Lauren's finishing the program long distance." The cover story sounded hollow.

Hannah didn't take the bait. She glanced around like she'd rather be anywhere else. "I just left a budget meeting. The science people and the administration."

Fabulous. Debi refused to wait around for Barry to publicly humiliate her. "I should probably let you go."

The other woman stepped up on tiptoes to peer through the crowd. "I wanted to introduce you to my boyfriend. Jack's supposed to meet me for lunch."

"Another time." The tight smile cracked her lips. "I need to get this in the mail to Lauren."

"Wow, she's already out of town?"

"I'll let her know I ran into you."

"Next time when she's in town, we should all meet up at the bar."

Ouch. The bar where Debi worked so she could serve everyone as a reminder of her diminished status. The mention of it was a direct hit. "Sounds good." Sounded like hell.

"Shit." Hannah turned and fully faced Debi for the first time. Her freckled face screwed up in a grimace. "That made me sound like such a bitch. I'm sorry. I'm distracted, but I'm not trying to rub your face in it. I just meant I'd like to see you outside of campus. You disappeared, but that doesn't mean you lost your friends here."

That's exactly what it meant. Their worlds no longer connected. They weren't even in the same solar system, but she smiled and promised Hannah she'd meet up later. Like in an alternate universe when people didn't want to kill her and she wasn't on the campus where Barry or her father could humiliate her. The urge to flee became imperative, hammering against her rib cage with the need to escape.

They separated, and Debi headed for the nearest exit. The early morning snow had already melted. The smudge of the mud coated Debi's soul, filling her with the desperate need to be quit of this place. She stepped down the stairs and around the corner where she landed in hell.

The thing that sent her running stood in the path to the staff parking lot.

"Barry." The one word burned her throat. Of all that she feared when she and Rose started the day, the near skeletal frame in front of her was the most omnipresent. He'd lost weight, his long fingers like bones wrapped around the handle of an artfully aged messenger bag.

The sneer marking his thin lips revealed big teeth. "Debra. I'm surprised to see you here."

She wasn't the least bit surprised. It was like the last week had sent her barreling to this precise moment. She gripped the folders to her chest, choosing to ignore Barry. "Allyson."

The mousey woman nodded a stiff hello. "It's been too long."

Debi wasn't distracted by Allyson's seeming kindness. She didn't take her eyes off the thin man. "I was thinking not long enough."

"I'm surprised to see you on campus." Barry's bushy eyebrow rose and a nasty glint lit his pale eyes. "In fact, I thought you were banned."

So much for an easy in and out mission.

"You thought wrong." Debi shifted her gaze to the mouse. "I'm surprised you're still working with this asshat."

"The pay's good. Now that he made tenure—"

"Tenure?" Debi spit the word like a curse. That was years ahead of his plan. "What did you do?"

"Fulfilled my destiny."

"You arrogant little prig. This has nothing to do with destiny. You stole research."

Allyson cleared her throat. "They never proved that. The student involved retracted his statement."

"The student was me," Debi laid it out for Allyson, because Barry would never admit it, but some dark part of her needed Allyson to know the truth. "Barry hasn't had an original idea in a decade. The only meaningful new research came from Hannah, Allyson, and me, and when I brought that to the attention of the head of the department, Barry covered his ass and set me up for a fall."

"The head of the department agreed with me. You broke protocol, jumping from animal testing to human testing without the proper approval."

Debi stepped into Barry's space. Wearing heels, she towered over the sniveling scientist. "I didn't take it to human testing. After months of successful animal testing, I knew it worked, but I didn't give it to some unsuspecting test subject. I took it, and the second you found out, you ratted me out to the head of the department."

"Your father deserved to know you exposed yourself to a medicine that hadn't been approved for human consumption."

"Bullshit." Debi shook, but she didn't back away. "Neither you nor the old man gave a whit about my welfare."

"I don't think that's fair," Allyson interjected.

"Really?" Debi turned on her former friend. "In the course of ratting me out *for my own good*, Barry also took credit for DV1028 and said I stole the proprietary compound for personal use. He threw me under the bus, ruining my career and helping his in the process."

Allyson glared at her brother. "DV1028 was Debi's research. You took credit?"

"Anything that goes down in my lab belongs to me. Read your contract," Barry snapped. "Debra was a hack, cutting corners and failing to follow procedure. I did what I had to do to protect the university from her ego."

"*My* ego?" Debi gripped the folder to keep from decking the little weasel.

"You're right. It wasn't your ego, it was you, you illegitimate bitch. The only reason you were accepted into the university in the first place was playing the daddy card against a brilliant scientist who probably isn't even your biological father."

Debi lurched for him.

———

"Hold on, sweetheart." Rose pulled Debi back so she didn't hit the man, breaking her hand in the process. He'd heard enough. This situation, whatever it was, might not be the danger he had anticipated, but the look on Debi's face said it was the explosion she'd expected from the minute her high-heeled shoes hit the ground. The woman liked heels, and God bless her, they made her legs look a mile long. Rose wrapped his arm tighter around her waist and felt her shiver in response.

Then he stepped forward and had the satisfaction of seeing Barry's pupils dilate in fear. "One more insult to Debi, and your sister will be calling an ambulance. Do I make myself clear?"

"Crystal." Blood rushed to his cheeks, reddening the mottled skin. "Dating a bouncer now, Debra? One with a black eye and dull intellect?"

"Is that supposed to insult me?" Rose asked.

Barry sneered. "A Neanderthal like you probably wouldn't understand a word out of my mouth. You're like Frankenstein's monster, a freak of nature. Debi, as you call her, is—"

Rose shoved the professor off the sidewalk and up against the nearest building letting anger fuel his movements. Blood and oxygen engorged his muscles as his body prepared to fight. "I'm all that and more." A science experiment gone wrong, more Frankenstein's monster than Barry could know. Big and bad and soulless. "I could kill you in a dozen different ways without leaving a trace of evidence, so before you open your big trap again, you might want to remember that an insult to Debi is an insult to me. I will end you."

Barry's grunts and struggles filled the space between the buildings. Rose let him drop to the ground. He hadn't even been aware that he'd lifted the other man off his feet. "Run, little man, before I change my mind."

Barry straightened his tie and jerked his head to the side. "Come, Allyson."

Allyson's face had gone pale and she glanced between her brother and Debi before casting an uncertain look at Rose. "Debi—"

"Allyson," Barry ordered. "Let's go."

"Call me," Allyson whispered before following Barry into the quad toward the modern building in the distance.

Rose took a deep breath. He'd threatened to kill a man he didn't know. His pulse and breathing were normal; no adrenaline flowed through his system. He might as well be looking at crafts at the state fair for all his body reacted. A knot formed in his gut like a chunk of ice keeping him numb. He turned to find Debi doubled over, her hands on her knees. "Whoa, what's going on?"

Breath panted out and the pulse in her throat thrummed like a hummingbird on steroids. "Panic attack."

"Yeah, I got that. Come here." He led her to a nearby bench and forced her to sit, and then he pushed her head between her knees for good measure. "Deep breaths."

Arms and legs twitched and she didn't bother arguing. Her back arched with every inhale and shook with each exhale. The movement drew attention to her frailty. The back of her ribs bumped through her shirt like waves as her back convulsed with uneven breathing. She was slight. He hadn't noticed before. She was such a big personality, her smart mouth making up for her slight physical presence. Wavy black hair cascaded down her back and veiled her face, making it hard for her to catch her breath.

Grabbing a hunk of silky hair, he sat next to her on the wooden bench and pulled the hair away to open her airways. Gradually, her breathing normalized. The shakes replaced the hiccups of her breath. "Adrenaline," he warned. "It's a bitch."

"Not my first attack." She lifted marginally, resting elbows on her knees and staring out at the parking lot. "Sorry."

Rose didn't want to relinquish the marginal contact, but sitting next to her holding the hair served no purpose, so he dropped the mass to her shoulders. "Sorry for what? Your ex-boyfriend? You don't owe me an apology for that asshole."

"No." A shallow laugh bubbled to the service. "The days of apologizing for his high-handed behavior are over. He knows exactly what he's doing and deserves whatever he gets."

"Then why apologize?"

"For, uh." A shiver shook her shoulders. "The panic attack. Sorry, I—"

"Apologizing for that is like apologizing for the snow."

Velvety brown eyes glanced up in question.

The vulnerability on her face stopped him short. She was beautiful, something he had noticed in the abstract, but this close, he appreciated the softness of her skin over prominent cheekbones with a sassy nose. Her full lips were another damn problem. "Not something you can control."

"Oh." She returned her gaze to the parking lot. "Most people don't get it, that I can't control them."

"Most people are idiots. What were you going to do before I got here?"

"Deck him?" Her answer was more of a question.

"If you're going to hit, do it right."

"Anything that caused him damage was right."

He rearranged her hand into a proper fist, without the thumb tucked inside. "If I train you right, you could break his nose next time."

"I'd pay good money for that."

"We'll work on it." The warmth of her hand tucked into his tugged at some lost humanity he didn't want to awaken. After Madigan, he'd worked hard to bury the links and connections to those he cared about. He couldn't afford to let her close when he wasn't sure he could control the angry monster inside. So he dropped her hand and glanced up, away from the intensity of their exchange. His silver pickup stood out in the faculty lot filled with sedans and the occasional SUV. Maybe he was too working class for the academics. Rose rubbed a hand across her shoulders, washing away the last of the shivers. "Are you cold?"

She straightened, holding his gaze. "Your hands warmed away the chill."

"That was the plan." It was more than warmth that passed between them, it was alchemy, that undefined something that turned a touch into fire, but if his truck didn't belong in the parking lot, his hands sure as hell didn't belong on her. He swiped his hand back. "Ready to go?"

"Sure, Rosie." She picked up the stack of files where she'd dropped them earlier and led the way to the lot.

Rose picked up the bags of water bottles and the rest of the evidence and followed her. They damn sure better get some good intel out of the bottles, considering the pain of seeing the source of her personal pain face-to-face. If she'd told him back at the motel about the ex, he would have suggested she stay back. Why had she insisted on coming if she knew her ex would be around to rub her nose in the past? Rose wanted to ask, but it was none of his business. They all had pasts they regretted. Debi was no different than any of the men on the team. The past haunted you, no matter how hard you tried to leave it behind.

Rose helped Debi into the truck and tucked the water bottles in the cooler behind the driver's seat. He started the engine with a rumble and pulled out of the lot. The roar of the truck drew a few stray looks from passing pedestrians, which he ignored. "I would rather have spared you that situation. You should have said no when I told you where the mission was."

"Why? Because of Barry?" She shook her head. "He's whatever. I needed to come."

"Why?"

"The motel was making me stir-crazy, you know that."

A group of cars pushed into line behind him, eager to leave the lot. "Was it worth running into Barry the Bastard?"

"Ha. I like that nickname."

"Enough to stop using the nickname you use for me?"

"Not a chance." She grinned at him, the smile warming the air.

Rose accelerated to move around a gold sedan and into the adjacent lane. "You didn't answer my question."

"Which one?"

"Was it worth running into Barry?"

Her smile faded. "It keeps my ego in check."

From what he'd seen, she didn't seem like an egomaniac. "That's not an answer."

"Best you're going to get."

He rode a few miles in silence. "You've got some sharp edges."

"You have no idea."

Rose watched the mirrors as he sped up the entrance ramp to the highway. An itch at the back of his neck said they'd gotten off too easy. "What's Barry's deal?"

"You've a lot of questions for a man who didn't say word one to me on the way here."

"Takes me a while to wake up."

"Didn't take long for you to wake up and scare the crap out of me in the dark motel room."

"Wasn't asleep yet."

"You need to sleep more."

"Said the pot to the kettle."

She curled a foot underneath her legs. "I took a job at the bar because I don't sleep much at night. Not since..."

The gold sedan that had been in line behind him in the campus parking lot still followed three cars back. It had been there since leaving campus. "Since Barry?"

"Not so much him as the whole sordid mess. There's not a single researcher in the lab that Barry hasn't poached. He takes the glory and does none of the work. He does luncheons and awards ceremonies and schmoozes the grant committees while the rest of us are... *were* doing the bulk of the work."

"How does a skater like him get rewarded?"

"Skater?" She'd never heard that term.

"Someone who skates by while everyone else does the work. Happens in every field, the Army included. Not on the teams, but in the regular Army. There's always some loser who skates out of the hard deployments while the rest of us do double time to make up for their lazy asses."

"And you take it?"

"Hell no. A blanket party is the preferred method of correction."

"I thought hazing was illegal."

"It is. Officially. Unofficially it's how shit gets done, although there are less physical means of getting a skater to pull his weight."

"Did you really beat some poor guy in his bunk?"

"Poor guy? Is it right or ethical for the go-getters to face nearly double the risk of death or dismemberment because a soldier who made a pledge and took a paycheck failed to deliver?"

The anger etched on his angular jaw surprised her. "You lost someone, didn't you?"

"We all lost someone." He forced his focus out the windshield. "Did you really take an experimental drug?"

"To think that on the way here, I actually wished you would talk more."

"Change your mind?"

"Absolutely."

"Too bad. Answer the question."

She rolled her eyes to deflect the emotion clogging her throat. "Barry made it sound worse than it was. I'd been working on a proprietary compound for nearly two years. I followed the protocol, and the compound passed animal testing with flying colors, but it can take years, years I didn't have, to get approval for human trials."

"You needed to succeed that badly?"

"God, I wish it were my ego, but no. I developed DV1028 for me. I needed—" She bit her lip. "I was an idiot. And I have no idea how Barry knew I'd started taking the compound. Couldn't wait to tattle to my father, the filthy little weasel. After accusing me of human trials, Barry took credit for my research, and said that my irresponsible behavior was putting his entire research program at risk. Jesus." Debi shoved a wisp of hair from her face. "Why do I spill my guts around you?"

"It's a gift." Rose shifted lanes to pass a slow semi. The gold car shifted as well. "I take it your father didn't take your side."

"I admitted to testing DV1028 on myself, and then told him in no uncertain terms that the research was mine, not Barry's. My biological looked me right in the eye and told me to prove it."

"Sounds like he's more of a bastard than Barry."

"And then some."

"Do me a favor." Rose pulled out his phone and handed it across the console. "Give Ryder a call."

Her face paled. "Why?"

"We've got company." He grabbed her arm before she turned. "Don't look. The driver isn't stupid."

"Echo?"

"Odds are high that the driver of the car is Team Echo." Her pulse beat rapidly beneath his touch. "Stay calm. We knew this was a possibility."

"We did?" Her voice squeaked.

"Yes, that's why we have contingency plans. Dial Ryder. While I drive, you're radio communications. Think you can handle it?" Challenging her gave her a job that forced her to focus away from the fear. She'd gone pale and frightened, two steps closer to another panic attack.

"I can handle it, Rosebud." The sarcasm made her voice stronger. She dialed and put the phone to her ear. He could have her put the phone on speaker, but relaying information would give her something to do. "Ryder, it's Debi. We have a tail."

CHAPTER FOUR

A whooshing sound strummed through her eardrum and she could see about as far as the dashboard. Debi held the phone to her head with the other hand over the opposite ear. "We picked up a tail when we left campus."

"Why didn't they attack when you were in the open on campus?"

"How the hell would I know?"

Ryder's warm laughter sounded tinny through the phone. "Relay my question to Rose."

"Oh." She turned her attention to the driver. Strong hands gripped the steering wheel with long, lean muscles sculpting up his arms. Everything about him screamed safe, steady, and calm, exactly what she needed. "Ryder wants to know why they didn't attack on campus."

"Best guess is this guy was a loner, set in place in the off chance we showed up there. He's waiting for orders."

"Is that good or bad?"

"Relay the information to Ryder."

"Right." Bad, it was probably bad, because once the guy had orders—

"I heard." Ryder's calm voice soothed the panic clawing her insides. "Ask Rose if we have enough time to get the primary plan into place."

"He wants to know if we have time for Plan A or if we need to go with Plan B?"

Rose glanced at the mirrors before signaling and getting off at the next exit. "I can make time. How long until they can get into position?"

Debi continued relaying information as they formed a plan. Ryder knew the perfect place for an ambush with high ground, whatever the hell that meant. The men seemed pleased and would be in place in thirty minutes, at which time Rose would drive them into position, drawing the guy on their tail into a trap. All Debi had to do was stay buckled in her seat. After hanging up the phone, she forced a deep breath to calm her nerves. "What now?"

"Now, we drive the long way to our destination, while avoiding high-risk areas."

"High risk?"

"Low traffic. Bad neighborhoods. Anywhere it feels like we're getting herded toward an ambush. This guy could have another team en route same as us."

"I really didn't need to know that." The idea of another team curdled the coffee and creamer in her stomach.

"Yes you did. You'll be fine."

"Easy for you to say." He was a tank that could survive a direct hit. She was like a porcelain doll held together with glue. All brittle edges and easier to break the second time around.

"How do you deal with drunks at the bar?"

The question threw her off. "With a bouncer."

"And when the bouncer isn't there?"

"With a smile on my lips and a big stick in my hands."

"Or a shotgun."

"That would be illegal."

"Not in Texas."

Debi choked out a laugh. It was still illegal to pull a loaded shotgun on a civilian, but she got his point. "So am I supposed to be the distracting smile or the shotgun?"

"This isn't a metaphor."

"But if it were?" She really needed to know where she fit into the plan, and better yet, where she fit into the outcome.

"You're the customer at the far end of the bar. I'm the distraction and the rest of the team is the shotgun. If we do things right, Echo will never see it coming."

"And what happens to the customer at the end of the bar?"

He turned to her, blessing her with a devastating smile that did funny things to the butterflies winging through her stomach. "The cute customer at the end of the bar will enjoy a second round on the house."

"Make it a double. Top shelf tequila. Proximo 1800."

"Sounds expensive," he teased.

"The customer at the end of the bar is worth it."

He winked. "Is she, now?"

"Definitely. Worth it."

"You and Lauren have a thing for tequila."

The first day Rose barreled into their lives, Lauren had been recovering from a few rounds with Jose Cuervo. "The tequila thing started as a dare years ago. Are you trying to distract me?"

"Does it matter?"

Not really. She needed a distraction. Rose was driving like a granny, making wrong turns and ending up caught in slow traffic that delayed progress, and all she could think about was the loser from Echo behind them. "What's he driving?"

"An ice cream truck."

She released tension with a smile. "Your humor always catches me by surprise."

"I'm not sure why. I'm told I look funny."

Not by any stretch of the imagination. "Do you have a girl back home? Because someone, somewhere has convinced you that you're charming."

"I am charming, and no, I don't have a girl back home." He took his eyes off the road long enough to smile, and he went from hard warrior to good-looking as sin. The smile could melt the ice cap. "What I have are sisters."

"God help 'em." She couldn't imagine overprotective Rose with sisters. He probably had them fitted for chastity belts when they hit puberty. "Did your poor sisters ever date?"

"Not when I was home."

"So they had you kidnapped and sold to the Army."

"No, but Iris—she's the second to the youngest—tried to convince me to run away and join the circus."

"She sounds fun."

"She's a pain in the ass. They all are, but..." He glanced back in the rearview mirror. "They're mine."

Antiquated and sweet at the same time. Debi turned her attention to their tail. "What's he doing?"

"Getting antsy. He's on the phone. We need to get back on the road. All this driving around has given our team time to get into position."

Nervous energy swirled like a low-grade twister in the cab of the truck. Debi tugged at the hair band on her arm, snapping it against the tender skin on the underside of her wrist. As distractions went, the little snip of pain did nothing to take her mind off the danger. They passed the city limits sign and traffic thinned as the surrounding area turned rural. Now even she could see the sedan in the side mirror. "He's getting closer."

"He's not trying to hide."

"Is that a bad sign?" Probably a bad sign, but Rose simply shrugged. Was the soldier from Echo that confident in his abilities? Did he know something they didn't? The truck's clock counted two minutes of absolute silence. Debi cleared her throat. "How old are your sisters?"

"Twenty-seven, twenty-six, twenty-five. Two of them are twenty-five. Irish twins. The next oldest is twenty-three. That's Iris. The youngest is twenty-two. Camy will graduate from nursing school in May."

The information slid through her ears like a vapor. Her breathing went shallow and she couldn't force enough oxygen through her lungs. A cigarette sounded fabulous right now. She snapped the band on her wrist. "Should I call Ryder? Let him know where we are?"

"They know where we are."

"How?" Right now she was having a hard time taking things on faith.

"They still have a tracker app on your phone, sweetheart."

"Oh." She'd be mad at the intrusion—Ryder had done the same thing to Lauren—but right now, that tracker meant the good guys knew where they were and when they'd arrive at the ambush site. Debi swallowed past the lump in her throat. "Wait, am I counting right? How many sisters do you have?"

"Six."

"That's... Six. Sisters? You're making that up to distract me."

"Nope. Six sisters. Lily, Daisy, Ivy, Marigold, Iris, and Camellia. Camy's the baby."

"Where do you fit in birth order?"

"Oldest."

Figured, given how he liked to control, plus the man had the first-born determination sitting in his square jaw. "The poor things with you for a brother." Debi rubbed an ache in the back of her skull. They were on the highway now, speeding to an uncertain destiny.

"Save a little sympathy for me. Six girls are hard to raise."

"And you did that?"

"Yeah. My old man left when Camy started kindergarten."

"How old were you?"

"Thirteen."

"Tough age to lose a father."

"Wasn't much of a loss. I was doing most of the work around the farm by then anyway. I helped Mom as much as I could. Joined the Army to make sure those that wanted went to college."

Where did that sweet edge come from? He was supposed to be a hard-ass. "Wait a minute. Ivy Rose, Lily Rose. Those are all flower names. What is your first name? Rosebud?"

"It's not a freaking flower name. My father named me." He sped around a slower farm truck, his eyes constantly flipping from the front to the mirrors, keeping his focus on the tail. "Mom named the girls."

"This is too good." She rubbed her hands together. "You shouldn't have given me this much ammunition."

He stomped on the accelerator as they climbed a hill. "If we survive the next fifteen minutes, you can harass me all you like."

"That's not funny."

"Wasn't aiming for funny."

The sudden rise as they crested the hill sent her stomach flying. Normally the tummy tickler at the top of the hill made her smile, but right now, she wanted to throw up. "Do you think he's going to make a move before we get to the ranch?"

"I would."

"You know you're supposed to lie to me to make me feel better?"

"Wrong. My job is to protect. Being unprepared will get you killed. You need to accept the reality of the situation."

The sedan hugged their bumper as they sped down the hill faster than the speed limit. "Reality sucks."

"It's going to get worse before it gets better."

"What are you, a freaking billboard?" The lake on her right barreled past, giving her a sense of vertigo. The curve at the bottom of the hill wavered in her vision. She dug her fingers into the armrest. "We won't make it at this speed."

"Won't need to."

She yanked on the seatbelt, locking it tight around her midsection. "I really don't want to end up in the same ditch as Lauren's truck." Lauren had crashed into that spot a week ago when men intent on kidnapping her cut her brakes. "There's not much left of her truck."

"Not planning on wrecking my truck." Rose released the accelerator as they approached the sharp turn. One wrong move would have them blasting into the side of the bluff. Or the lake.

Debi's heart pumped like a windmill drawing blood painfully through her veins. The sun dimmed and her vision blurred. The lake was murky this time of year. Cold. Her breath sputtered. She'd gone swimming in the lake since she was a kid, but she'd rather not dive in car first.

Echo slammed into the truck from behind, and the truck fishtailed. Rose straightened it out. "Damnit. I'm still paying on this truck," he muttered. "Come on, Fowler." The sedan hit from the side, pulling more low curses from Rose. "Fucker."

"Is this part of the plan?" She really didn't remember this part of the plan.

"Wait for it." He slowed the truck at the curve.

The sharp report of gunshots echoed. Debi ducked. She tried to drop to the floor, but the seatbelt locked her in place. Rose braked and shifted the steering wheel. The move slammed her into the door. They wheeled around the curve before Rose yanked the emergency brake, forcing a skid that spun them in a half circle. They slammed to a stop in the center of the highway, facing the opposite direction. Dizziness spun her head in a loop. Her vision fogged and she welcomed the blackout that threatened.

"Deep breath, sweetheart. We're not finished."

CHAPTER FIVE

Shots fired at the perfect moment. The gold sedan swerved, missed the curve, and crashed into the cliff. All according to plan, but Rose wanted to catch the bastard. It was time to figure out what the fuck Echo wanted and why the hell they didn't back down, but a panic attack had Debi in a tight grip. A thin glaze veiled her eyes. If he left her like this, she'd be an easy target for anyone on Team Echo. Keeping an eye on the car embedded in the hillside, Rose slid across the seat. He released the buckle on her seatbelt and lifted her to his lap. "Deep breath." He demonstrated and watched her chest rise and fall as she complied. "Listen to my voice. You're safe." He rubbed a hand up and down her back with each inhale and exhale. "The danger's past."

"Liar." Her tone held the bite of humor despite bending over like an old woman. "Reality, remember."

"Ok, it's not past. I need to go make sure we have this guy on lockdown."

"Where's the rest of the team?" She barely got the words out past the panting breaths. Sweat coated her skin.

"Fowler and Craft were at the top of the cliff."

"Snipers?" she guessed.

"That's right." Rose didn't see Ryder, but he had planned to hide in the ditch on the approach to the lake. "I need to make sure you're not a sitting duck before I leave you alone."

"Not helping. Thinking about some loser." Shuttering breath. "Attacking while I can't see. Definitely not helping."

"Embrace reality."

"Ass." She lifted slightly. "Did your sisters try to kill you in your sleep?"

He chuckled, working to distract her, to get her attack under control so he could get Echo under control. "No, but Mari painted my fingernails while I slept. Once."

"What did you do?"

"Went to her parent-teacher conference with hooker-red fingernails."

"Hard to live. That kind of thing. Down." Her words came out breathy. Short.

"Wasn't a thing for me."

"Sure. Big guy. Like you. Who would tease you?"

"Mari on the other hand." He scrubbed a hand across her quivering shoulders. The sedan hadn't moved, and he hadn't seen the driver exit, but that didn't mean the guy wasn't loose. If Echo bolted, Ryder might be in a position to intercept. "Mari never did anything like it again."

"Did I hear gunshots?"

"The shots were our guys. All part of the plan. When Lauren wrecked here, Ryder recognized the location as the perfect spot for a sniper."

"Which one? Fowler or Craft?"

"All of us have sniper skills, although Fowler has the best accuracy at greater distances." A shiver passed from her body and into his and the vulnerability kept him rooted. Despite training. Despite mission. Gradually the tremors passed and the tension in his gut eased. "You good enough for me to leave?"

"Peachy." She straightened, the movement sliding her butt across his thighs.

Beside them, someone pounded the door panel.

Debi's scream nearly shattered his eardrum.

"Let's go, let's go, let's go." Fowler jumped up and slid across the hood.

"Watch the truck," Rose muttered. "Asshole."

Debi collapsed against his chest. "Jesus, that scared me."

"Don't think about it. Listen to the sound of my voice. Just be in the moment."

"The moment sucks."

He smiled against her hair. "The moment's not so bad." Nestled like a gift in his arms, she smelled of strawberry shampoo. "Reinforcements have arrived. You're safe."

"We're safe."

Rose was never truly safe. Those he loved were in danger, so he stayed away for months on end, but he couldn't get away from the woman whose smell filled his head. "You know, this wasn't really a panic attack."

"Nice try, Rosie. Definitely panic."

Ah, there was the bite of sarcasm he enjoyed. "A panic attack is the fight or flight response at inappropriate times due to a perceived danger. This was the real deal."

"Marginal difference." She continued to lean into him, her

breathing evening out. She snuggled into one side and breathed deep. "Besides, I'd like to think when the time came, I could defend myself rather than cowering."

"You can. You have. The night the two soldiers from Echo tried to infiltrate your house. You walked out gun in hand to take any comers."

"Pure adrenaline."

Man, Rose missed that. The way adrenaline hyped you up for battle. Fear had been a motivator. "Adrenaline works. Trust it to do its job the next time."

She shifted against his shoulder to peer up at him. "Were you a psychiatrist in another life?"

"No." But he understood fear. He had watched a soldier try to climb under a dead body to get away from the gunfire in his own head. *That* was the type of panic that made the fearless experiment seem like a reasonable alternative. "You good to go?"

A shaky breath rocked her body. "I'm fine."

They sat close, her pressed tight against his chest, and her lips were... Right. There. Shit, he needed to get his head on straight. He pressed a kiss to her forehead, the desire too strong to deny. She needed comfort. The situation they were facing was a million miles out of her league. And the smooth, soft skin combined with her scent made him want to stick right there and let the team handle the shooting and the accident. That insidious desire wrapped around a man's soul and helped him straight into the grave. A woman complicated things. He eased her off his lap and resumed his position behind the wheel of the truck. He drove closer to the wreck and moved to the side of the road.

Ryder marched up from the ditch that went under the

highway to the lake. Craft and Fowler swept the area around the sedan, guns at the ready.

Rose stepped out of the truck. "Stay here," he ordered Debi. He joined the team between the wreck and his truck. "Echo got away?"

"No thanks to you, dipshit," Fowler taunted.

"I'm not the one who missed the shot," Rose answered.

"My orders were to take him alive. If the rules of engagement have changed, you be sure to let me know."

"Knock it off." Ryder's voice rose above the bickering. "We need information. Craft and Fowler, go retrieve the asset. The blood trail leads up the crevice." A thick bandage covered his hand as he pointed to the washed-out gully between two bulging bluffs. "Rose, you're on babysitting detail."

Staying near Debi, discovering her vulnerabilities and fears, put him at risk of attachment. They both needed some distance. He wanted an active assignment. "What's your plan, boss?"

"Calling my wife. Make sure everything is all clear." In the past week, Lauren had been kidnapped, beaten, and drugged. Team Echo had used Lauren as bait to lure Ryder to his death. Echo wanted to end Team Fear and remove all evidence of the experimental program they'd volunteered for. Team Fear lost two good men before they figured out Echo's deadly plans. Not a one of them was going down easy.

Calling Lauren wasn't something Rose could do in Ryder's place, so he was stuck with the temptation for the time being.

"Wait." Debi hopped from the truck, her heels sliding in the gravel. "Are you going after the guy in the car?"

Craft and Fowler nodded.

Rose nailed her with a glare. "I thought I told you to stay in the truck."

"The truck was starting to close in." She moved her hands close to her head like it was being smashed between the walls. "Staying active helps."

She was right, but that put her close enough to get hurt.

She turned her gaze to the rest of the team. "If the, uh, guy doesn't make it—"

"He'll make it," Ryder assured her.

"But if he doesn't." Debi ducked her head, her face pale at the thoughts she kept inside. "A blood sample would help."

"I like the way you think." Fowler reached over to give her a fist bump. "Rose, you have any syringes?"

"Shit. Yeah. I should have thought of it." He opened his medic kit and pulled out syringes. "Along the same lines, I'll search the car. See if he left any clues behind, maybe some meds. I can swab the blood spatter."

"That'll help, but I really need more material to work with." A skeptical quirk caused a lift in her eyebrow. "You know how to draw blood?"

"Oh, yeah." Fowler gave her his best shit-eating grin. "I believe I drew first blood this time around."

"I mean with a syringe, Dr. Kevorkian?"

"I can get the job done."

She looked uncertain. "Maybe I should go—"

"You're not going," Rose insisted. Where the hell had that come from?

"Taking blood is delicate work, and I—"

"I got it." Fowler tucked the syringe in a pocket of his cargo pants. "But I didn't say it wouldn't hurt."

He and Craft laughed as they double-timed it up the side

of the bluff. A hiccup shook Debi's shoulders as she drew in a shallow breath and watched them climb. A shimmer of uncertainty in her wary gaze drew him. Her eyes squinted against the sun, but the shuttered lids couldn't hide her fear. She still wasn't over the panic. A long-buried instinct wanted to give aid and comfort. Contrary bastard that he was, the desire to soothe sent him in the opposite direction, toward the car Echo had used to follow them.

Ryder's plan had been solid. A week ago, someone had sent Lauren on a collision course with this hill at the bottom of the lake. At the time, Ryder had recognized the spot as the perfect place for an ambush. They put Fowler at the top of the hill and lured Echo into position. If Rose had done his job, he'd have captured the driver before he could escape up the hill, but Rose hadn't been able to desert Debi, another reason to stay the hell away. The attraction screwed with his focus. He didn't have time for sex, games, and rock and roll, and he damn sure didn't have the right to paint a bigger target on her chest.

He turned his gaze to the gold sedan. It was late model, with dents along the front panel. The front windshield was shattered, likely from the bullet. Despite the shot and the high-speed chase, Echo had prevented the car from flipping when it hit the curve. The other soldier was well-trained by the same assholes who had trained Team Fear. Behind him, Ryder spoke in low rumbles on the phone. Debi had gone back to the truck to get something from the medic pack. Rose dropped to the ground to search under the car.

Debi's heeled boots returned and crossed his line of sight. Damn woman had legs for miles and those slim black heels gave her an extra four inches of pure sass.

"I got the swabs and some Ziploc bags. I can—"

He gripped her ankle to lock her down. "Hold up." Her foot blocked a rectangular protrusion on the undercarriage that didn't belong there. "C4," he yelled. "Everybody back." He jumped up to hustle her away from the car bomb. She was already moving. They made it a dozen steps.

CHAPTER SIX

The concussion blast split the air like dry thunder. The pressure in her ears expanded until an ache in her head threatened to explode. Sound ceased. Debi tumbled in a vacuum surrounded by light and debris and the terrifying absence of sound. Flickering electricity danced on her skin.

She flew faster than pain. *Whoosh*, her back hit before she crumbled against the side of the bluff. Rose landed against her. The bruising impact of solid muscle moving at the speed of C4 hit like a second blast. Air compressed in her lungs before they dropped the rest of the way down. He twisted as they rolled, taking the brunt when they hit solid rock at the bottom. An unnatural silence throbbed in her ears.

She fought the cocoon of his arms, struggling to regain her feet. Fight. They needed to get up and fight. She was no tactician, but they were easy pickings. Rose's eyes focused on hers. His mouth moved, but she didn't hear the words. Panic welled up in her still tender chest. "Let me up." She didn't hear her own voice, just an echo of pain in her eardrums.

He used his body to contain her struggling limbs. Once he had her tied down, he gave her shoulders a hard shake. His lips moved.

Tears dripped from the corner of her eyes. "I can't." She couldn't what? Think? Hear? Speak?

He gave her another solid shake before turning her head to meet his gaze. "Stay. Down," he mouthed.

She nodded and the back of her head scraped gravel. She struggled to see around him, to know what had happened, but he had her wedged into the ditch like a coffin. The lines of his face warped as her vision blurred. *Coffin*. Not helping. Sweat slicked her skin.

His body settled over her and he loosened his grip to run a finger along her jaw. The gentle touch against the backdrop of the explosion stopped her mid-breath. Blinking away the fog, she focused on his face. Tan. Golden. And his dark eyes were blue this close, like a midnight sky with the barest sliver of a moon. A deep well of emotion hid in the depths.

Deep breath. She couldn't hear him, but the words from earlier were locked in her memory. The way he'd talked her down. No one had soothed her in the middle of an attack before. The memory helped her focus. *Deep breath*. The way he'd taken a breath with her, counting ... *one, two, three, four, and exhale*. The tactile imprint of his large palm brushing over her back stayed with her, down her spine and across her shoulders. Calm. His voice was like water over rocks, rough against smooth, a kind of meditative focus.

The intensity of his gaze froze the fear. There was no other word for it. Everything inside her froze, waiting for his orders. He moved his lips in slow, exaggerated movements. "Ready. To. Go."

The words were more vibration than sound. The words stayed trapped in her throat, she was afraid to speak. She nodded instead.

He counted down this time. "Three. Two. One."

He lifted her to her feet and shoved her toward the twisted metal of his truck. Her boots slid in the gravel, seeking purchase. He didn't give her time. He lifted her and tucked himself around her. The driver's door flung open and he shoved her across the seat. She didn't have time to strap on the seatbelt before the truck rumbled to life. The windshield shattered as Rose slammed the truck into reverse.

A scream scratched her throat, tore free, but she didn't hear more than an echo. Rose spun the car in a one-eighty, heading down the highway as fast as her grandpa chasing a hooker. They made the turn away from the bluff, away from the lake, and Debi dropped slowly back against the seat. Relaxing her muscles brought every ache to the fore. Her head pounded and her entire back throbbed like a nasty bruise, which it probably was. She reached up to pull her seatbelt on, but her arm wouldn't move. A burning pain spiked through her shoulder. Her opposite hand reached to rub away the ache and came up bloody.

Crap. Debi closed her eyes. Took a deep breath, but a breath wasn't going to cut it this time. The seeping wound forced her into the flaring reality of pain. Was it shrapnel or a gunshot? She hadn't heard gunfire, but she hadn't heard anything since the bomb bruised her ears. "Gunshot?" she asked, but she couldn't hear her own voice. Could he? She glanced across the seat.

The anger in his gaze went so deep it threatened to draw her into the black hole of his soul. He reached across with one hand and pulled her seatbelt over her body.

Some words you didn't need to hear. The injury was bad. Moving jolted pain through every nerve ending. Hell, having a cow knock the wind out of her was playtime compared to the stretch and burn slicing through her body right now. She closed her eyes and let her head fall back.

Breathe deep. One, two, three, four, and exhale.

He counted like a dance instructor, with a silent beat between each count. His calming voice, even one she couldn't hear, sent her inward. Tingles spread down her arm to her fingers. Blood oozed down her chest. Damn, she'd liked this shirt, although, truth be told, she'd worn it one too many days. Ok, she was seriously losing it. She tried to open her eyes, but the heaviness was too much to push past.

Passing out right now would be great, because good God-awful son of a Texas steer, this hurt. But she stayed awake, each jostle of the truck sending spasms through her trembling chest. Gradually, she became aware of wind swirling her hair around her face like a whip, and then, a whisper of the wind, a mere snap pierced the silence.

Sound. Thank God. At least the hearing loss had been temporary.

Minutes or hours later, the wind stopped smacking her and went silent. She opened her eyes to see the metal sign and family brand that spanned the driveway to the ranch. Home. Tears burned the back of her eyes, but she sniffed them away.

If she started, she might never stop. She focused on the details so she didn't panic. Didn't fall asleep and never wake up.

Red paint was weather rough on the side of the barn. Rose pulled in front, jumped out to open the garage-sized double door before backing inside. The dim light made it possible for her to fully open her eyes.

Red stained the right side of her body. Pebbled glass covered the dash and floor. Debi brushed remnants of the windshield from her legs.

"Stay still," he barked. He stood outside the driver's door, pulling his medic bag from the back. If she'd ever believed him peaceful or kind, the look on his face disabused her of it. Anger lived in the hard line of his jaw and the muscle ticking in his cheek. "Ornery woman going to bleed all the hell over my truck," he muttered.

"Just so long as I don't die in your truck."

He shoved the bag over his left shoulder. "Don't move."

"Good idea. Don't know why I didn't think of it."

"You know how to shoot a handgun?"

"What about my shoulder?" She didn't want to sound like a wimp, but the pain escalated like some savage creature trying to eat her from the inside out. "Remember, I don't like blood." Actually, the sight of it made her want to lose her lunch. Or whatever meal she'd last eaten. She was starting to lose grasp of reality.

"Gunshot wound. You'll live. I'm sorry, sweetheart, but I have to make sure we're not walking into a hot zone. The barn provides cover, but there's only one way in or out. We need inside the house for me to patch you up right. Now, answer my question. Do you know how to shoot a handgun?"

"Grew up on a ranch."

He pulled a black handgun from his pack. A semi-automatic, probably a Glock, although her vision was foggy. Rose racked the slide to chamber a round. "The barn is empty, but I need to clear the house before I take you inside. Understand?"

"Sure."

He handed her the weapon. "Anyone comes through the door, shoot first, ask questions later. Got it?"

She gripped the weapon in her left hand, careful to keep her trigger finger positioned to avoid accidentally discharging the weapon. "Sure, Rosie, go clean the house."

"Clear the house."

"I'd rather you cleaned it, but you do you."

A muscle twitched above his lip. "Stay alert." Bag slung on his back, he marched to the open barn doors. He closed one and with a final and intense look, he was gone.

Debi lifted her gun arm to brace the butt of her hand against the dash. She was a righty, and at the moment, her right side had all the mobility of a rusted tractor. The odds of hitting the side of the barn while in the barn were unlikely with her left. Come to think of it, she was an easy target. The idea sped panic through her pulse. She was strapped into her seat with the passenger door closed. Trapped. The sides of the truck closed in on her like a carnival fun house. There was nowhere to run if anyone came through the door. She may as well paint a bull's-eye on her chest. Although the blood was doing enough of that, seeping through the thin cotton. Cold made her fingers tingle.

Pain kept the panic in check, but she needed free of the restraint. She set the gun on the dash and lowered her hand to the seatbelt. Her fingers tracked down the belt to the locking mechanism where she mashed the button to release the clip. The belt retracted, slipping across the wound. "Holy mother."

Pain zipped through her body like aftershocks. Sweat dripped down her face. The *what ifs* of the situation kept her moving. She needed to get free of the truck in case something bad went down, so she reached across her body and popped the door open with her left. The door gave and her body lurched with the sudden jolt, more pain spiraling from the wound. She eased her legs around to the opening and scooted to the edge of the seat.

"Jesus H Christ." Rose's tone had bite. "You had one job."

Startled, she slid off the seat and had to catch herself with her left. Her right arm dangled like cooked spaghetti.

Rose grabbed her before she slid to the hard-packed ground. "What if someone from Echo had walked in the door?"

"Then I'd be gone and you'd have to forgive me for bleeding all over your truck."

"Not funny." He grabbed the Glock, set the safety, and tucked it behind his back. "Wasn't worried about the truck. You've lost a lot of blood, sweetheart."

She twisted to get a look, but he maneuvered so her good arm faced him, and just like that, he had her up in his arms. He paused long enough to close the barn. Moments later, he had her in the shelter of her house. The deadbolt slammed home with a solid click. He wove a path through the house to set her on the sofa.

"Wait. Blood will never get out of the microsuede."

Rose rolled his eyes. "Where do you want to do this, Princess?"

"Take me to the bathroom down the hall."

"This isn't some scratch we can bandage up in the bathroom before you hop in the shower."

"Oh." Last night's dinner agitated in her stomach. "Hospital?"

"First place Echo will look."

When a hospital was unsafe, she'd fallen pretty far down the rabbit hole. "Doctor?"

"Mandatory reporting on gunshot wounds. The police will get involved, which will draw Echo right to us. Don't worry. I'm trained in battlefield triage, you'll—"

Something pounded on the front door. Rose transformed. An invisible shield covered his expressions as he went warrior strong before her eyes. He set her on the couch and pulled out the Glock. "Stay here."

Like she could get up at this point. She didn't hear him move, but moments later the door clicked open and voices filled the emptiness.

"What the fuck happened?" Rose's angry voice followed by something or someone smacked into the wall. Granny's china cabinet rattled with the pounding noises in the other room.

"Get the fuck off,' Fowler answered. "We didn't know about the bomb. Found the detonator minutes after the car blew sky high."

"What about the shot? The bastard tagged Debi. You should have had him contained before he could take a shot." Rose's voice lifted in anger.

Fowler's angry voice shouted right back. "Wasn't the asset who did the shooting, asshole. There was another shooter, so get the fuck off."

The china cabinet rattled and something clattered to the bottom shelf, the broken glass like a mini-explosion in the tense room. "Maybe you should take this outside." She wanted her voice to be stern, but it came out a mere whisper. Neither of the men responded as the argument escalated. Debi stood to make her point, but the ground wiggled underfoot. She dropped to her butt. The soft cushion called.

Let go. Drift.

CHAPTER SEVEN

Boom, one minute she was upright and snarky, the next she dropped to the couch like a medicine ball. Rose dislodged his elbow from Fowler's throat and raced around the couch. "Grab my kit." He eased Debi's head down and lifted her feet onto the couch. "A little hydrogen peroxide will get the stain out," he assured her.

"S'okay," she mumbled. "Barry sat here. We could burn it. Isn't that your specialty?"

"Incendiary devices. I prefer blowing things up." He put a pillow behind her back to keep the wound elevated. "But I could branch out; help you start a Barry the Bastard bonfire later."

"Sounds like a plan. We had a barn fire here last year."

"So I heard. Maybe fires are your specialty."

"Wasn't me. I think Barry started it."

The runt from campus had lit her barn on fire? That was more than a bad breakup. Rose grabbed her boots and yanked them from her feet.

"You cut off my boots and I will haunt you."

"We don't do that." He let his eyes show a humor he didn't feel. Color drained from her cheeks, leaving her skin a sickly grey. "The ER likes to cut off your clothes. I think they get kickbacks from the clothing industry."

Fowler grabbed the medic bag and setup on the opposite end of the couch. "Field dressing or are we stitching her up?"

"How much time do we have?"

"Ryder's on the hunt. The bastard won't get anywhere near here. We've got time."

That gave him time to assess, something he'd wanted but couldn't do until they were secure. "Compression." Rose warned Debi before he put a clean dressing and pressure over the wound.

Debi hissed breath between her teeth. "What happened? I thought we set a trap?"

"We did." Fowler pulled a medicine bottle and syringe from the kit. "The guy on your tail set the bomb and hightailed it up the hill. We were right on his ass when he blew it. Took him down."

"Then how the fuck did he get off a shot?" Rose scrubbed his hands in the kitchen sink. He glared at Fowler from across the room.

"Wasn't him." Fowler injected Debi with a painkiller. "What's your pain level?"

"Fifteen."

"One a scale of one to ten."

She grimaced. "My answer remains the same."

"Lucky it wasn't me doing the shooting. You'd be dead."

"You didn't kill the soldier in the car behind us."

"I had orders. We needed information." Fowler drew liquid into the syringe. "Which is why his partner took him out."

"There were two?" Her words started to slur.

Rose shook clean water from his hands. "We went over this once, sweetheart. Keep up. Bad guy one hightailed it up the cliff when Fowler shot him. Bad guy two shot him so we wouldn't capture him."

"The second guy killed the first guy." Her eyes alternated between wide open and long blinks. "To shut him up. You think he would have talked?"

They were good at their job. "He'd have talked," Rose said. There was no end to the pressure they'd exert to get the information they needed. Rose grabbed the Celox applicator from the kit. The blood-clotting agent stemmed blood loss.

Fowler frowned as he finished the story. "What I don't understand is how Echo Two took out Echo One with a damn-near perfect shot, but managed to miss Rose's big ass in the truck and hit Debi instead."

"Distance. Rapid movement. Not everyone has your skills." Rose frowned down. Her color hadn't improved and her face was pinched in pain. "How's the pain?"

"I think it's gone down. To a fourteen."

He rubbed her good hand so he didn't jostle the wounded side. "We got you covered, sweetheart. You'll be feeling no pain before we get to the end of the story."

"Promise?"

"Oh, yeah. Saved the good stuff for you."

"Top shelf, huh?"

Rose laughed. "Proximo 1800. Only the best." He glanced over Debi to meet Fowler's gaze. "We can stabilize and slow the blood loss, but she needs a surgeon. Doctor at the least. Help me get her patched up, and then we need transport."

Fowler tossed the morphine back in the med kit. "Echo had a man on surveillance here at the ranch. They must have been communicating, because the second man was moving to intercept when the bomb went off."

Rose prepped the Celox. The plunger distributed blood-clotting agent into gunshot wounds, which saved lives and limbs. Fowler peeled back the compress so Rose could work. The wound flooded with blood. Torn flesh on soft skin. Blood coated the entire sleeve of her cotton shirt and her black hair matted around the entry wound. A rock the size of a mountain settled in his gut. He'd never triaged a woman before. "I can't see shit in here. Grab a light."

Fowler flipped on the overhead, and then brought a large lamp as backup. He set it up to focus on Debi's shoulder. The compress had soaked more blood than she could afford to lose. He needed to slow the source of the bleed, but first he needed to get as much foreign material out of the wound as possible.

"Hold this." Rose handed over the still covered Celox. He slipped the hair band off Debi's wrist and pulled her hair from the wound. Then he grabbed a scissor from his kit.

"Cut my hair, Rosebud, and I will kill you on the spot."

"Relax. Your hair is safe. The shirt, not so much." He and Fowler switched places and he cut the shoulder of her shirt to get a better look at the wound.

"I thought only the ER cut off clothes."

"Guess they have their reasons. Going to lift you now." He gave her two seconds to process before he lifted. "No exit wound. The bullet's embedded."

She cursed at him as he jostled the injury. "Maybe Fowler should take over."

"Trust me, you don't want this guy cutting into you."

"Who said anything about cutting." Debi struggled to sit up.

Fowler pressed on the compress to keep her seated. "I practiced on goats, so I'm sure it's the same thing."

She dropped back on the sofa. "You're kidding?"

"Nope." He glanced up at Rose. "Blood pressure's dropping."

"The meds should take the edge off in a few." He glanced at Debi. Her eyes were open, but starting to dilate. He needed to keep her engaged, like he had while Echo had followed them. "Don't you want to know who shot you?"

She nodded, and then groaned.

Fowler pulled out more clean compresses as he spoke. "Echo fought like a feral cat when we captured him. His eyes were fucking crazed. Next thing we know, he's taken a shot between the eyes." Fowler wiped at the blood spatter under his chin. "Second guy took him out. No mercy, man, that shit was cold."

"Did you get his blood?" Debi asked.

Fowler swiped at his face again.

"Not that blood. A sample. In the syringe."

"Oh." Fowler tapped the Velcro pocket on his upper thigh. "Got it right here."

"Go put it in the fridge," she insisted.

At least she was still engaged. Actually, she was still a smartass, which he truly appreciated. "We're not staying, sweetheart." Rose used a smaller needle to numb the injury site.

"Put it on ice, then." She glanced at Fowler. "Before you and Dr. Frankenstein knock me out."

"You're right," Fowler answered. "He is like the monster."

"If Rose is a monster, what are you?"

Fowler grinned. "I'm the good-looking one."

"Not so much. He's built like Thor." Her gaze slid between the two men before landing on Rose. "Neither of you are monsters."

A moment later, Rose injected the Celox, cutting off the most severe blood loss. Debi grunted and bit back a curse. Rose squirmed away from her gaze. The woman thought he was some comic book hero, but that was the painkiller talking. Rose and the rest of the team weren't some medical mutation that made heroes. They were more of a warning against man's hubris. Monsters created in a lab by someone with a God complex. "Fowler, you grew up around here, didn't you?"

Fowler grunted noncommittally. "I'm not from anywhere."

"Don't give me that shit. I don't care if your hometown is fucking top secret. We need a doctor, say within a two-hour radius? If not, we're going to have to risk the questions and take her to an ER."

"Hold on, let me think." Fowler moved to put the blood sample on ice. Something alerted him and he pulled his Glock and approached the kitchen door. Ryder and Craft burst in.

"Second man is down. Put himself out of his misery. These guys are crazy as fuck," Craft said. "They keep self-eliminating, we won't have to kill them. We got four at Ryder's townhouse. These two today. Leaves six if they had twelve on their team."

"Unless they're self-duplicating." Rose had a bad feeling about the way the men had gone out. What the hell kind of information were they trying to protect that they were willing to kill one another, kill themselves, to protect? Or had the drug cocktail finally driven them out of their minds? He thought back to the number of times he'd promised to end himself if he became a threat to others. Maybe these guys took the same vow if they became a threat to their twisted mission. "Fowler, think faster or we're going to the ER."

Ryder scrubbed his hands in the kitchen sink soaking his bandages in the process.

"Keep the wound clean," Rose ordered. Ryder had taken a solid stab to the palm in the fight a few days ago. They couldn't afford an infection.

"We had to bury them in a shallow grave, didn't have equipment for much else. Coyotes will get 'em before anyone else ventures up that bluff."

"I'm more worried about their reinforcements."

"Roger that." Ryder dried his hands on a cloth. "We need to get gone."

"We have time to finish this?" Rose asked. Debi's health trumped the mission.

"We can keep guard while you stitch her up, and then we're out."

"Ry, I can triage, but she needs a real doctor." He didn't want to screw up. A soldier, no problem. He could get them back to fighting shape, but Debi deserved a legitimate doctor who could keep her stable, limit scarring, and prevent infection. "Plus she needs blood and IV antibiotics."

"Wait." Debi's words started to slur. "As long as we're here, I need clothes. And take the food. And—"

"We got it." Rose assured her.

"Wait." She blinked several times and struggled to lift her head off the couch. "Ryder."

Ryder stepped closer. She pulled him down to whisper in his ear. He smiled and squeezed her hand. "Thanks."

"What was that all about?"

Ryder stepped toward the back bedrooms. "You'll have to ask your patient."

Rose looked down but Debi was fully out. The hair that normally flowed down her neck was in a lopsided ponytail away from the wound and her navy blue shirt had a hole cut in the shoulder to reveal the ragged wound filled with blood clotting agent. Blood flow was down. "When I'm done here, I want you to lift her while I put her in a shoulder sling. I want to keep her unconscious until we get to an ER." He didn't want her to feel the pain, which was why he'd waited to finish dressing the wound.

"We're not going to the ER," Fowler insisted.

"The hell we're not. You want to keep your sorry ass secure, you can hold back, Sally, but I'm—"

"Just shut up for one damn minute." Fowler yanked out his cell phone, cursing like a Basic Training Instructor. "Craft can be your surgical assistant, Dr. Frankenstein. I've got some calls to make." Fowler crashed out the front.

Craft scrubbed up at the kitchen sink like he knew what he was doing, cleaning all the way to the elbows with soap and water. Rose prepped the bandages he needed, but his gaze kept straying to Debi's still form. He'd spent his whole life protecting women, and somehow he'd still ended up here. A complete failure with Debi's injury on his shoulders.

"She looks so small," Craft said, coming over to stand next to Rose. "Fragile."

A knot the size of a walnut lodged in Rose's throat. "Six

sisters, and not once did I have to take them in for stitches or broken bones."

"Because you're an overprotective asshole and they now hate you." Craft shoulder bumped him, keeping his hands clean. "Get your head in the game, brother. She needs you focused."

Rose packed the guilt and the shame and the anger in a box. "Let's do this." He tapped another compress against the wound. Even in sleep she moaned against the invasion. Shit. His hands shook. He wanted to shove them in his pockets so no one noticed, but he had work to do. They covered the wound, added the sling. Before they were done, he'd had to cut her whole shirt off. Ryder came from the back carrying a duffel bag.

"Bring me a blanket we can wrap her in. Maybe some slippers or wool socks," Rose said.

Ryder dropped the bag and headed back to the bedrooms. Craft and Rose wrapped the sling around her shoulder so movement wouldn't aggravate the pain. The morphine and compresses must be doing the work, because she didn't make a sound.

Fowler slammed back into the kitchen, the amount of noise he made an indication of his frustration. "Saddle up. I got us a doctor. Ryder, you and Craft finish getting supplies and anything you need from here. Rose and I will head to the doctor. We can meet up after the doctor finishes."

"You giving the orders now?" Ryder's voice lowered. "Because splitting up is a shit idea."

"Wasn't my idea for one of us to take a hit." Fowler's tone bordered on insubordination. "You want to leave Lauren back at the motel alone?"

Rose stepped between the two soldiers. "Debi can't wait for us to backtrack, so unless the motel is on the way—"

"It's not," Fowler answered.

To Rose, that left one solution. They weren't in the desert with the Army at their back. They didn't have a base to fall back to and get medical attention. No reinforcements would dig them out of this mess. They had four men and zero intel to guide their movements. They'd lost all focus and cohesion in the months since they'd left the team.

"Fuck." Ryder draped a blanket on Debi and put slippers on her feet.

Ryder's gentleness in the midst of their anger settled Rose more than anything. The tension existed still in the tightening muscles of his shoulders and back, but anger diminished to be replaced by guilt and frustration over Debi's injury. The bloody wound fell one hundred percent onto Team Fear and the clusterfuck of their current mission.

"Did you pack her comfortable clothes?" Rose asked. The woman wouldn't be wearing her typical skinny jeans and t-shirts until she healed.

"I packed a bunch of Lauren's stuff. The women can share."

Debi was taller and leaner than Lauren. "You know dick about women." Rose took off down the hall until he found a room full of sunshine and light. The clean, cheerful lines matched Debi's personality. The walk-in closet was filled with more shoes than he had clothes, and every single one had heels. Not a sensible shoe in the bunch. He grabbed several pairs of jeans, workout clothes already stacked in sets, and anything else he could lay hands on. A lone pair of tennis shoes was tucked into a gym bag in the far corner. He tossed the rest in with the shoes and headed out.

Walking back into the room was like a bomb ticking down. If anything, the men looked angrier despite the extra time to cool down. They were all feeling caged by a situation out of their control.

Craft tossed pantry food in a box while he and Fowler groused back and forth. Stress vibrated off Ryder. The anger flowing through them individually and as a team was a byproduct of the conflict between them and Echo. It was the reason he'd slammed Fowler into the wall. The reason Fowler and Craft were fighting like teenagers. They had survived, but pieces of the team were starting to unravel.

Rose understood Ryder's dilemma. Splitting up was a dumbass move, but it was the only play they had. The argument between Craft and Fowler escalated so Ryder finally whistled long and loud.

"Shut. Up." Ryder twisted his neck to relieve the tension. The click of his vertebra popping filled the new silence. Finally, Ryder shifted. The anger visibly faded and he faced them much as he had when they were active duty. "The side effects suck. The anger fucks with us every damn time and we need to figure that shit out. We need to turn our anger on the enemy, not each other. We're still a fucking team."

Craft stopped tossing canned goods and stood. Fowler nodded sharply. Order fell over them. Anger drained from faces. Shoulders snapped back to the position of attention. Ryder had reminded them of who they were. Team Fear.

"We can't take my vehicle," Rose said. Echo's actions continued to diminish their options, which accounted for some of the earlier anger. "I'll leave the truck in the barn."

"We can lay down the seats in my SUV." Fowler cleaned up

the medic bag and zipped it closed. He carried it in one hand and grabbed Debi's bag in the other. "Let's roll."

Rose lifted Debi, careful to keep the blanket wrapped tightly over her shoulders. She weighed less than his sister Ivy, who he'd had to carry when she sprained an ankle last year. Debi was out cold, not simply fragile, but completely at his mercy. She was breakable and still in danger. The rock in his gut churned into gravel. This was why a smart soldier stayed the fuck away from civilians. Collateral damage was unavoidable, and from where Rose stood, unacceptable. Debi didn't deserve to get drawn into their world. He should have left her at the motel. He marching behind Fowler out the door, and grief and regret followed like a shadow.

CHAPTER EIGHT

A pounding headache and dry mouth woke Debi from the sleep of the dead. Every muscle in her body protested when she tried to shift positions. She opened her eyes to a dark room and a monster-sized silhouette sitting upright in a chair next to the bed. The size of the shadow caused her heart to seize. She tried to sit up, but a zap of pain at her shoulder reminded her of the gunshot. Everything flashed through her brain and panic threatened.

"Give it a minute." Rose's big hand pressed her gently back to the bed. "You really awake this time?"

"Have there been false alarms?" The frog in her throat sounded more like an ugly old toad with a frog in his throat.

"This is round three."

"Lucky three." Debi struggled to move, but her body didn't respond. "Where are we?"

"Motel number three, about four hours from the last one you remember."

The math didn't add up in her addled brain. "I missed one?"

"We're moving every day, paying cash, and staying off the main roads."

"Seems wise," she rasped. With a cough that jarred her shoulder, she tried to clear her throat. It was hard to believe that they'd moved locations multiple times and she'd been that unaware. The last thing she remembered, she'd been at the ranch, and he and Fowler had given her an injection of something. "Blood loss?"

"Significant, but not life threatening."

"Did the couch survive?"

A slight smile broke the solemn line of his lips. "The Barry couch is toast."

"Finally some good news. Did you burn it?"

"I figured you'd want the honors."

"Oh, I do." Not really. She'd rather not face the reminder of the shooting, although she'd probably have a scar. A big one. "Did you really stitch me up?"

Rose shook his head. "Found a doctor who was willing to patch you up without any records. You want water?"

She licked her chapped lips. "Wouldn't refuse."

He reached to the nightstand and grabbed a bottle of water with a straw through the top. "We stemmed the bleeding and got the doctor to do the deed." He pulled the bottle back when she'd taken a sip. "Met back up with the rest of the team. There's safety in numbers. Your little incident scared the crap out of Lauren. She wouldn't leave you for the first twenty-four hours."

"It was my turn." Lauren had taken enough damage when

she'd been kidnapped. Debi took another sip, but when she tried to get a good gulp, Rose pulled the straw away.

"Keep it down and you can have more."

"How long have I been out?"

"A couple days. Lauren comes over in the daytime. She left a couple hours ago."

To spend the night with her husband no doubt, leaving Rose on bodyguard duty. Again. Poor guy. "Help me up?"

"Stay put."

"Dude, I've been out of it for days. I need a trip to the restroom. Help me up or I'll go alone."

He glanced at the door to the outside. "Did you call me dude?"

"If the flip flop fits, big guy." Debi turned to her good side and used her free arm to brace herself into a sitting position. Her injured arm was in a sling, tucked tight against her body.

He stabilized her before helping her to her feet. The feet currently wearing Goofy slippers. "What's with the slippers?"

"Got them from your closet. Lauren said they were your favorite."

"That's because she has a warped sense of humor." Debi had threatened to bring Goofy slippers and a housecoat the last time Lauren needed a change of clothes. Holding onto Rose, Debi stepped free of the top-heavy footwear. "They're likely to trip me if I try to walk in them now."

"You walk in sky-high heels and you're worried about Goofy?"

Debi used Rose's arm as a crutch to help her hobble to the bathroom door. "You don't like my heels?"

"I like them fine, but you're off heels until you're done with physical therapy."

She frowned. The entire time she'd dated Barry, she'd been forbidden to wear heels that made her taller than him. Now all bets were off. She wore them whenever and wherever. They were a piece of her daily armor. "I don't think so, Rosie. I don't own anything but heels."

"You own Goofy slippers—"

"Not a chance." The day she left the house in slippers and a housecoat was the day she went for a psych eval.

"I brought your gym shoes."

She owned gym shoes? "I appreciate it, but—"

"Doctor's orders."

She released his arm and leaned heavily against the bathroom's doorframe. "Doctor or medic?"

"Right now, they're the same thing. Besides, I didn't bring any other shoes for you."

"I was wearing boots when it happened." Threatening Rose if he cut off her boots was one of the last solid memories before waking up.

"I took them off, left them behind."

An ache formed at the loss. The heels were a little thing, comparatively, but they were a defensive weapon, much like Rose carrying a gun. "You are a cruel, cruel man."

He reached in to flip the bathroom light on for her. "How do you feel?

"Like I've been shot."

"You have been shot."

The light stabbed her eyeballs. "Thanks for the reminder."

He leaned against the opposite jam. The light from the bathroom showed eyes rimmed with an exhaustion that went deeper than the dark circles.

"When's the last time you slept a full night?"

"The night before Mad Dog took his life."

PFC Madigan had killed himself because Team Echo dosed him with something and then convinced him that he'd killed his wife. The rest of the team had believed the lie, when in reality, Echo had killed Madigan's family and let him take the blame. "Call me crazy, but not sleeping doesn't sound healthy."

"We're trained to fight on very little sleep."

They'd been used and abused and spit out, and yet all the Team Fear men held on to their time in the service. "You're not in the Army anymore."

"Thanks for the reminder," he said, mirroring her earlier response, but no emotion crossed his features.

"But you're still a warrior." Only an idiot would think otherwise.

He stretched his spine along the doorjamb and grabbed the top of the trim, the move drawing attention to his height. He absolutely filled the doorway. His biceps flexed, or maybe they were always so defined. Debi swallowed. Her inappropriate libido was working overtime, but Rose was tired, she was still drugged up, so now was not the time. And wasn't that a sad state of affairs? She turned and presented him her back. "Would you untie the sling?"

"Leave it."

"I don't think you want me showering with this thing on."

"Wait on the shower for a few days."

She snorted. "Not a chance." She felt like the bottom of the bar's dumpster. "Undo the sling."

"No."

"This isn't a power struggle." Although, crud, it probably was, and right now, she didn't have any power. "The shower will help clear my head."

"You need sleep."

"I'll sleep better after a shower. Plus I'm betting you don't want me tearing things apart if I try to do it myself."

"No." If anything, his tone grew more uncompromising.

She turned to try to gauge his mood by his expression, but his hard features were unreadable. "Don't bet against me, soldier boy."

The vibration of his sigh ruffled the hair on the back of her neck. "Women," he mumbled under his breath, and then he undid the sling and removed it from around her right shoulder. "Do not use your right side until the doctor looks at it tomorrow, and keep it dry."

"That defeats the purpose of a shower." Her injured arm was against her skin rather than through the armhole. It probably was too hard to dress an unconscious woman without aggravating the injury. The yellow wash they used to clean the wound was visible through the neck of the shirt.

"I'll cover the stitches so they don't get wet." The air of resigned acceptance was in every syllable he spoke. "Take off your shirt."

She choked on her own spit, and sputtered and coughed like an empty water line.

"I've already seen you shirtless, if that's what you're worried about."

It wasn't her bare breasts so much as the reality that she looked like death warmed over. The idea of Sergeant Sexy checking out her assets while she was literally at her worst didn't go over well.

"Relax." With the one word, he left the doorway, which gave her space to breathe. She really wanted a shower and a chance to brush her teeth. His warmth hit before she heard him return. The silent moves from such a big man were hard to get used to. He lifted the back of the shirt. "I can cover it from the back." He lifted the side of the t-shirt over the wound, and taped something around the wound. "I've got pain pills if you need them."

Need was relative. "No thanks."

"You're a terrible patient."

"What can I say? I don't have experience getting shot." This was the first she'd ever needed a caregiver.

"I can give you a few pointers."

"You've been shot?" That surprised her. The soldier seemed bulletproof.

"Even the best quarterback gets sacked sometimes. All of us have had our share of injuries. First rule of wound care, listen to the medic."

Right. If and when he got shot, she'd bet good money that he went right on working. "I'll take a pill when I get out. I don't want to get woozy in the shower."

"Getting behind the pain is a bad plan. Once you get out of the shower, you'll wish you took one before."

"I'll take my chances."

"Your choice."

The acceptance gave her pause. He had the power to force her to do things his way, but he presented his side of the argument and let her make the choice because he was a good guy and not just a sexy one, which made it that much harder to keep her emotions out of it.

With an offer to help when she needed it, he stepped from the room, closing the door behind him.

Debi took the first full breath since she'd woken. The intensity he exuded dissipated once he'd gone, leaving her feeling deflated and strangely alone. Her shoulder started throbbing the instant he'd taken off the sling. Pulling the t-shirt off the rest of the way, she avoided the reflection in the mirror. The shower was quick, because he was right. It hurt like hell without the sling or a pain pill. She combed her wet hair one handed, and then stared with distaste at the clothes she'd shed. They were dirty and smelled like antiseptic.

"Debi?" Rose knocked lightly.

Her pulse spiked. The door separated them, yet his voice rumbled through the wood like an audio aphrodisiac. He was big, bad, tall, and gorgeous. He had a tattoo—and she still wanted a good look at that—his voice got her worked up, and he was the most considerate man she'd ever met. All that goodness wrapped up inside a soldier. The attraction made sense, but the slow roll of her heart had her leaning weakly against the sink. Too much. He was too much and she was too vulnerable right now.

"Clean clothes."

"Oh." Relief washed away the fear that started inside, the kind she didn't want to examine. It wasn't the panicky kind. It was more like a big freaking warning label that should be tattooed across his chest: Proceed with caution. The towel wrapped around her didn't feel thick enough to buffer against the feelings running through her. The hollow door wasn't enough to protect her from the temptation, yet she shielded behind it as she opened it a few inches to take the clothes.

"Don't try to put your arm into the shirt. Leave it off that side and I'll put on a fresh bandage.

She nodded, the movement pulling her neck muscle and stretching the stitches. "Thank you."

The one-armed thing made it hard to dress, and she had to

yank and pull with her non-dominant hand to get the sleep shorts from twisting at her waist. The shirt was three sizes too big, and had a strong, masculine scent, the kind that promised life-altering sex. After sharing a motel room for days on end, she'd recognize his scent anywhere. Dropping the shirt over her head, she left the injured arm under so she didn't have to fidget with it too much. When she finished, she stepped from the room, feeling unusually shy. She'd been alone in a motel with him for a week or more, but the wound put her on the defensive. She didn't want a man to take care of her. Yet here she was, taking his help because she didn't have a choice.

"Don't argue." Rose held out a pill the size of a quarter. "Take the medicine."

"Wasn't going to argue." Their fingers brushed as she took the pill. The burn of attraction was instant, and completely unnecessary. As long as she needed him to take care of her, she wouldn't make a move. Not until they were back on even footing. Even then, there was something about him that made anything more than friendship a gamble. Debi had walked away from Barry with everything but her pride intact. Rose had the ability to turn her inside out until there was nothing left.

He handed her the water with the straw. "Turn around. I'll put a clean bandage." The slow and economical movements he used were clinical, impersonal yet gentle as he tucked the soft cotton of the shirt between her side and her arm so she didn't flash him. He didn't rush, nor did his fingers touch anything inappropriate. She was relieved and a little disappointed. Debi focused across the room on the bed that was all but calling her name.

"I think I'll..." She nodded at the bed.

"Wait." He slid the sling over her shoulder and made a few adjustments. "You should eat."

The last thing on her mind was food. "I'm pretty sure this motel doesn't have room service."

"No, but I made you a sandwich." He gestured to the table under a weak overhead light. "We got groceries and a cooler, so we're not dependent on fast food."

She followed him to the table, feeling petite next to his massive presence, and overwhelmed by his continued generosity. It had been too long since anyone had done for her. The seat opposite—the size of doll furniture in comparison to him —groaned when he sat down to his plate of food. A thick sandwich filled with meat, cheese, and sliced tomatoes was cut into identical wedges on her plate. She couldn't remember a time when someone had cooked for her, and the simple sandwich was more than that. It was one more thing this sweet man did without being asked. "You'll make someone a good wife someday."

"I'm not getting married," he said around a bite.

"Really?" A man like him with six sisters and a caregiving soul? Oh, he'd get married as soon as some smart woman figured out how to rope him. "Why's that?"

He shrugged. "Don't plan to live that long."

A pang hit her chest more painful than the gunshot wound. "Ryder isn't convinced that this fearless thing is a death sentence."

"He's seeing things through the eyes of a husband. He wants to believe he'll be around for Lauren." Rose grabbed a chip and chewed on it thoughtfully. "I hope he's right, but I'm not banking on it."

"You don't strike me as a pessimist."

"Vegas odds are about five to one against us living to see next year."

That kind of realism hurt as bad as getting shot. "I'll take that bet. If you die, I owe you twenty bucks, but if you're around to see the ball drop New Years Eve, you pay me one hundred."

"Must be new math. Don't you mean twenty?"

"Nope. You said five to one odds."

"If I lose the bet, I won't be around to collect. Seems win-win for you."

Nothing about this was a winning situation. Water and pain pill swished in her agitated gut. "Guess you'll have to stick around."

He finished his sandwich before he spoke again. "Eat up."

She shoved the plate halfway across the table. The talk of death and dying didn't do much for her appetite. "I'm really not hungry."

"Eat half. You need something in your stomach with the pain pill I gave you."

Her stomach was pitchy, but that had more to do with the topic of conversation than the medicine. Still, she didn't argue. She put her half on a napkin. "You can have the rest."

He reached across the table as she pushed the sandwich toward him, and their hands brushed. An instant flare of feel-good nerves shot up her arm. A chemical reaction, the right compounds in the petri dish of their tiny motel room. Add time, plus the catalyst of that one brief touch. Boom. The result was combustible. Neither controlled the reaction, but neither had to act on it. Better for both if they kept that mess of hormones locked up.

She stared at the Formica tabletop and chewed her sandwich in silence. When her eyes drifted closed, she placed the last few bites on her plate. She didn't say a word as she climbed into bed, but she couldn't prevent the sense of loss eating her stomach lining. She'd never had Rose, but the thought of losing him left her empty inside. She'd find a way to cheat death and the men hunting Team Fear.

CHAPTER NINE

A lump the size of a super soldier lay prone on the bed nearest the door. Unable to sleep, Debi stared at his profile in the dark. The ache in her heart matched the constant throbbing in her shoulder. She tried to adjust the pillow, but the sling kept her arm immobile.

"Get some sleep." Rose didn't move, but he didn't drift to sleep either.

A sliver of light filtered in from the bathroom, but otherwise the room was dark. "You on guard duty or medic duty?" When he didn't answer, she punched her pillow. There was no position that was remotely comfortable. "How long have I been out?"

"No time at all." Rose cleared his throat. "It's the middle of the night, and you need rest. Take another pain pill or I'll give you a shot."

She was set to argue on principle. The injury wasn't what kept her awake. Plus, obedience wasn't her thing. Until she remembered how he'd taken care of her, and not just during the shooting. He had talked her down from the panic attack rather than do his job. Tonight was the first night he'd had a chance to sleep. She owed him, for far more than the last few days.

She opened the bottle using her good hand and swallowed a pill with the last of the water. Before he'd gone to bed, he had made sure everything was on the nightstand where she'd need it. Who was this guy? He was supposed to be a big, badass soldier, but he had an unexpected depth. He was self-less and kind and... That was the pain medicine talking.

She glanced at the other bed. He lay facing her, his jaw lined with whiskers, and his eyes closed as if his order should have been followed already.

Let him sleep.

"Fine," she whispered to herself, but when they were both back to full speed, the soldier needed to learn a lesson about women and the tragically overused word *obey*.

"What's the problem?"

Debi was startled to realize he'd opened his eyes and was staring at her. "A minute ago, I took a horse tranquilizer. I'll be fine. Get some sleep."

"Six sisters, remember? Fine has many definitions, and not one of them means everything is okay." He sat up and dropped his legs over the side showing too much bare skin. He'd stripped down to boxers again. A fine mat of hair covered legs corded like tree trunks. The ball of muscle at his calf looked stronger than all the muscles in her body combined. He scrubbed hands through his short hair, making it stand on end. "Having a hard time getting comfortable?"

He was up now and digging in. Telling him she was fine

wouldn't cut it, so she went with honesty. "I can't sleep on my back, but when I lay on my good side..."

"The injury feels unsupported?"

"Exactly." Every time she had a nap jerk on the way to sleep, her shoulder twitched, pain zipped, and she was awake again.

The dim light didn't show his features, but he stood with fluid efficiency. He brushed a hand over her temple. "No fever."

"Opposite actually. My toes are freezing."

He pulled something from his bag and shifted the blankets off her legs. The warmth was instant when he slipped oversized socks on her feet. The shivers were already fading when he pulled the sheet and comforter back over her. He grabbed both pillows from his bed. "We can prop the arm for you. Scoot back." When she complied, he dropped the pillows in front of her body, and then gently lifted her arm to rest on the pillows.

The absence of stretching pain was instant. "But I don't want to steal your pillows."

"You won't." He walked around the bed, pulled back the covers, and climbed into bed with her. The bed dipped with his weight and she started rolling back until he braced his body behind hers. "Now you won't roll back and your arm is supported. Better?"

Better was subjective. "The shoulder feels much better." But now she had a whole new reason not to sleep. She was in bed with Rose, a man she'd spent the last week fantasizing about in graphic detail, but none of it compared to the solid wall of muscle at her back. The man was seriously hot, and he was draped over her like a blanket. If she had a free hand, she'd push back the bedspread and let some cool air in.

He punched the pillow under his head into a ball. One hand slid under her neck while the other draped lightly over her waist. "This okay?"

Okay? Her heart about jumped out of her chest. The strength of his arms was nirvana. The gears in her head turned overtime, and she still couldn't process a proper response. The timing of their little snuggle fest couldn't be worse. "Perfect." She cringed. Being in his arms was perfect, but did she have to blurt it out?

He didn't move. "Go to sleep."

"Is that an order?"

He tucked himself tighter around her.

"If I could stay awake just to spite you, I would."

Rose chuckled. "Try it, sweetheart, and I'll have a shot in you faster than an undergrad on spring break."

"That's not a very evolved mentality. Aren't there laws about that?"

"Sweetheart, we've broken more laws than Bonnie and Clyde. And I'm doing it for your own good."

"Fair enough." The meds made her eyelids heavy, but there was something she needed to say first. Maybe it took the medicine to force the words out. "Thank you." The silence was as absolute as the dark. Debi cleared her throat. "I don't know a single person who could have kept a clear head after a bomb and a shooting, so thank you."

"Don't thank me." The pad of his thumb rubbed circles over her hipbone. "I'm the reason you got shot in the first place."

The loopy feeling of the drugs couldn't hide the anguish in his tone. "Team Echo is the reason I got shot."

"We're one and the same, Team Echo and Team Fear."

"Not even close." Rose and the rest of the team were good men in a bad place.

"Trust me, when it comes down to it, we are."

"You're wrong." The *whoosh* of a truck speeding down the highway interrupted the silence. As the truck disappeared into the night, she relaxed against him, the pull of the medicine undeniable. "But I do trust you, Rose." The only man she'd ever entrusted with her life. He was a good man, and without a doubt he would protect her. She took a deep breath and her back brushed his chest.

The mattress cocooned her side, and Rose enveloped the rest. The rubbing continued, oddly hypnotic and soothing, so she let her mind drift into numb oblivion. "A girl could get used to this." Cocooned and feeling no pain. "Goodnight, Rosie." As her mind fogged, she heard his faint *goodnight*, and didn't know if it was real or a dream.

———

As a soldier, Rose had slept wedged between rocks in the middle of the Afghan mountains, but curled around a soft woman kept sleep at bay. He had meant to offer comfort and a secure place to rest, which she desperately needed. He hadn't anticipated the way they fit like two mismatched puzzle pieces. Her drying hair tickled his nose. Each breath brought the smell of strawberry shampoo and woman. His head was screwed.

Debi said she trusted him. What the fuck was that? He'd

nearly gotten her killed. He never should have let her leave the motel room. The results of his piss-poor judgment could have been catastrophic. And then he'd multiplied his sins by failing to get Echo One locked down after Fowler had taken the shot. Rose couldn't think of a single mission where he'd so royally fucked up and failed to do his job.

And she trusted him. She'd wedged her sweet ass against him, tucked her toes between his legs, and drifted to sleep. He was wrapped around her, his head wrapped up in her sassy attitude that outshone her silky black hair. The pert lift of her nose was more saucy than cute, and her soft lips were most often lifted in sarcasm, her go-to response to maintain emotional distance. She was too damned smart for him. Too good. He rolled onto his back, careful to keep his body solidly against her so she couldn't roll over and hurt her healing shoulder. The soft snuffle of her breath was the lullaby that sang him to sleep.

The *snick* of the exterior door to the adjacent room brought Rose fully awake. Light shifted through the curtains. Dawn, so he'd gotten a few hours of rack time. He jumped out of bed at the same time someone tapped lightly against the door three times. "Briefing in three minutes. My room," Ryder whispered through the door.

Rose heard it and opened the door. "I don't want to leave the patient unprotected."

Ryder peered over Rose's shoulder into the dark room beyond. "I'll be quick, but your ass better be there." He moved down the hall and tapped on Craft and Fowler's door, relaying the same message in low tones not to be confused with soft. Rose dressed in the dark, careful not to wake Debi. In three minutes, they were all crowded around a crap TV set. Lauren's features were stark as she sat at the end of the bed staring at the screen.

A news show broadcast pictures of both Ryder and Lauren, wanted for questioning in regards to an explosion in an El Paso townhouse. The townhouse had been theirs until some slimeball had stolen it from Lauren in Ryder's absence and used it as a meth house until Ryder returned and put that shit to rest. Unfortunately, they hadn't done the job cleanly. There were bodies in the rubble—four men from Teach Echo and a couple drug dealers—that they'd covered with an explosion. "It was only a matter of time," he told Ryder.

"Yeah." Ryder brushed his good hand over Lauren's hair. "I wish I could have kept you out of this, baby."

She reached up, grabbed his hand, and held it between both of hers. "We're together. That's the important thing."

Rose turned to see their photos still plastered on the right half of the screen. "You think this is the police or Team Echo?"

"Either way, we're fucked." Ryder stared at the ceiling like it held the secrets of the universe. "We better hope the desk jockey that checked us into the motel last night is too busy watching porn to see the news, but we need to move. This time, Lauren and I stay out of sight. Even then, we need a long-term plan. We can't keep changing motels. Running doesn't work. We're not getting anything done."

"Where exactly do you have in mind?" Frustration made Rose's tone harsh. "Your place is in ashes and crawling with cops. My place is an eighteen-hour drive away." And no way did he want to bring this shit to his mother's door. "Craft, you got a hidey hole close by?"

"There's a safe house in El Paso, not far from base in the warehouse district. It's where I keep my equipment, but it'd be a helluva tight fit, no kitchen, and it's a risk. Echo might have found it already. Fowler?"

"Fuck, fuck, fuck." Fowler kicked a boot into the exterior door, which rattled against the frame. "You don't know what the fuck you're asking."

"Brother, we haven't asked a damn thing, but I think you have a place in mind. One that has you ready to crawl out of your skin."

Fowler ran his hands through his hair until it stood on end. "You don't know what it's like. I'm trying to keep those I care about out of this."

Rose thought about Debi sleeping in the other room. About his sisters. About Lauren sitting on the bed with wide eyes staring at the photo of herself on the screen. "I get it. We can find another way without bringing more innocents into this."

"No. Shit, this is what we built it for." He circled a tiny patch of carpet before meeting Rose's gaze. "I have a place, but we follow a strict protocol. Every vehicle gets scrubbed for bugs and trackers, as does every man or woman before we even get close. No cell phones. No GPS. Nothing electronic."

"Brother, I'm bringing my computers."

"I have equipment," Fowler insisted.

"Nothing like this. This is next-level shit. If we need to hack into government files to figure out this clusterfuck—and we all know that's where this is headed—we need equipment."

"Not until—"

"Yeah, we'll clear your screening first. I'll head back to El Paso and meet you guys—"

"No." The thought of Craft going solo made Rose's skin

crawl. Last man who took off on his own ended up dead."

"Not alone."

"Lauren and I can't risk going back to El Paso. Not with the cops and Echo on the hunt. Fowler has to take us to the safe house, so we split into two teams." Ryder's solemn eyes filled with responsibility.

"Looks like you're on babysitting duty." Rose relaxed for the first time that morning. A mission without Debi sounded like cake. He'd gotten too wrapped up in caring for her. His head was jacked, something time and distance would cure. "You can hang with the women while I go with Craft to get his supplies."

"Make a list of everything we need," Craft said. "As long as we're making a run, we need to get everything we can so we're not in the open again."

Rose moved to grab a notebook, but Lauren beat him to it and started writing. "Groceries," she said. "First priority."

"Guns, ammo, counter-surveillance, comms." Ryder pointed to the top of the list. "That's first priority."

"I've got—" A knock on the door stopped Craft's sentence. He pulled out his weapon and moved to the door.

"It's me." Debi's strained voice sounded through the door.

Craft motioned her in and resumed his list. "I've got surveillance, counter-surveillance, and comms."

Rose lifted his eyebrows. "Because?"

"These kind of toys are their own reason."

Fowler leaned his back against the closed door. "You can take guns and ammo off the list. I got it covered."

Ryder scrubbed a hand over his jaw. "We're not talking about a hunting rifle and a few rounds."

"As I said, I've got it covered. More than. Going into a gun shop requires a background check, and we don't know if any one of us would pass. Plus, it would alert anyone looking for us. Where we're going, there's plenty to go around. Trust me."

Debi sat next to Lauren on the bed. "What did I miss?"

"We're going to a safe house?" Lauren's voice wavered with uncertainty as she attempted to keep up with the briefing.

Ryder nodded at Lauren's questioning glance. "We're headed to somewhere we can set up a base camp. Craft and Rose are headed for supplies."

"What kind of supplies? Because I need my lab equipment."

"Put anything you need on the list," Rose offered.

"The supplies I need aren't available at the local supermarket."

"Where do we get it?" Because no fucking way was she going back into the open.

"You don't. I do," Debi insisted.

"Oh, hell no." The hardheaded woman was still recovering. Warning explosions went off in his gut. "The last time did not go well. You are not mission critical."

The group disintegrated into verbal chaos. Finally, Ryder whistled and the noise lowered. "Lab equipment is mission critical. Knowing what the fuck was done to us is mission critical."

"You got that right, brother." Craft's eyes sparked. "I want to destroy the fucker who did this."

"Tear him limb from limb," Fowler agreed. "The Army did this shit, but there was a person, a living, breathing responsible party. That's who I want to see hang."

Rose thought about seeing Captain Johnson on campus, but bit his tongue. The women had been too involved in the process, and Johnson was one of their own. They would take care of him or die trying.

"I want them as much as anyone." Ryder nodded in agreement with the rest of the men. "We need to test the blood from Echo and the water bottles from the night they dosed me, which means a science geek." The look he sent Debi was as close to an apology as Ryder got. "No offense."

"None taken," Debi assured him.

"If we had the fucking Army at our back, we could handle this in-house, but we don't. We can't." Ryder gave Rose a hard glance. "We need experts, so like it or not—"

"Not," Rose voted. He didn't want Debi anywhere near their mission.

"Duly noted. Debi's going with you."

"Looks like you're on babysitting duty," Fowler mocked.

Shit.

CHAPTER TEN

Rose's phone rang like a radio contest help line. Six times he ignored it. The seventh time, Debi wanted to brain him. The instant Ryder had ordered Rose to take her along, he had gone silent. Not a word the entire time. She sat on the bench seat between the two big men and she may as well have been an ornament for all they acknowledged her. They stopped at Dr. Branson's office for her follow-up and to replenish medical supplies before loading Craft's computer gear in the back. It was afternoon by the time they headed to the bar to pick up her lab equipment, supplies, and research notes. The number of books she had in storage was unimaginable. And absolutely necessary.

When the phone rang yet again, Debi gave up playing nice. "Your girlfriend is persistent."

"Not a girlfriend." Rose hit the ignore button. "Sister."

"Have you considered it might be an emergency?"

"No. Crap." He pulled the phone out of his pocket, but it had already gone to voicemail.

Debi watched as he typed a short text.

What?

One-word texts marked the end of civilization. "Which sister?"

"Camy."

"Camy is short for... Camellia?"

He nodded.

Geez, was a single syllable answer too much to ask? She turned her attention to Craft. "He has six sisters, all named after flowers." And then she realized— "Do you know Rose's first name?"

"No." Craft grinned down at her. "But it's got to be something girly with a last name like Rose."

"Flowery is what I think."

"Maybe not. Could be something like pine cone or Kentucky blue grass."

"Lotus Blossom." Debi warmed to the subject, but Rose didn't react. They tested a few radical theories without a single muscle twitch or eye roll. The man had silence down to an art.

He pointed to a building on the corner a block away. "Pull into the bank, there."

"Easy to trace," Craft warned. "Pulling money out of the bank is a time and date stamp. Location."

"Which shows where we were, not where we're going. And where we're going, we can't use cards. Cash is a necessity we'll need soon. Best to get it before we go underground."

"Roger that." Craft pulled into a parking space and rammed the gear into park. "Can I trust you with my baby while I get cash?" he asked Debi. The wink and teasing grin seemed as natural to the man as fighting.

"Your baby? Would that be the truck or your computers?"

"Yes," he answered with a sarcastic grin.

"Go on," Debi offered. "I'll guard both with my life."

"Don't even joke about it." Rose pulled his wallet out of his pocket and grabbed a red and gold ATM card. "Lock the doors. One of us will have eyes on you at all times."

"Relax, Rosebud. It's an ATM, not Fort Knox. I'm sure it's fine."

Still, he waited for her to hit the lock button before he stepped up to the machine. The phone he'd set in the drink holder slot started ringing as he slid his card in the machine. Debi looked between the phone and his massive back. Craft gave her a questioning look, but she shrugged him away. She was one itchy palm away from answering the phone when the ringing went silent. Rose was tucking money into his wallet when he came back to the truck.

"She tried again," Debi told him.

He lifted to shove his wallet into a back pocket. "She'll give up, sooner or later."

"And what if it is an emergency?"

Rose shook his head. "Unlikely. This is Camy's M.O."

Craft returned to the truck and put the gear into reverse. "Where to?"

She gave him an address.

"The bar?" Rose asked. "Not the ranch?"

Keeping the supplies and her notes at the ranch was a risk. "Not after the fire last year."

"The one that Barry set?"

"Yeah, that one." At the time, she figured he had wanted to destroy her research. "I had a lab setup in the barn. Nothing fancy, but someplace I could work in peace. I miss it." Like a runaway child. "Anyway, I moved the equipment and my records to the bar. No way is he destroying the evidence that he stole my work."

"Why didn't you show your father the proof?"

"Pride." A part of her still hurt, no matter what her brain dictated. "He didn't give me a chance. We haven't spoken face-to-face since the day he kicked me out of the program."

Craft parked on the street in front of the bar. "Sounds like a real winner."

"Yeah, my life is filled with them." Truer words had never been spoken. Rose slid out of the truck and held the door open for her. She glanced back at Craft. "You coming?"

"Staying on guard duty. Do you have much?"

The men were either very good at their job or paranoid as hell. "Couple of boxes. I'm sure Rose and I can handle it." Debi led the way into the bar without checking to see if Rose was behind her, because she felt him at her back. The hair on the back of her neck stood at attention around the solid soldier.

At the bar, Frank stood a few hairs shy of six feet and three hundred pounds. A pronounced tire lapped over his belt, but he was faster than he looked and scared the bejesus out of anyone foolish enough to start a fight. She waved as she moved past.

"Hey," he hollered at her. "Where you been?"

"Not here."

"I got that." He pushed his bulk through the narrow opening and followed her to the back. "What happened to your arm?"

"Car accident." Close enough to the truth.

"Sorry to hear it, but we got problems enough here. One of the vendors is threatening to stop deliveries if you don't catch up with the invoices and another waitress quit. With Lauren out and you a no-show for the last week, we're understaffed."

"So hire someone. That's why I pay you to manage."

"You want to add me as an authorized signer on the account, I can pay the bills. Otherwise, that's on you."

Not a chance. She wouldn't give someone free access to steal her blind. Frank was a good guy, but she'd thought the same of Barry. She glanced at Rose. "It's going to be another twenty minutes while I write some checks."

"You're not the bartender." Rose said it as a statement.

"I am the bartender." At the raised eyebrows and his dubious stare, she corrected herself. "But I'm not *just* the bartender. I own the place. And that stays between you, me, and Frank."

Rose's phone rang before he could reply.

"For the love of all things Texas, would you answer the blasted phone?"

He answered the phone with a terse "What?"

Debi shook her head and headed to her office. She could really use a cigarette right now.

––––––––

Camy bit the tip off her thumbnail. Her brother was currently chewing her ass, which was his default mode with any of the sisters.

"What do you mean you're in El Paso?"

That was complicated. She glanced at the boy on the computer who typed faster than most people could think. He moved his hand in a tight circle. *Keep him talking.* "You weren't answering phone calls. The letters we sent came back undeliverable, so Mom and the rest of the girls elected me to come find you."

"Find me? Stay the hell away. And why aren't you in school?"

That was a subject for another day. Preferably never. "I need to see you." She even added a little please at the end.

"I'm getting ready to leave on a deployment." The stress in his high-pitched voice was off the charts. Not an emotion she recognized in her brother.

"If you're leaving on a deployment, why do the people on base say you're discharged?"

"You went to base?" He mumbled what might have been curses into the phone. "Stay put, you hear me? Do. Not. Move. I'll call you back in ten minutes."

He clicked off without warning.

Camy glanced at the boy on the laptop. A wicked grin lifted his normally serious features. He straightened his glasses. "Got him."

———

Rose walked into Debi's office like a charging bull. "Time's up."

She jumped to her feet. "What's wrong?"

"My dumbass sister followed me to El Paso. Anything besides those boxes that you need loaded?"

She clicked the laptop closed. "My computer—"

"Not happening. You heard Fowler. No electronics in or out. Leave your cell phone, your laptop. You can pay bills online. We'll find a secure computer." He bent down to hoist the large box she'd had Frank pull from storage. "Let's go."

The rush inherent in his attitude stole her breath. "You go. Load these. I'll come out with the last box."

"Do not lift anything," he ordered.

Once he was out the door, she forced a deep breath. Focused on the way his voice had sounded when he'd talked her down from the panic attack last time. Deep inhale. Count. Exhale. Her hand shook as she grabbed the USB drive with all her financial records. The anticipation of something bad happening was nearly as frightening as something bad actually happening, but when Rose came back for the last box, she was ready to go. They stopped at the bar where Frank was pouring one of the regulars another beer.

"Hey, Frank," she called, but he didn't hear her above the country music. She walked around the bar with Rose on her heels. "Hey, Frank," she repeated.

This time, he and the customer both looked up.

"Hey," Wade said. "If it isn't my favorite bartender. Looks like you're on the injured reserve list."

Debi ignored the affable drunk who flirted with any female within a ten-yard radius, but Wade tried to intercept. Practiced at avoidance, she skirted a bar table and ended on the other side closer to the bar manager.

Wade shoved into Rose, because he was either inebriated or had a death wish. Rose waved him off like an annoying insect.

Wade pushed back. "Watch where you're going, asshole."

Fabulous. Picking a fight with a man the size of a Humvee was about as stupid as you could get. How much had the rancher had to drink? One more thing to mention to Frank, because the cowboy was getting more territorial over the bar and its inhabitants than was strictly healthy. She moved closer so she didn't have to yell over the music. "Frank, I'll be gone for awhile. If you need anything, send an email."

She leaned closer to talk to him about the problem customer when Wade slammed into Rose, knocking the box and its contents clattering to the ground. "That better not be my microscope."

Rose crossed his arms over his chest, a move that spoke volumes about how much he'd like to pound Wade into the ground, but he held back. The anger that was an ever-present side effect remained banked, but for how long was anyone's guess. Another reason to leave quickly.

Debi leaned over to check the contents of the box. Notebooks spilled onto the floor, and she had to dig to see what else was damaged. A few broken petri dishes. Jerk.

Wade crowded closer, and when she ignored his presence, he reached down and rubbed his palm over her ass. She didn't have time to react.

"That's it." Rose's voice sounded more resigned than angry.

Debi glanced up to see Rose clock Wade. One hit and the cowboy dropped.

"What the hell? You can't hit one of my customers." Although—and she'd deny it until she died—she was happy to see Wade lying prone. He had groped and offended every waitress who ever worked for her.

"No man has a right to touch a woman without permission. Period." An angry red flush climbed Rose's face. "Now move. Get your ass in the truck."

"River Rose, is that any way to speak to a woman?" A petite blonde stepped closer to the bar. She looked like an elf with hair in a cute pixie cut and silver hoop earrings dangling from her ears.

"Camellia." The horror in his voice was matched by the slack-jawed horror on his face. "I told you to stay put."

"If you were looking for obedience you should have called Lily." She marched forward with a beauty pageant smile and offered her hand to Debi. "Hi, I'm Camy."

Debi introduced herself, reached out and shook the other woman's hands, a little dumbfounded by the ball of energy that seemed to light up the bar around her. "Did you just call him River?"

"What else would I call him?"

Indeed. "The list is long, but I'm partial to Rosie."

"Sure, that's a natural." Camy sat down on a bar stool and faced Frank, who had been mesmerized from the moment Camy walked in. "Can I get a draft?"

Debi and Ryder spoke at the same time.

"Are you even old enough?"

"We're not staying."

Camy folded the square napkin Frank had already placed in front of her. She nodded her head toward Wade. "What's with the dead guy?"

"He's not dead." At least Debi hoped not, and he was going to be mad as hell when he woke up. Maybe he'd find another hangout. "Your brother clocked him."

"Act first and ask questions later." Camy took a long drink of the beer Frank placed in front of her. "Sounds like River, although he's usually too controlled to deck someone. That implies an emotional connection."

Rose moved the beer away. "Get your ass back in your car and go home. To college. Wherever the hell you're supposed to be right now."

"Definitely not college. I quit last semester."

"You did what?" Rose roared, but he turned to the door when a shadow moved.

A man stepped into the room carrying a chip on his shoulder. As tall as Rose but not as wide, the man blocked the sunlight from the entry way, and the energy flowing off him promised he was as deadly as any of the men from Team Fear. Rose had his gun out before Debi could blink. The men stared at each other for a long minute. Debi focused on her breath. Her bar was not the site for the next mass shooting.

Camy pulled her draft closer and sucked it back. With a last gulp, she slammed the empty onto the bar. She had obviously excelled at drinking in school, which was probably why she hadn't finished.

Frank reached for the phone, but Debi placed a hand over his. Whatever trouble this new guy represented, she didn't want the police called. Rose could handle it, as long as he asked questions first.

Camy spun on the barstool until she noticed the man in the entry. "Oh, hey, Dean."

"You know this guy?" Debi asked.

"Sure. We picked him up hitchhiking outside of Ames, Iowa."

"Stills, you lousy mother—" Rose swallowed the curse and moved in like he wanted to deck the new guy. "You stalked my sister?"

"You weren't answering your phone. I figured she'd find a way to reach you, and when she headed to Texas, I knew she'd reach you before I did."

"We're radio silent. And for the record, you told us to fuck off, so we don't owe you a damn thing."

"Changed my mind, but we've got bigger issues right now."

Debi eased closer. Maybe she wanted to eavesdrop. Maybe she needed to plant herself between two adversaries. The men knew each other, but that didn't mean Rose wouldn't strike, and she couldn't afford another fight in the bar. Frank was one wrong move from calling the cops, and they would have to explain Wade and this other guy. Assuming Rose hit him, which looked likely by the bunched fists and glare. Stills, as Rose called him, leaned back with his hands on his hips like he had nothing better to do than pick a fight with a man the size of a tank. The flush on Rose's face suggested he'd be happy to give him one.

Debi slid between the two men. "Gentlemen, let's discuss this somewhere more private."

Rose bodily lifted her—careful not to touch her injury—and moved her behind him. "Do not walk into the middle of a fight. You own a bar. You should know better."

Camy stepped up and smacked Rose on the arm. "Mama raised you better than that. You don't order a woman around like—"

"I'm ordering you, Camellia Marie Rose, to get in your car and head back to Iowa before I put your skinny ass on a bus."

Stills whistled a high-pitched note until they all turned to him. "Fight later, move now. Your sister picked up a tail when she started asking questions."

Rose straightened and turned back to Stills. Everything about his demeanor changed. His lips drew into a deep frown and his body seemed to grow, the muscles bulging through his shirt. "How many?"

CHAPTER ELEVEN

"Two-man surveillance team. Camy was dropped by a friend, so no car. The tail stayed with the girl not the car. Good thing for you, my ride is out back. So if we can delay the bickering, I highly recommend we move out."

Rose dialed his phone while he herded Debi and Camy away from the doors. "Echo is here. Bug out. We've got a ride. Rendezvous at the set point when you're sure you got away clean."

Debi veered toward the bar. "My box." Before Rose could argue, she tossed the contents back inside. "Lab equipment is mission essential, remember."

Rose brushed her aside and lifted it one handed while keeping the gun in his dominant hand.

"Bye, Frank. Sorry about the trash," Debi said as she stepped over the cowboy. Debi led them through a dark hall to a back door.

Stills pulled a shotgun from his coat and chambered a round with a solid *ker-clunk*.

"Damn thing should have been chambered," Rose said. Time mattered, and the difference between having a round chambered or not made a difference.

"I was in the car with your sister. Didn't think I'd need it."

"Wait, what? You had the shotgun in the car?" Camy yanked her arm from Rose's grip. "Not cool, dude."

"That's why you don't pickup hitchhikers." Rose took point and stepped from the door. No movement. No shadows. The alley was clear except for a beater that looked older than dirt. Peeling green paint and rust. "Tell me this piece of shit isn't yours."

Stills cleared the car before opening the door to let Camy and Debi slide in the back. "Had to acquire it rather quickly from someone who wouldn't report it stolen."

"Drug dealer?"

"Don't ask, don't tell."

Rose dropped the box in the deep trunk. "I don't like it. Only two doors means it's hard to get the women out in an emergency."

"Not going to be a problem, because we're not going to get caught."

"He's cranky because his truck is totaled," Debi said.

"Not totaled." Rose took a seat in the front and slammed the heavy metal door closed.

"May not be beautiful, but she's fast. Guaranteed."

Right. Stills had a way of exaggerating things, but he was damn good at acquisitions. At least there was plenty of legroom. Actually, the bucket seats were new and wrapped around him like a favored recliner. The dash gleamed and the carpet still had vacuum marks. Smelled perfumed, but other than that, it seemed like a decent ride.

Stills started the engine on a roar as loud as a jet taking off. The chrome gear shifted into drive and eased down the alley like a red carpet unfurled beneath the tires.

In the back, the women bonded over Camy's shoes. Her presence was pretty much his worst nightmare. So far, Echo hadn't gone after extended families, but Rose wasn't taking any chances. He had friends watching over his sisters, and he stayed the hell away. After what happened with Maggie Madigan, Rose couldn't bear to be around his family. If Echo knew about Camy, they'd exploit it. Hurt her to get to him.

They made it a block without a tail, but had to stop at a red light. Before the light turned green, a tall, thin man on a street corner raced toward them. "That's my car, motherfucker—"

Stills ran the light, turned right from the left lane, the tires squealing over the man's swearing. The car was in fifth gear and on the highway in record time. "Told you. A getaway car has to be fast."

A chuckle came out of nowhere as the tension eased. "Stills, you dumbass, you stole that car from less than two blocks away."

"Didn't have much time." Stills grinned. "I improvised."

"Improvise, adapt, overcome. That's the Marines, idiot."

"I was a marine before I joined Team Fear."

"No shit. How did I not know that?"

"Because you walk around in a cone of silence."

Debi leaned between the bucket seats. "You got that right. I'm Debi, by the way. Thanks for the assist."

"My pleasure. Camy didn't tell me Rose had a woman."

They both answered. "Oh, I'm not..."

"We're not together."

"Right." Stills let the word hang, but neither picked it up to fill the silence. Finally, he shrugged. "Someone want to tell me what we're running from?"

"Boredom," Camy answered with a bright smile.

Debi shook her head. "My past."

Rose frowned. Neither woman belonged in Team Fear's problems, but Echo knew about Debi's ranch and her bar. No way could he leave her without Echo using her. Now Camy was in the same position. He wanted her the hell away from the fire that was about to rain down, but sending her home would lead Echo right back to the rest of his sisters. "Camy, call Mom. Tell her you found me. I'm leaving on a deployment and you're heading back to school."

"You want me to lie?"

"Did you tell her you quit college?"

"No."

"So you already lied. Pick up the phone and dial before we have to toss it." Where they were going, there were no phones. The cone of silence was a very real thing. It was the only way to protect the team and separate them from those they loved. Anyone close to them was a target. While Camy sweet-talked their mother via telephone, Rose gave Stills the lowdown. "The plan was for you to join Santiago's team once you pulled your head out of your ass."

"By the time I surfaced—"

"Where were you?"

"Me, a southern sweetie with a bottle of Jack, and an open playing field, given the fact that I was the only sober male able and willing to satisfy. When your bat signal came I was sitting down to..." He glanced back in the rearview mirror to make sure the women were occupied. "Two fine-looking females. By the time I surfaced, Santiago and team were so far underground I couldn't get a scent. Sticking close to El Paso was a mistake," Stills added. "If your teenage sister could find you—"

"First of all," Camy interjected. "Not a teenager. Second, what I did wasn't easy. I had an alarm setup for his ATM card, so when he used it, it flagged me and I was able to move closer. When he finally answered my call, all I needed was enough time to triangulate his position."

Rose twisted to eye his sister. "Where did you learn to trace calls?"

She crossed her arms over her chest.

"Doesn't matter," Stills said when she didn't answer. "Echo has access to that much and more."

"That was a risk we were willing to take. We need cash, and we're not coming back to El Paso, at least not until we have enough information to track down these assholes."

"Where we headed?"

"Fowler won't tell us, yet. In case..."

"In case Echo caught up with you."

"Exactly. We're meeting at a set point." He glanced at his watch. "In an hour." He pulled up a map on his cell phone. "Think you can get us here in an hour?"

"No problem." Stills took the next exit at the speed of a race car driver. "Hang on."

———

They pulled into a dusty ranch as the sun dropped off the horizon. A rusted sign over the long, winding driveway read Mesquite Manor. Manor was a fancy name for big ass house on the prairie. The surrounding desert had burned away all but a few hardy patches of prairie grass and mesquite lined up on the ridge behind the house. The only thing blowing in the breeze was a row of wind turbines that gave off a high-pitched whine as they drove past.

Fowler waved them to the drive in front of the house to offload supplies. "Keep the computer stuff in the truck. Everything else goes in."

Rose glanced in the back seat where Debi was sacked out and leaning on Camy's shoulder. They'd had a hell of a day, and he'd forgotten to stay on top of the pain meds. Sleep was probably the best thing for her. He pushed the seat forward and reached back to lift her from the car. The slight weight of her didn't slow down his climb up the grand steps to the wide front door. When she was awake it was easy to forget how delicate she was, because her personality made her seem sturdier, but she was breakable and in a situation way over her pay grade.

Camy watched the careful way he carried Debi, and a mischievous look passed over her elven features.

"Not a word," he warned her.

Debi moaned when he shouldered through the front door. With a gasp, she started, jerking away from Rose. "It's fine," he assured her. "We're here."

"Where's here?" she croaked. She struggled until he set her on her own two feet.

Together the three looked around what looked like a large waiting room, the kind you expected in a large mountain lodge not on a derelict spit of land in Texas. Tables and chairs were in groupings on one side while the other had a smattering of mismatched sofas and chairs. A giant fireplace sat in the center, the chimney climbing into the ceiling above. The space was large enough to seat forty or fifty people comfortably.

A woman with a long, dark braid down her back stepped from a doorway in the back. "We thought you'd never get here." She stepped forward. "I'm Janet Fowler. Jake's mom."

No wonder Fowler hadn't wanted to bring them here. They were raining their shitstorm down on his mom. "Ma'am. Appreciate you helping us out."

"That's why we're here, but we can talk about that in the morning. Right now, let's get you settled in your rooms."

"If it's all the same, ma'am, I'd like to keep the patient on the bottom floor."

"I can climb stairs, Rosebud."

"You're the medic?" Janet asked.

"Yes, ma'am."

"You're not what I expected, but then, Jake is hush-hush about his military time. As it happens, Jake warned me about Debi, right?"

She nodded, but for once kept her mouth closed. The pain level had to be high to keep her normally chatty self in check.

"I have rooms setup down here for you. Although Jake didn't warn me we had another female."

Camy grinned. "I'm a stowaway."

"I can't wait to hear that story. These guys don't seem all that open to surprises."

"Oh, well, I'm also River's sister, so he couldn't dump me on the highway."

"No matter how much I wanted," he added. Any minute

now, Debi would latch onto that name and harass him. The potential conflict built up in his mind. He looked forward to sparring with her. A little too much.

"You two follow me." Janet pointed to Debi and Rose before she headed through the kitchen and down a narrow hall. "These rooms once belonged to the on-call doctor and nurse. You'll find they're bigger than most. The nearest exit is down this hall another twenty feet. Both windows are barred, but the release button is to the right of the frame."

Debi ran a hand over the empty walls, the wallpaper yellowed with age.

The first door creaked as Janet opened it and motioned them inside. "Debi, I thought this one for you. The pink would hardly do for a man like Sergeant Rose."

"His ego is pretty solid. I think he could pull off the pink."

"This bed is bigger," Janet added.

"Sold." Debi sat and bounced on the end of the king-sized bed. "Now, what is this place?"

"Mesquite Manor was a home for the criminally insane in the 1920s and 1930s."

"We're sleeping in an insane asylum?"

"Oh, don't worry. The staff slept in these two rooms, so you should be ghost free. The rest of your friends are in patient rooms, however..." Janet shivered. "Follow me, Sergeant Rose."

"Just Rose."

Janet didn't even pause for a breath. "There's a bathroom between the rooms for you to share." She led him to the room next door, this one closer to the exit.

The room was plain with a simple bed, brown bedding, a chair, and a desk. A fireplace stood against the wall to the bathroom, and next to it a closet. The window looked out on a hidden grove of trees behind the house. The release for the bars over the window looked new, as did the windows.

Rose tested the release latch and saw the bars swivel free like shutters caught in the breeze. "I get what this used to be, but out here in the wilderness isn't the place for bars on the windows. So tell me, what is this place now?"

"Your home for the foreseeable future. Jake will show you around while the girls and I eat."

"Did someone say food?" Debi leaned against the open door frame. "I could eat a horse. Or a ghost horse." She laughed at her own joke. "Seriously."

"Dinner's ready and waiting. Lauren wouldn't eat without you. I thought we girls could eat and get to know each other."

"As long as there's food." She glanced over her shoulder at Rose. "You eating with the girls?"

"Oh, I think the boys are headed out to the barn," Janet answered. "I'll keep the stew warming for you."

"Thank you, ma'am." When they reached the kitchen, Rose pulled Debi aside. He pulled a prescription bottle from his pocket and handed her a pill. "Take one of these with dinner."

She shook him off. "I'm fine."

"I see the way you're holding your arm. And you'll delay the healing if you get behind the pain."

"Yo, Rose," Fowler hollered from the other room. "Let's roll."

Rose held the pill out on the palm of his hand. "Take it."

She took it and shoved it in a pocket. "Have fun in the barn, Rosebud. Sounds like some sort of weird initiation to me."

"So long as we get some answers." The place oozed creepy

serial killer. It wasn't the ghosts or potential for ghosts that got to him. He couldn't figure out what kind of country inn, or whatever the hell this place was now, needed bars on the windows. Rose and Fowler walked around the house to a big weathered gray barn. He didn't see the vehicles anywhere. "What is this place?"

"I'll brief everyone at once," Fowler answered. They stepped through a small door to the side of the big-assed barn doors. The lock had a keypad. "375842. Don't get it wrong."

Rose filed the number away for future reference. "All the keypads the same?"

"What kind of idiot do you think I am?" Fowler asked.

"Fair enough. Every door have a keypad?"

"Most." They strolled through the door and into an alternate universe. The missing vehicles were parked in what was the biggest garage Rose had seen in the private sector. In the back, stairs led to an office with big windows looking down on the cars. Doors led off to either side. Their boots echoed on the polished cement as they walked up the stairs to the office where the rest of the team worked in silence.

One wall was lined with electronics. Monitors and displays straight out of NASA mission control. Craft supervised the unpacking of boxes while he setup computers along a long low run of countertop designed for that purpose.

Rose gave a long, low whistle. "This is a serious investment." The computers and electronic toys were on the high end of too-damned-much. He walked the length as if inspecting the troops. "You spent your signing bonus on toys, didn't you?"

Craft rubbed his hands together in unfettered glee. He jabbed a thumb in his chest. "Only child. My parents are retired and living in Boca. Of course I spent it on me. Fowler spent his on this place. Ryder used his to buy the townhouse for Lauren."

Most of that was lost to fraud. A group of unethical men— a banker, a realtor, and a lawyer—had illegally foreclosed on the townhouse. Anything Ryder had left was spent on the Team Fear investigation, because none of them were truly free until they eliminated the threat against them and their families.

Craft pulled out a monitor and set it up on the nearest vertical space. "What did you spend your signing bonus on?"

Rose ignored the question as he turned a circle at the end of the control room. The other wall was covered with surveillance equipment. A large screen split into eight divisions that looked like surveillance videos spread across the property. Fowler hit a button on a control panel. The top screen shot showed the front gate clatter closed.

"What the fuck is this place?"

"The command post. Come on back." Fowler led the way to a briefing room complete with enlarged computer display, white board, and other electronic gadgets. They took chairs around a central table that would have made the Joint Chiefs proud.

Ryder sat, turned to the side, and put his boots up on the adjacent seat. "Nice setup. Want to tell us why you have it?"

"Ten years ago, my granddad left this place to my mother," Fowler started.

"Because he was a ghost hunter?" Craft teased.

"No. Big Jake liked to be prepared." Fowler paused for emphasis.

Didn't take mental calculus to solve that equation.

"You're a fucking prepper, aren't you?" Craft exclaimed.

CHAPTER TWELVE

"As in doomsday" Debi leaned on her good elbow and stared at Janet. This petite woman had prim hair shot through with silver and ran a survivalist training camp for doomsday preppers. "How do you even start something like that?"

Camy and Lauren added their voices to Debi's question. The three women wanted to know where they'd been transported. And wondered if it was a good move.

"Family business. I was a single mom, so when Jake came along, we stayed here and helped out. When Big Jake passed, I took over, but we ran into financial troubles. Big Jake had big plans, you should see the command post, but he wasn't much of a businessman. Little Jake joined the teams to help pay off some debt and modernize."

"He's been training his whole life. That's why he's such a good shot." Debi pushed her dinner bowl away. The stew had been amazing, and now she was stuffed to the gills. It was the first home cooked meal they had had since the chaos began.

"How do you know he's a good shot?" Janet stacked their bowls and set them in the farm sink.

"I'd say he's more of an expert shot," Debi answered. Once she'd had time to think about it, what Fowler had done, what all the men did was exceptional. "Fowler positioned himself at the top of a bluff. He shot the driver of a moving vehicle traveling sixty miles an hour."

"The boy does his granddad proud." Janet smiled and patted Debi's hand. "But I think that's enough for one night. You look beat."

Camy stood, her eyes glittering with excitement. "I'm not the least bit tired. This place is beyond, just beyond anything."

"Then you can stay and help me with dishes before I show you to your room. There's no cable, no cell service, no Wi-Fi."

"No worries. Fowler already confiscated my phone."

"Jake would see to it, I'm sure. Don't take it personally. Anyone wanting to train at The Manor has to leave all electronics before they pull through the front gate."

"No kidding. That little wand he has do a bug check is like something out of science fiction." They had parked out in the middle of nowhere in a pullout off the main highway. Fowler had checked for bugs and trackers on every person, every piece of luggage, and every vehicle before he'd led the way to The Manor. "God help the poor sap with a metal plate in his head."

"We take OPSEC serious around here." Janet stacked the dishes on the table. "There is a wall of books in the great room that should help occupy your mind when you're not on duty. Take the night to get acclimated. Lauren, can you help Debi get settled?"

Lauren held out a hand to pry Debi out of her chair. "Got it. Thanks for dinner, Janet."

"My pleasure. Really. We don't get many females around here, at least not civilians."

Lauren grabbed Debi by the hand and led her down the hall. When they reached Debi's room, Lauren turned and locked the door. "Do you get the feeling we're not going to be civilians for much longer?"

"God, yes. As much as I like the idea of defending myself, I'm not sure if this is a good thing or a bad thing."

"Ryder's all for it. He had me training in self-defense before any of this went down. After the problems with Echo, he wants me to know how to rope a dirtbag from fifty yards and then truss him up like a calf at the rodeo."

"Don't put me down for that." Debi's whole body ached. "Where did they put my lab equipment?"

"Janet said something about the basement. We can look in the morning. Right now, you need a long bath and a nightcap."

"How about a quick shower and a pain pill."

"I think we can arrange that." Lauren searched through bags the men had delivered earlier. "No pajamas. That's what happens when men pack for you. Sweats?"

"Grab the gray shirt on the top."

"An Army of One?" Lauren pulled a giant shirt from the bag. "You wearing Rose's t-shirt to bed? Or are you wearing Rose to bed?"

"Just the shirt. The large size makes it easier to get on and off with the sling." The warm flush on her cheeks promised she was blushing, and Debi didn't like it one bit. She nodded at Lauren's hand. "I see you got your wedding ring back."

"I did. Thanks for telling Ryder where to find it." Lauren dropped the shirt to hold her left hand to the light. Lauren had removed the ring when Ryder disappeared to protect her from the fallout from the fearlessness experiments, but his absence hadn't kept Lauren free from harm. Echo had ultimately used Lauren as bait to try to trap Ryder, who had nearly snapped when they had dosed him with more of the experimental drug. Now that they'd survived, Ryder and Lauren were stronger than ever and needed the ring and everything it symbolized. That was the secret Debi had told Ryder before they'd knocked her out. Lauren's ring had been in a jewelry box at the ranch. Lauren rubbed the glistening gemstone. "Is it stupid that my heart about beat out of my chest when he put it back on?"

"Not stupid at all. You guys have earned all the happiness you can get."

Lauren twisted the ring around her finger. "He worries."

"About?"

"Nothing. Everything. He worries that Echo will find us, or that he'll have a psychotic break and kill me. You know, typical married stuff."

The laughter jarred Debi's stitches. "Nothing normal about our situation."

"I'm sorry I pulled you into this."

"About that..." Debi wanted to tell Lauren the truth, but settled on a partial truth that was a long time coming. She cleared her throat. "I have a confession. You know how a new owner bought the bar awhile back?" When Lauren nodded, Debi continued. "Well, the new owner was my father."

"The world's biggest academic snob owns the bar?"

"No, he bought it for me." Debi swallowed. "It was a guilt offering after he kicked me out of the program and banned me from the research labs."

"What, he's trying to buy your affections?" Lauren's voice

rose at the insult. "That dirty son of a carpetbagger. Why didn't you tell him to shove it?"

The instant outrage warmed something cold inside. "I knew you'd see it my way. And I didn't say anything because I was hurt and offended. The little weasel didn't even have the decency to offer it to me in person. He sent a lawyer. I didn't want a part of it, refused to do more than make deposits and pay bills until Ryder left and you were hurting for money." She'd wanted to help her best friend without it seeming like a handout.

"You're the reason all of us waitresses had to wear skimpy outfits?"

As lies went, this was big. "Your tips went up, though, right?"

The deep bruise on Lauren's cheekbone flexed with a frown. "You are so not forgiven."

"I know." Debi stood and headed toward the bathroom. "I didn't know what to do. Thanks to Barry and darling Dad, I will never work in a lab again." She flipped on the bathroom light and was treated to a ghastly reflection of herself in the medicine cabinet mirror. She glanced away. The pain of her father's disloyalty hadn't eased with time. "He didn't believe me. Part of me wanted to tell him to shove his guilt offering up his tight ass, but the other part figured he owed me for ruining my career."

"Both reactions were right." Lauren gave her a one-sided hug to avoid the injury. "So I guess now that you've spilled your guts I have to forgive you for keeping something this big from me."

"Sorry." Debi tilted her head to the side and put on her most innocent expression. "It's not you, it's me?"

"Please. Don't use that tired excuse." Lauren helped Debi remove the sling and get ready for the shower. "Need anything?"

Her toiletries were waiting for her in the shower. "I don't think so. Give me a few minutes and I'll holler when I'm ready."

Lauren stood at the door with a fierce expression, a look made tougher by the fading bruises on her face. "For what it's worth, your biological is an asshole, and he was wrong. He should have listened. Taking Barry's side over his daughter's word was a dick move."

Tears stung, but Debi battled them back. "Thanks for being my friend."

"Well, it's a hardship, what with you being so ugly and mean."

Debi choked out a laugh. "We don't have to hug it out or anything, do we, because I'm half-naked here?"

"Nah, save the half-naked hugging for the owner of the king-sized t-shirt."

"We're not—"

"Keep telling yourself that." Lauren slammed the door closed on a laugh.

———

"I always knew shit was hitting the fan." Fowler stood at the head of the table, one hand in a pocket and the other holding a stale cup of coffee. "I joined Team Fear for the signing bonus. Used the money to upgrade what Big Jake had already started. I'm not going down easy."

Rose leaned back in his seat. This place was a lot to take in.

"For a safe house, this place is stellar, but we can't bring our shit to your door."

Fowler nodded. "Appreciate it, man, but I gave Janet the choice. She wants us here. What's more, it's the best place to set up shop. The Manor is completely off the grid. The power comes from the wind turbines. The name on the title of the land is a dummy corporation, so there's no tracking it that way. Janet doesn't even have a social security card."

"Internet?" Craft asked.

"IP address traces to Singapore. If you do any high-level snooping, you need to run it deep. This place is mostly off the grid and I'd like to keep it that way. All the satellites see when they pass is a torn-up barn and a condemned building. That's what we want them to see. We have regular survivalist groups who do their annual training here, but we rescheduled everything for the next few months. Winter is slow anyway. Things keep going into the summer, we're going to have to reevaluate."

"Cops ever come out this way?" Ryder asked. He and Lauren were on the wanted list, so having the cops snooping would be hell.

"If they do, they're looking for people or product coming in from Mexico. For the most part, we're the forgotten out here."

Ryder leaned forward, all deep focus. "You said survivalists train out here, so how are you setup for training?"

"Shooting range is two stories beneath our feet. There's a tunnel from the main house to the range, so after today, no outside walks where you can be seen and/or identified. The armory is down there, away from the main house in case of an accidental explosion, although there's a gun safe on the house side of the tunnels, just in case. PT and hand-to-hand training rooms are in the basement under the house."

"Brother, you spent your entire fucking signing bonus outfitting this place." Craft looked around with a new set of eyes.

"The bonus and every paycheck before and after. I was raised to believe in Armageddon, but I never figured to be a weapon for the other side. The fearless thing seemed like a good idea when I signed. Imagine a rebel armed with a military-grade armory and no fear."

Rose had listened to the briefing in silence, but all he heard was how to defend their position on this plot of land. Rose wasn't looking for another Alamo. He wanted answers. "Since you weren't planning for medical experimentation, I don't suppose you have a lab?"

Fowler shook his head. "We have a clinic, downstairs in the former nuthouse. And don't use that phrase around Janet. She's a mite attached to the ghosts."

Rose let that one pass. "You got a place Debi can set up a lab? She brought equipment, we still have the water bottles to test and Echo's blood."

"She can set up in the clinic waiting room. Not sure what else to call it. It's creepy as fuck down there, but all stainless steel, even some outside ventilation if she wants to get cosmic."

"How about we start with whatever the fuck they shot into our veins." Rose's temper bloomed out of nowhere, out of one long-assed day that bled into the next. "Because as fan-fucking-tastic as this place seems, I'm not hearing anything about how to get out of this situation. They come looking and we can defend. Great. For how long before they bring in aircraft and turn this place into a motherfucking crater?"

Ryder braced an elbow on the table and gripped his forehead with two fingers like he was rubbing out the mother of all headaches. He was still bruised and cut up from his last altercation with Echo. His dominant hand was cut to shreds. "I hear you. This isn't about World War III. Lauren's here. Other civilians." He nodded at Fowler. "You got an exit plan for your mom and the women?"

Craft shook his head. "Brother, they hear you talk like that, they'll have your balls."

"If I can't protect my woman, I don't have any in the first place. So what you got, Fowler?"

"The place is riddled with tunnels. Some end up absolutely nowhere. You ask me, the staff were as imbalanced as the patients here. We can study the schematics. Make sure the women know the exit strategy. There are two crappy vehicles waiting on the other end, but the engines will outrun anything outside of a race car. Janet knows the plan. She can train the other women."

"It doesn't suck." Rose stood, went to the white board, and grabbed a marker. He started to write notes as the spoke. "First priority, exit strategy." He marked that with a giant checkmark. "What's next, boss?"

Ryder grabbed a pen and notebook from the center of the table. "Two-pronged approach. First, we need to know what they did to us, if it's reversible, and if we're as unstable as they want us to believe."

"Second." Craft walked to the mini-fridge and pulled out water bottles, rolled them down the table for the rest of the men. "Who are we dealing with? We need a file on every surviving member of Team Echo, but they're not working alone. They've got someone inside the Department of Defense. Who funded the research? Who were the assholes poking and prodding us before they cut us loose? And where the fuck is Captain Johnson? Because I don't have a clue as to his level of involvement. Whoever is involved, we're talking high-level black ops shit, and they'd rather bury us than own up to the program."

Stills sat quietly at the end of the table while they discussed strategy for the next hour or more, watching the interaction in silence, but he leaned forward as Rose finished writing notes on the white board. "You boys have bigger problems than you think. When I crawled out of my very pleasant distraction, I tried to look you up, but no dice. Called on a buddy who was on Team Delta, and he's dealing with his own shit. These other teams, they're not all good guys. The ones that are clean are dying off faster than an epidemic. Car accidents, drunk drivers, and a heart attack in a healthy thirty-one-year-old soldier."

"You know, we always assumed that Lauren's accident was caused by the guys who kidnapped her."

"Good point, Rose." A muscle ticked in Ryder's jaw. "But it could have been Echo, given everything we know now. Were they trying to draw me back to the local area or kill her outright?"

"Four of them were in the bar that night. They might have taken it as an opportunity and assumed you were in the truck with Lauren."

"Fuck." Ryder threw his empty water bottle at the wall where it crashed into the waiting trashcan.

"Three points," Stills joked.

The room went silent with the implications. Ryder nailed Stills with a glare that would shrivel the balls of a lesser man. "Stills, not that long ago, you told us to fuck off. You wanted to go your own way. There's no fence to straddle here. You're either in or you're out."

"I humped it down to Texas as fast as I could, which ought to tell you where my loyalty lies." Stills leaned forward, his eyes narrowed and tight. "But given the fact that these fuckers killed one of my best friends and they'd like to do the same to me? I'm in."

Ryder tapped a pen against the pad, the only sound in the room besides the soft whirr of the ventilation system. "We're on lockdown here until we have a solid plan to take these assholes out for good. Rose, you take point on the scientific aspect. Figure out who and what and how of this designer drug. Craft, you're on the intelligence gathering. Use your magic fingers to dig into some classified files. Who, what, when, why, where, and how, but especially who. Who funded the program? And if you come across any medical or scientific research, hand it off to Rose and Debi."

"I'm not sitting on my ass out here in BFE," Stills said when he didn't get an assignment. "Give me something to do or I walk."

"Stills, you have a contact on Delta, so start there. What's the deal with the other teams? Who is involved? Are there any potential allies out there? Anyone with more information we could use? I want dossiers, locations, pictures. Strengths and weaknesses."

"You want to know if they're naughty or nice?" Stills asked, his stern features belying the joke.

"I want to know more than Santa Claus."

Fowler stood at the opposite end of the table, legs braced apart. "I'll take point on security. I know the layout and can keep us off the grid."

Ryder nodded agreement. "I'll coordinate big picture, reassign personnel as needed, pull in the women for anything that doesn't require loss of life or limb. And if any of you fuckers tells Lauren I'm giving her light duty, I'll slit your throat in your sleep."

Craft chuckled. "It's good to be back."

Craft was right. They'd all gone separate ways after the Army had discharged them—medically unfit—and they hadn't accomplished anything on their own but getting two good men killed. They might be in a world of hurt, but they weren't alone. They were a team. Rose finished writing out duty details and tossed the marker to the table. "Live by the team, fight by the team."

"Hooah," the rest agreed.

"Now let's grab some chow and get a solid night's sleep." Fowler led the way out of the room, shutting off lights as he went. "I'll show you the main tunnel back to the house. We've got perimeter guards that roam the property every night. There are alerts in place if anyone crosses the gate, touches the fencing, or comes within fifty yards of The Manor or the barn. Electronics alert in the command post, my room, and Janet's. We'll know if anyone comes at us tonight. Not that I expect anything."

"Too soon," Ryder agreed. "But don't get complacent."

"Speaking of complacent." Rose gestured to the dirty bandage covering Ryder's palm. "Now that we're settled, you need to clean that up. Stop by and I'll make sure it's clean and put on new bandages."

"There's a clinic in the basement of the main house," Fowler offered. "I'll show you when we get to the other side of the tunnel.

The tunnel was one of those horror movie deals with painted concrete walls and a light every ten feet that flickered. Craft raced ahead, jumped up to *clang* one of the hanging lights so it swung back and forth on rusty, creaky hinges. "Asshole," Rose muttered. Last thing he needed was the thought of this damn tunnel when he was sleeping in a haunted freaking hotel for the criminally insane.

The tunnel ended in the former root cellar. Fowler pointed the opposite direction. "Clinic's down that way. If you come down here on your own, keep to the central hallway until you've studied the blue prints."

A short set of steps led to the back pantry of the kitchen. They dished up stew and buttermilk biscuits and sat down for chow like they'd never left the team. Rose scarfed down a bowl before he realized how much time they'd spent on the other side of the compound. He glanced at his watch to make sure the clock was right. Debi was long past due for another pain pill. "Shit." He scraped back from the table, put his bowl in the dishwasher, and headed out.

Craft intercepted him at the doorway. "Where are you going?"

Hell, he knew that look. Craft was digging in, ready to screw with him. "My room. Move."

Craft's forehead wrinkled as he thought long and hard. "Isn't there someone else's room down that way?"

"Yes, dumbass, I'm going to check the patient before I hit the rack."

"Patient? You mean Debi?" Craft looked around Rose to

the audience still sitting at the long farm table. "Do you suppose he thinks that calling her *the patient* makes her less hot?"

"I think they're playing doctor," Stills suggested from the safety of the kitchen.

"Laugh it up, dickhead."

Craft shrugged and moved to the side. "I was just seeing what was what. Because if you're not interested, that bartender is one fine—"

"Shut it." Rose body checked him into the nearest wall. "One more word, and we're taking it to the mat."

"My bad." Craft raised his hands in surrender. "Rose has called dibs."

"Can't call dibs on a person." Ryder took a sip of sweet tea. "At least that's what Lauren tells me."

"Amateur. You can't tell a woman you called dibs. Defeats the purpose. Take me for instance, if I called dibs on Camy..."

Rose crossed his arms over his chest. He didn't need to threaten. There were rules. Sisters were off limits. Period.

"Why you gotta be like that?" Craft asked.

"Didn't say a word."

"Exactly. The eyebrow thing and the arms. A threat was implied."

"Bet your ass."

Craft frowned at Rose's response. "O-kay. Different example. Take Rose here. If he called dibs in front of *the patient*." Craft added the emphasis to the word and waggled his eyebrows. "She would have him by the balls."

"Fuck off." Rose stormed down the hallway to the sounds of the team laughing it up at his expense. He let it roll off, because he had bigger problems to worry about. Craft was right. Rose was a walking hard-on around the bartender, but he damn well knew better than getting involved right now. Anyone close to him was a target. His future was not bright, and Debi was a non-combatant. Still, one look at her and his dick stood at the position of attention. The woman had him by the short hairs. God help him when she figured it out.

CHAPTER THIRTEEN

D ebi zoned out in the dark, not quite awake, not asleep. The giant divot in the center of the bed said some big dude had slept there, leaving a superhero-sized imprint large enough to swallow her whole. She rolled downhill every time she was almost asleep, pulling the stitches and yanking her awake.

A sliver of light under the door widened as Rose peeked into the room. "Why aren't you asleep?"

Debi blinked against the glare. As her eyes adjusted, she pushed off on her good side to sit up, then scooted back to lean on the pine log headboard. "Lauren and I are planning an all-nighter. Booze, friends, a couple strippers."

"Why is every answer sarcastic with you?" He stepped inside and closed the door, leaving them with only the sliver under the door for light.

"Sarcasm works for me." The inability to see his face brought out something unexpected. Honesty. Maybe it was the pain pills. "Because the truth is often hard, and most people are looking for an easy answer. Sarcasm lets them laugh and move on without getting involved."

"Your father?"

Well, wasn't he a perceptive one? "No. Every drunk who ever walked into my bar."

"Your old man a drunk?"

"I have no idea." She'd never seen him outside of the university. Never been to his house. There was no fake family Christmas. They didn't even share a last name. "Sarcasm is my native tongue and the world has given me a plethora of material. Hate to waste it."

"You're not as tough as you want to believe." His voice sounded nearer, but the deep darkness made it impossible to see the outline of his large frame.

Her heart beat against her chest, which was still bruised from the panic attack. Every breath hurt. "I'm not as weak as you think."

"I don't think you're weak." The bed dipped under his weight.

"No?" Her voice came out breathy. She lifted her knees to rest the sling against. "I do. Think I'm weak." Damn, the truth spilled from her mouth like coins from a slot machine. She'd sought out her father, because she hadn't been enough on her own. She'd wanted, needed maybe, her father's approval. And that ship had sailed. The panic attacks that had haunted her youth had only gotten worse around her father, and in the end, the attacks were one more reason he despised her. Her screwed-up parentage was a Freudian wet dream.

"You're not weak."

The tone flat warned her not to argue, but the darkness pulled the truth from the depths of her soul. "I'd have done anything to win his love." To her, that was the definition of weakness.

Rose ran a finger along her good arm causing a shiver to run through her body. "It should have been the other way around. He should have moved mountains for you."

The knot in her throat was too large to speak around. A single tear dripped down, but she didn't swipe it away, because it would mean losing Rose's gentle touch. She could smell him now, masculine and sexy. She'd never been closer to another human soul, or more certain that she didn't deserve it. A dozen sarcastic comments crawled up her throat to push him away, but she swallowed them along with the lump that never truly left.

She twined her fingers through his and held on, because she needed his warmth, his touch. She needed him. They stayed that way, holding hands across the big bed, until a nap jerk twitched her body and yanked their hands apart.

"You should get some sleep," he said, his voice rough with sleep.

Her body said yes, while her mind said hell no. She couldn't be alone with her thoughts right now. "Rose, will you sleep with me?"

Crickets.

"Oh, God, I didn't mean..." She smacked a hand on her forehead. At some point she wanted the soldier in her bed for something more than sleep, but tonight she simply needed company. "I mean—"

"I know what you mean." The box springs squeaked when he stood. "I'll make you a deal. Take another pain pill, and I'll stay and keep the pressure off your injury."

"Another pain pill. Afraid I'm going to take advantage of you?"

"Don't fall back on sarcasm."

But it was the one thing she was really good at. "Look, the last pill made me the most morose human being on the planet. Another one might turn on the waterworks." And the last thing she wanted was to cry all over Rose. She wasn't a pretty crier.

"Tears aren't a weakness. Take the deal."

The image of him standing over her, bulging arms crossed over his massive chest was born out by his shadow at the end of the bed. "Fine, but if I cry on you, you've got no one to blame but yourself."

"I've got six sisters. Tears stopped scaring me years ago."

"Oh." That made sense. He'd probably seen some ugly tears, too. She reached out a hand toward him, a risky move since she could have touched any body part, but finally found his hand. "I'll take it if you stay."

The rattle of pills forecasted his movements before he handed her a pill and a bottle of water. She swallowed it while his clothes hit the hardwood floor. The sound was quite possibly the sexiest thing since a striptease. He settled into the center of the bed and eased her next to him. Quick moves had one pillow rolled under her sore arm to take the weight off. One of his arms curved under her head while the other cinched around her waist drawing her close to his tight body. The musculature against her back was the stuff of dreams and she was too sore to take advantage of it. The universe had a cruel sense of humor.

She wiggled to get her body into place, her legs brushing

against the cotton of his boxers. "Are you wearing the green and blue paisley?" She licked her lips. "Those are my favorite."

"Go to sleep."

"If you insist." She didn't need the pill. His body wrapped around hers and her eyes blinked closed. "Rose?"

"Hmm?" His breath fluttered in her hair, raising goose bumps.

"Thank you." It helped hearing the words from a man. Her father should have moved mountains to win her love and affection. A fist unknotted in her chest as she drifted to sleep. She wasn't as strong as she wanted to be—yet—but she wasn't defective either. There was still time to fix her mistakes.

———

The basement hallway stretched like an abandoned subway station with benches set into alcoves. Rose didn't want to think about who had sat on those benches and what they'd waited for. Thick beige subway tiles covered the walls and floors, and the same drab hanging lights from the tunnels flickered every ten feet. Narrow archways turned off at random intervals, rabbit holes Fowler had warned, so Rose kept going forward, his footsteps echoing in the cavernous basement. The hall turned off to the right and landed without ceremony in an open room the size of the upstairs great room. On the far side were closed doors leading to a hospital clinic. The cool air stuck to Rose's skin, reminding him of a morgue.

Debi yanked supplies from a box on a counter under three windows cut into stone at ceiling height.

"You should have waited for me," he said, stepping into the room.

Petri dishes clattered to stainless steel. The crash echoed like waves through the interior space. "Crap." Debi leaned heavily on the counter. "You scared me."

He moved closer to help her place everything in order. "I can't imagine why."

She lifted her head to peer around the room. "I'm convinced Fowler hates me. Of all the places to put me..." She pointed across the room, deeper into the dark. "Can you believe this place?" A portable hospital bed was parked against the far wall, tucked neatly into place and left to gather dust. Restraints dangled against rusty legs. "I'm a scientist. I don't believe in ghosts or spirits or energies, but this place flat unnerves me."

"Seen any ghosts yet?"

"Honey, if I see ghosts, Echo won't have to find me, because I'll have a coronary on the spot." She turned back to the box and grabbed out something with her good hand.

"Here, let me." He slid the box closer and started pulling out parcels and envelopes and wrapped supplies. "I'd have carried this down for you. Helped you set up."

"Oh, I didn't want to wake you. You were sound asleep when I woke at the crack of dawn."

Not asleep. He'd needed time to get his head on straight and convince his body that the soft woman in his arms wasn't meant for his morning pleasure. The six hours wrapped around her made up both the longest and shortest night of his life. Debi had fallen asleep instantly and he hadn't wanted to wake her, which was a damn lie. He'd wanted to keep her up all night, and not by holding her hand. The silky strands of her hair had wrapped around his arm, filling his head with the smell of strawberry shampoo. Add the curve of her fine ass against his skin and he'd been sunk. Desire was a cruel bitch. He wasn't a monk, and after so many nights of sharing the same motel room, knowing the little hum she made as she drifted, knowing she woke when the sun peeked through the curtains. All of it added up to temptation incarnate. None of which he could tell her, so he grabbed a microscope from the box and set it on the counter. He had no idea what equipment like that cost, but it was a good bet they wouldn't find a replacement out here.

Debi pushed the microscope several feet down the counter. "Anyway, I didn't carry it down. Craft hauled for me and helped me set up."

Craft. Asshole. Rose just bet Craft was helpful. A surge of anger flooded his veins at the mention of Craft. Rose wanted to deck him for no good reason other than what the other man had said about Debi the night before. Yes, she was hot, and no way in hell was Craft good enough for her. Neither was Rose. "Where did he run off to?"

"Training. Apparently there's a schedule."

"There always is. PT first thing in the morning." He spiked his fingers through his hair, still damp from the post-workout shower. "Puzzles the rest of the day."

"Will there be croquet later?"

"This isn't summer camp. The sooner we solve the mystery of Team Echo, the sooner you get your life back." He hoped for her sake, for all the women, that they could solve the problem, but the idea of Debi leaving put a hurt on his chest. "Dr. Branson called earlier. He wants me to take a look at your stitches and see if you're ready to start moving the shoulder more."

"Does that mean I'm joining the ranks of PT in the morning and hand-to-hand in the afternoon?"

"Not yet, but if there's no seepage and no sign of infection, you can start physical therapy today. The clinic is down here. We should take a look."

"That's a very disgusting image you put in my head. Seepage. I think we can skip the wound check." Disgust turned her frown into a grimace.

"No. We can't. Into the clinic, Debi."

She set the petri dishes near the microscope and a tower of bins. It was the second time she'd stacked and unstacked them. "The light's good if I work during the day, but we're going to need better task lighting at a minimum."

He recognized avoidance when he saw it. He set a hand at her elbow and slowly turned her toward the clinic. "We can probably make the lights happen. I'll talk to Fowler. But for now, let's go into my office and look at the stitches."

"I'd rather learn hand-to-hand. One handed." She dragged her feet as they neared the back.

"Come on." He led the way to the closed doors that supposedly housed the clinic. "If you're good I'll give you a Hello Kitty sticker when we're finished."

She stopped dead at the door. "I'm holding out for two Hello Kitty stickers and one My Little Pony."

"Sure, but I'm all out of stickers. How about a rain check? I'm good for it."

"I charge interest."

"How much?"

The edges of her lips curved into a smirk. "Depends on how bad this hurts."

The reply spilled from his lips without talking to his brain first. "If it hurts, I'm doing it wrong."

Surprise widened her eyes before mischief glinted there. "Then I guess we'll have to see if you deliver."

"Oh, I'll deliver." Shit, what the hell was wrong with him? She was a patient. He opened the door and ushered her in front of him.

She stopped cold in the doorway. "Well, this is unexpected."

Rose eased in behind her. The room looked like an actual clinic, complete with examination table, supplies, and a locked medicine cabinet. Debi opened the opposite door and it linked to an identical room. Beyond that was another exam room with a portable x-ray machine. "Shit, he really has been preparing for Armageddon."

"Do you think he has a doctor on staff?"

"Wouldn't surprise me. My bet is Dr. Branson. Explains why he was willing to help and keep things off the books." Rose led her back to the first room and patted the paper covering the table. "Hop up. Let's take a look."

She climbed up using the little stool, putting her eye-to-eye with Rose. The velvety brown of her doe eyes gazed with longing at the back door and the rooms beyond. "Fowler really does hate me. Putting me out in a dim, creepy space with torture devices—"

"There's only one torture device."

"That you saw. I'm out there in the dust and dirt, with or without torture devices, and he's got all this antiseptic, well-lit space in here. I have room envy."

"We can move you into one of these rooms if you want. If

we need three exam rooms, there won't be enough of us left to fight anyway."

"You're mighty cheerful, Rosebud."

"Reality." He shifted the shirt off her shoulder and tried to ignore the pleasure at seeing her in another of his t-shirts. The worn fabric sported the U.S. Army emblem front and center, right between her full breasts. Not that he noticed. And he also shouldn't notice the way her long neck stretched out like a dancer's, not nearly as tempting as the long legs which parted slightly on the exam table. Damnit.

Right now he was her medic. He peeled back the bandages to look at the damages. The skin was cool to the touch with no sign of infection. He'd seen worse. The skin around the wound was soft. Female. The muscles in his hands twitched involuntarily. Not for the first time, he wished he'd been the one to end the shooter.

He stepped closer to get a good look. With an absent gesture, he moved the light closer to make sure none of the sutures had pulled. The doctor had done better than Rose expected from a country doctor. There was a pattern to the stitches that reminded Rose of the work done by surgeons during the Iraq war. He'd have to look it up.

Debi cleared her throat. "Hey, Rose?"

"Hmm?"

"If you're done staring at my chest, can I get dressed?"

"I'm not." He yanked his hands back like she was a hot skillet. His head smacked the light with a loud *ping* that had him biting back a curse. "I wasn't."

A sexy chuckle escaped her lips. "You're easy to tease. I like it. Teasing you."

He focused on the white gauze and the tape, because

everything out of her mouth was starting to sound like an innuendo. And it worked him up. He had to step back so his growing erection didn't touch her as he finished applying clean bandages. Maybe it was the brush of her hair over his arm or the smell of strawberries. His hands nearly shook as he finished. "The doctor did a good job."

"So I'm cleared for duty?" She wrinkled her nose as she shrugged her shoulder and righted the shirt. The reaction showed she still had pain, but that was inevitable.

"No duty. You're cleared for physical therapy. I'll run you through exercises later today." He pulled together all the soiled cotton and tossed it in the red bin attached to the wall. They really had thought of everything. "All done."

"Good." With the speed of an explosion, she lashed out and wrapped her legs around his waist, pulling him close. Eye to eye, their breath mingled. "I have a confession."

"Hmm." Hell, he'd lost his voice. Maybe his capacity for thought. They were headed where his body had wanted her since the day they met. Blood surged to his groin, leaving his brain defenseless. "What's that?"

She rubbed a finger across his lower lip. "Do I make you nervous?"

She threw off his equilibrium, but he could work with that since he was trained to adapt to new and dangerous situations. He licked his lips, letting his tongue brush the finger she still pressed against him. "I can handle you."

"Oh, sweetheart, I doubt it."

"That's my line." A part of him doubted he knew the first thing about handling Debi. She had him spun up tight and she wasn't even operating at top capacity. God help them both when she was back at full speed.

The erotic brush of her fingers skimmed his jawline. "Remember that first morning when you made me coffee with Irish crème?"

"Hard to forget." Team Echo had just handed him his ass. One of their members attacked from behind, so quietly, so unexpectedly, that he'd be dead if Echo were armed. Afterward, they'd regrouped in Debi's kitchen. She'd dropped her coffee, shattering the glass and her nerves. The start of a panic attack he hadn't recognized. "You were afraid."

"I'm not afraid now. Since that morning, I've been wanting to do this." Her lips trailed her fingers, moving like a whisper across his. The soft tease skimmed the surface of his desire.

"Not enough," he muttered around the edge of the kiss. Not nearly enough. Fingers wrapped around the base of her skull, he maneuvered her where he wanted her. Head tilted to the side, he dove deep. The moan at the back of her throat encouraged him to lose himself in the taste of her. Temptation whispered at the edge of the kiss, pulling him deeper, into more than a first kiss. Deeper. Tongues tangled, teeth nipped, and the pull traveled straight to his groin.

The loss of fear meant the normal filters that kept him from going too far and too fast were obliterated by the soft curves of the woman he wanted to own. He stepped forward into the vee of her legs. His hands wandered her body, memorizing the swell of her chest, the indention at her waist, the delicious flare of her hips. The woman was built for his hands.

Those long legs he admired wrapped around his hips and yanked him closer to home. His lips controlled hers. His hands roamed her, lifting to brush her... bandage.

Guilt like ice washed over him, drowning the need. He stepped back before he took her right there on the exam table.

Quick breaths lifted her chest. Keeping her eyes locked on his, moving slow to draw attention to the moves, she unlatched her feet, scooted to the edge of the table, and dropped to the tiled floor. The move brought her so close he nearly wore her as a second skin. "That was the interest payment. I still expect my Hello Kitty stickers."

CHAPTER FOURTEEN

"Are you sure it was Captain Johnson?" Ryder stood at the far end of the room, his legs braced apart. He had one hand around a mug of coffee and the other tucked into his pocket in true military briefing style. The discussion was overdue, but with all the chaos raining down plus Debi's injury, they hadn't had a chance.

"Hell if I know." Rose prowled the command post. "Looked like him. Our eyes met for a fraction of a second and then he was gone."

"I can't imagine a student losing you. Even in a crowd." Fowler hopped up to sit on the counter near the surveillance monitors.

Stills dropped into a swivel chair. "Unless you've lost your touch."

"Could be a student. Prior military." Craft was parked at the computers like his ass was cemented to the chair. "I can tap into the campus security cameras. See what I see."

"That's a good place to start, but that kind of surveillance is slow. If Johnson thinks you identified him, he won't be easy to find." Ryder sipped his coffee. "Hard to believe it's a coincidence."

"Unfuckingbelievable, actually," Rose said. He'd had time to think while monitoring Debi's recovery. "If Johnson is on campus, there's a damn good reason. There has to be a link to the company or the military. Johnson went underground the second the Army released us, and he shows up on campus. Why?" Rose's brain worked faster than his mouth, so he jumped from one subject to the next, trying to get his teammates to help connect the dots. "We assumed that Echo traced Ryder to campus through Lauren, but what if that's where they originated. What if that's where *we* originated?"

"That's a huge leap," Fowler said.

"Think about it. Why El Paso? There are no Special Forces teams. We didn't fit into the mission or command structure—"

"That could have been reason enough, to keep us off the military grid," Fowler said.

"You'd believe anything with a conspiracy in it," Stills said to Fowler. "What Rose is talking about is a giant fucking conspiracy."

"Doesn't make me wrong. Why recruit us and move us away from all our military connections? Why go where they had to build a special training facility when the Army had that elsewhere?"

"Because El Paso is where the quacks are?" Crafts offered.

"Exactly." Rose stabbed a finger in his direction. "The campus has a world-class research lab with plenty of funding. Anyone want to bet that some of their research is funded by grants from the U.S. government?"

Stills leaned back in the office chair. "Grants mean a paper trail. Even if they don't detail the experiments or the drug protocol, there has to be a way to track the budget expenditures."

"Budgets and grants have contact names. It's a place to start." Craft tapped out several lines on his computer keyboard, the sound angry in the now silent room. "I want to destroy the people who set this shit into motion. The company—whoever the fuck that is—started an experimental government program and bailed on us when things went south."

"We were expendable. Still are," Ryder said. "We signed on the dotted line and drank the Kool-Aid."

Anger welled up, filling Rose's soul like a blood blister that burned and grew with each new revelation. He'd signed, true enough, because he had needed money for his sisters' education. Fearlessness was the bonus that finally lifted the mantle of responsibility that had settled on his shoulders at thirteen. No more worries over the girls. He'd been able to handle them with logic and not fear over an unknown future, but there was a cost. To save his family, he had to leave them. The reality burned. "I want the quacks to fry for what they did. They played God because they could, without comprehending the cost in human terms."

"Hooah," Craft agreed.

Debi stepped through the doorway, her face pale. "Sorry to interrupt. Rose, you said to get you for physical therapy, but you all sound busy. It can wait."

"No, we're done," Ryder said. "Craft, find Captain Johnson. Stills, you track the money."

"I want in," Rose said. "I want to destroy the doctors." They were the true monsters.

Ryder nodded his understanding. "Work with Debi on the science. We'll meet again in the morning."

Rose reached for Debi and led her from the room. "Come on, sweetheart."

———

Rose braced his legs apart and faced Debi. After the kiss, he'd given them both space, avoiding the basement until it was time for her physical therapy. The room was outfitted like a small gym. Treadmills lined one wall and weights on the other. The mats in the center could be used for hand-to-hand, but right now, he used them for her daily torture. She pulled back on a resistance band until her lips twisted in pain. Mobility on the right was limited. "This is too soon," she mumbled. "Way too soon."

"The injury damaged the rotator cuff. Movement is key to maintaining mobility. It'll hurt, but Doc said you should start physical therapy."

"That's not the way I remember it. I believe he said I *could* start therapy, not that I had to."

"If you want to regain one hundred percent mobility, you start now."

"Who says I want that?" She puffed a breath through tight lips. "I'll get one of those nifty grabber thingies to reach the top shelf."

"Those grabby thingies are made for retirees. You'll thank me one day."

"Don't hold your breath."

The anguish on her face churned in his gut. He got no pleasure from the workout, but if she were one of his troops, he'd tell her to suck it up. "One more set and we'll switch to weights."

"Why does that not sound easier?" She counted to eight between gritted teeth. "Ahhh, that burns."

Rose twisted to get the weights so he didn't have to watch. He grabbed two cans of soup he was using as improvised dumbbells. "Swap these for the resistance band."

She shrugged her shoulders before grabbing the cans. "I knew at some point you'd revert to type and ask me to cook for you."

There was the sarcasm. The smile lifting his lips caught him off guard. Demonstrating the movement he wanted her to make, he answered her unspoken question. "The other weights are too much for starter exercises."

"Doesn't feel like starter exercises." Her left arm went up like a spring while she tilted her body to try to use momentum to swing the right up. She finished the first set, her face red with the effort. "This is cruel and unusual punishment."

He glanced at the clock on the far side of the room and gave her two minutes between sets. "Did you make progress in the lab?" He should feel guilty for avoiding her. His job right now was to work on the drug angle.

"Some. Tested the cup given to Lauren and me. Started work on the water bottles. It's tedious work."

"Figure out what they gave you?"

White teeth bit into her bottom lip. "GHB."

"The date rape drug?"

"Yes." A hiss whispered between her gritted teeth. "It's a good thing we shared the tea, or they could have easily over-dosed Lauren."

"Didn't you notice anything?" Shit, he didn't want to sound

like he was blaming. They'd all been taken surprise by Team Echo.

"The first tea tasted off, but it was an herbal tea blend, so we didn't think anything of it. The second tea tasted fine. GHB is colorless and odorless for the most part, and can come in a liquid." Tension drained from her shoulders as she talked about the science. "I don't know if we were knocked out or we lost the memory of them moving us. I remember throwing up in the parking lot, and the next thing I remember is waking up in Lauren's guest bedroom with two dead bodies."

"Fuck." Rose didn't want to ask. None of them had considered what had been done to the women when they'd been in Echo's hands. "Did they..."

"I don't think so..." Her eyes squeezed closed. "I'll have to ask Lauren first. Alone. I can't spring it on her in front of everyone in case...but I don't think so."

"Oh, sweetheart, I'm sorry." He brushed a wisp of black hair from her face. "How are you holding up?"

She leaned into his hand. "This happened days ago, feels like weeks considering all we've been through. I'm fine."

Probably not fine. The female heart was a tricky beast, one he'd navigated with six sisters, but Debi had never had anyone to help her. "Do you want to go talk to, uh, Lauren or Janet or someone?"

"There weren't any signs. I have to assume they used the drug to overpower us, not..." She rubbed a knuckle against the corner of her eye. "I'm fine."

"That word doesn't cut it with me. You know that."

She shrugged away from his touch. "Let's finish this." The right arm shook as she lifted straight up and down with the can of soup in her hand. Muscles worked in her jaw and cheek as she ground out the movement, determined to finish therapy, maybe get the crap out of her head for a minute.

"Seven more. Lift as high as you can."

She did three and paused with her hands hanging. "You're an ass at training."

"Thank you. Four more."

Without a word, she pushed through the final set. When she finished, she let the cans hang down and stretch the muscles.

"Nice work, sweetheart." He took the Campbell's soup cans from her and set them on the mat. It had to hurt, no way around it, but she'd done every exercise he led her through without complaint. Her arm trembled, though, and he'd worked it hard. He patted the nearest weight bench. "Take a seat."

She frowned like she wanted to argue, but sat instead.

"Too tired to fight, sweetheart?" When she lifted her nose instead of answering, Rose walked around the edge of her seat and rested his hands lightly on her shoulders. "Relax." Using light strokes at first, he massaged the muscles at the top of her shoulders to ease the stress the training had caused. She needed to work the muscles, but she needed to recover as well. "Ice them when you get upstairs." He worked his way to her bony shoulder without interruption, but when he hit the wounded side, she flinched.

"Watch it," she warned.

"I'm not going near the stitches, but I want to work the muscles to avoid undue pain." The last thing he wanted was to hurt her. The skin closest to the wound was warm, probably from the exertion. "Feel better?"

A muscle twitched under his fingers, and after a moment,

she closed her eyes and leaned back into his touch. "Too soon to tell. You should keep at it."

He chuckled. She needed the comfort of touch. Maybe they both did. The thought of what Echo could have done, the power they'd had, twisted something deep in his psyche. He had six sisters. Statistically, that put at least one of his sisters at risk, which meant he'd had to work hard to keep them protected. Trained. Educated.

They'd suffered from their father's abandonment, but damned if Rose was going to give some lowlife the chance to use daddy issues against his sisters. He made sure they knew their worth. Debi hadn't had anyone to look out for her, so she'd ended up with some asshole who burned down her barn and stole her research. The father had failed to give her a solid sense of her value, which set her up for a bad cycle. Rose itched for five minutes alone with her old man to beat the ever loving shit out of him.

"Ouch." She jerked away from him. "Too hard."

"Sorry." Thoughts of her old man had made his moves too rough. He closed off those thoughts—for now—and concentrated on working the tension from her tender flesh. When the muscles relaxed under his touch, he eased down the front of her arms away from the wound. At the elbow, he switched to the backside of the forearm to follow the single thick tendon that ran from elbow to wrist.

She gave a soft moan, more pleasure than pain. Both arms hung limp from her shoulders like they were weightless. No matter what she said or didn't say, the massage helped ease the pain. And it was the least damn thing he could do, considering.

The bones in her wrist were fragile, dainty in a way he'd never noticed before, and her skin was intoxicating enough to tempt a reformed alcoholic. He switched to the other arm, circling his thumb up the long muscle. At her bicep, her arm twitched like he hit a nerve, but he kept on until she jerked away. Her eyes popped open.

The underside of her bicep was ticklish. The temptation was too great. "Problem?"

"Nope." She twisted her lips into a frown.

Rose rubbed the knot on the front of her arm before softening his touch at the underside of her arm, smoothing feather light touches to her tickle spot.

She jumped this time, and his fingers brushed her chest before she slid out from under his arms and stood. When he persisted, tickling along the underside of her arm, a laugh bubbled up.

"Ticklish?"

She twisted to frown at him. "Did you do that on purpose?"

Of course he had. She needed the laughter and he'd needed to hear it. "Feel better now?"

She reached as if to cross her arms over her chest, and then winced when it pulled her injury.

"Here, let's get you strapped back in." He snagged the sling and eased it around the outer edge of her elbow. And it was too damned close to her chest. Her breath hitched as he moved, drawing his eye right where he shouldn't want it, on either side of the Army emblem.

"That's probably good enough." Debi turned so he could loop the sling around her neck. She lifted her hair out of her way with her good hand, exposing her neck. For the first time, he noticed the long slender line, as delicate as her wrist. He rubbed a knuckle down her spine from her nape to the edge of the shirt. Her breath hitched, but she didn't step away.

The silk of her skin drew his touch. He bent low to drop a kiss to the tender skin under her hairline. His nose nuzzled her neck, drowning in her scent. The breath strangled in his lungs. The chemistry between them had been instant, from the moment he tucked her curvy body into his and dove for cover when Echo had tried to infiltrate her ranch house. He'd wanted his hands on her, but he wasn't in the position to act on those desires. They were at war, and she was injured. His hand stilled. He stepped back, physically and mentally.

A groan loaded with frustration climbed her throat. "Rose, the thing with Echo that could have happened, but *didn't*," she emphasized, "doesn't change a thing. The attraction is mutual."

Over her shoulder, he could see her chest rise and fall with each shallow breath, and the sight left him speechless.

"I'm not sorry about what just happened," she continued. "I'm not sorry about the kiss in the lab. We're going to have to deal with it. I'm betting on soon." Without looking back, she made her exit to his silence. The clock ticked off the seconds, and then minutes, since her departure, and still Rose didn't move. The chemistry was like the weather outside. Undeniable. Unchangeable. He wouldn't even if he could, because it was the first thing in months that made him feel alive. He welcomed it like a lost limb at the same time as he caged it.

No one had watched out for Debi, so he'd do what others had failed to do. He'd protect her, from himself most of all.

———

Debi walked in on the most laughter she'd heard since a Saturday night at the bar. Camy's howls turned a snort, which sent her into another spasm of giggles. The counter held her as she leaned over and attempted to stifle a serious case of the giggles.

Stills had his hands in a sink of suds, but when he saw Debi, he pulled both hands up in a sign of surrender. Suds dripped down his corded arms. "I didn't touch her."

"It's not me you have to worry about."

The words sent Camy into another raucous round until she finally dropped onto the floor. "Oh my God, you have to tell her. Dean tells the best stories." She swiped moisture from her eyes. "About River."

The mind boggled. Why Rose had a problem with his first name was still a mystery.

Stills shook his head. "No way in hell am I repeating that story." He rinsed off a large pot and set it to dry on the counter. "Dinner's in five minutes. Debi, do you mind letting everyone know?"

"I don't mind if you tell me where everyone is."

"Oh, they all trooped up to their rooms about a half hour ago."

"That's great. Where are their rooms?"

Stills dried his hands on a nearby towel. "That's right." His grin grew. "You're down here. With River Rose."

"Not *with him*, with him. In the same hall." Oh, yeah, now that she heard his name in Still's teasing voice, she totally got why Rose didn't want his buddies knowing. "I'll figure it out." Debi didn't have a clue where the staircase was hiding, but didn't want to stick around and explain her relationship with Rose, because obviously there was no relationship, and after she spooked him earlier today...

"I'll come with you," Camy said. She reached a hand out. "Help me up."

Debi reached out with her free arm to give Camy a boost, and then followed her down a narrow hall to a set of stairs. Rose's little sister had the same blonde hair, cut into a pixie style that showed off high cheekbones and a delicate nose. "Those are some pretty fabulous genes you Rose kids share."

"How's that?"

"You know, blonde hair, blue eyes." Gorgeous.

"Not so great when you grow up in a small town. Every year, my new teacher said the same thing on the first day of class. Look at you. Spitting image of your sisters. You've gotta be a Rose girl."

Debi climbed, but damn the narrow set of stairs were long. "Doesn't seem like such a bad legacy."

"That's because you haven't met my sisters. Not a rule breaker in the bunch."

"I'd bet good money that you're a troublemaker."

Camy turned, her face in a radiant smile. "Thanks. Nicest thing you could say." She pounded on several doors and kept walking. "Dinner," she hollered. She pounded on a few more before they came out at the top of a staircase leading down to the main room. "Are you sleeping with my brother?"

Holy cow, the girl moved fast. Debi stepped to the left side of the stairs and held the rail on the way down. "Um, no."

"Why not?"

Wow. "Um..." Debi stumbled her way down the rest of the stairs and came to a rest at the bottom. It usually took more than a vivacious twenty-something to make her stutter. Finally, she pointed to her sling. "I got shot. That's why."

"Oh, well, good reason. Hold up. Let me show you something." She slipped an arm around Debi's and pulled her next to the fireplace that stood in the center of the room. "We're about to get a dinner show."

Craft was the first to hit the stairs, his normally light brown hair wet and tousled, looking like a runway model on steroids. The breadth of his chest nearly matched Rose, who had him beat in height and width. He jogged down the stairs before he caught a glimpse. "You two coming?"

"In a minute." Camy smiled and waved like a pageant contestant. "Girl talk."

He skipped out like he'd rather clean toilets than sit around and listen to girl talk. "Get's them every time," Camy said. "So, are you planning to make a move on my brother?"

Debi's head spun. Maybe she'd entered an alternate universe where sweet-natured Camy was about to go all Rambo on her ass. "Would that bother you?"

"Not at all. Hold on." She touched a hand to Debi's shoulder. "Here comes contestant number two."

Fowler took the stairs two at a time, showing his familiarity with his surroundings and his outstanding physical conditioning. A dinner show indeed. The way his arms moved brought attention to his biceps. Drool worthy. He took one look at Debi and Camy and swiped a nervous hand over the tips of his spiked hair. He took the quickest path to the kitchen.

"Talk about gifted genes." Camy fanned her face. "Where in the name of God's earth did the Army find these men? Because men built like this do not exist in the real world."

"I see your point." Debi had an idea about that, but she'd wait until they were all together. "Was Rose always so... built?"

"Mostly." Camy frowned as if trying to recall. "I mean, he was always so much older, he seemed like a giant. Sure, his suit coat keeps getting wider, but he's still the same. I mean, he worked on the farm until he joined the Army, so his body had to keep up with the chores."

That was one way to think of it, but she'd love to see proof. "You don't happen to have any older pictures of him, would you?"

"Like blackmail pictures." The hint of sibling rivalry showed on her delicate features. "I'll check my phone... Oh, crap, Fowler confiscated it, but I'll see what I can dig up. Wait, here comes contestant number three."

Ryder preceded Lauren down the stairs, holding her hand in his bandaged one. Even without his leather jacket, he looked like a badass in a skin-tight black t-shirt and jeans. The thick biker boots made an intimidating clunk on the stairs.

"Oh, well, I know he's married and all, but it can't hurt to look. Do you think the Army did some genetic manipulation or something?"

"Definitely not genetic manipulation." The science wasn't there yet. At least she didn't think so.

"But something, right?"

Ryder pulled Lauren into him at the bottom of the stairs. Lauren tilted her head and whispered something they couldn't hear. Ryder responded by dropping a gentle kiss to her lips.

"God, isn't that the sexiest thing?" Camy whispered.

Debi held her words until Ryder and Lauren disappeared into the kitchen. "How did you figure out about the runway show?"

"Oh, you mean the view from the fireplace? Caught it by accident this morning. Was having a little bit of a pity party with my first cup of coffee and they started down the stairs like contestants from *The Bachelorette*, you know, that reality show?"

First cup of coffee? "How much coffee have you had?"

"I don't count. Some things in life should remain a mystery."

Now that the show was over, Debi stepped around the fireplace. "Maybe you should cut back?"

"On coffee? Not a chance. Before we go eat, answer my question. Are you going to make a move?"

As if her thoughts had conjured him, Rose stepped through the door and peered around the fireplace. "Let's eat, girls." He glanced between the two as if trying to decipher the situation. "Now."

And like that, he was gone. "Is he always so..." There were no words for how he messed with her head.

"Bossy, short-tempered, and protective." Camy nodded her head solemnly. "Fair warning."

Debi glanced longingly at the kitchen. The last ten minutes had been a Camy-sized tornado. "Are you trying to warn me off?"

"Not at all. I figure if he finds himself a woman, he'll have less time to harass me. I swear to God, all I'm asking for is one day without him hounding me."

"So all you want is one day to yourself?"

"Oh, honey, I'm hoping you can distract him for longer than that." Camy pulled her into the kitchen.

Debi was halfway into her spaghetti pie before she regained her equilibrium. That's when she realized Camy had maneuvered her onto the long bench sitting thigh-to-thigh with Rose. She definitely needed to keep an eye on Camy. She was chipper and sweet and sneaky as hell.

CHAPTER FIFTEEN

News of the GHB had made the rounds, so it was a somber dinner. Rose ate his spaghetti pie in silence. It was the only thing Stills knew how to make, but they each had to take turns according to the chart by the pantry that put Debi and Craft on cleanup after dinner. The idea of them spending time together gnawed at something inside he didn't want to examine too closely. He stuffed another bite in his mouth.

Beside him, Debi's hand twitched. Most of her food was still on her plate where she'd twirled it into endless circles.

"You okay?" he asked under his breath. "And don't say fine."

She peeked through thick lashes. "The preliminary results are in on the water bottle, but I don't know how to..." She gestured in a circle around the table.

"Get their attention?"

"That, plus I'm not sure how to start."

"Easy." He whistled until every eye was looking at him. "Debi has more results."

"You have the subtlety of a tank," she muttered behind a smile.

"You're welcome."

With fork in hand, she lowered her arm under the table and stabbed him in the thigh. "You know about the GHB." She cast a glance at Lauren before she continued. "But I also ran a screen of the water bottles until I found the one I believe was used to dose Ryder."

Rose removed the fork before she pierced his skin. "What did you find?"

"There are compounds I couldn't positively identify without further tests, but the predominant toxins found in the water were amphetamines combined with a high dose of anabolic steroids."

Curses were muttered around the table. Rose set the fork onto his plate. "I specifically asked the doctors. Before I signed the papers. I was told no steroids."

Debi rested her empty hand on his thigh. "We don't know if they were included in your original compound, but I wonder if you noticed a change when you started the program. Did you start to bulk up? Temper shorten?"

"Roid rage is a myth." Stills pushed back from the table. "And I for one didn't notice any changes. You guys?"

The word no was tossed around, but the doubt on Debi's face was obvious. "We couldn't help notice that you guys are built..." She used her left hand to mark one side, while Camy used hers to an exaggerated distance away. "Big. We'll call that outside the range of normal."

Fowler stood and took his plate to the sink. "They picked us for our size, or that's one of the reasons. Our loyalty and dedication were another."

Janet kicked back from her seat at the head of the table. Her gaze traveled around the room for silent moments. "I see what you're saying, but Jake was more or less this size before he joined the teams."

"I don't think we should discount it," Debi insisted. "The addition of steroids would make the teams more aggressive, which in battle is a positive, but they'd also explain the anger issues."

"The aggression and anger issues are things the Army would want. Hell, I know some survivalists who use it for those same reasons." Janet helped Fowler clear the table. "Improved muscle mass, performance, and strength."

"Increased risk taking," Debi added. She nibbled uncertainly on her lower lip.

"You're talking impulse control?" An angry flush covered Ryder's face. "The all-out need to succeed at any cost. Bold, violent, no pain."

Debi nodded. "Isn't that similar to what you experienced that night they dosed you?"

"I felt mindless. Impulsive." He nodded, not looking too happy about it. "But that could have been the amphetamines. Arriving at the proper dosages for the experiments was hell, but I don't remember ever feeling as out of control as I did the night Echo took you and Lauren."

"The situation of Lauren in danger could have been a catalyst unlike any we experienced in the desert," Rose offered. They'd barely made it to Ryder in time to prevent him from going in without backup or weapon. "The drugs pushed you the rest of the way."

"It worked with Mad Dog and Gault." Stills swirled tea in

his glass. "We have to assume they'll try again, given the opportunity."

"I think we should work very hard to deny them the opportunity." Debi twisted in her seat, trying to get free but was trapped between Rose and Camy. He slid out of the way and let her free. "The long-term side effects are severe. Liver and kidney damage. At the dosages in the bottle, and we don't know if that's within the normal range, you could see heart attack, stroke, or seizure. I would never..." Her free hand shook as she walked to the sink and refilled her water glass. "The careless mixture of different classes of drugs is irresponsible. They could have had no idea what the mixture would do. I would never do to another human being what they did to you. There are compounds in the water that I'm assuming are the propriety formula they used for the fearlessness. I want... No, I *need* to go to the university lab to test so I can figure out what they used."

"No." Rose stood, his heart racing.

"We need to discuss it." Ryder stood and rested a hand on Lauren's shoulder. "The whole point of this is to find out what the fuck they did to us. If the university has equipment that can reverse engineer the compounds, then it's worth the risk."

"That's easy for you to say." Because his woman would stay in the secure area of The Manor. Shit, Rose couldn't use that, because Debi wasn't his woman. He moved closer, the need to smash something an impulse he didn't want to deny. "I pushed for Lauren to go into the bank, and she ended up getting hijacked by the meth heads, so we made a deal, then and there. The women don't go into danger."

"The women have a voice." Camy stabbed a finger at him.

"You're not everyone's surrogate father, River. You don't speak for everyone."

His gaze whipped to his sister. "Camellia, we're not talking life and death here, although that's enough to give me veto power over you. We're talking torture, mutilation, and pain beyond what your comfortable little life could possibly prepare you for. Extended pain." The sight of Maggie Madigan still haunted his restless nights. No way would Camy or Debi or any of the women be put into that position. Not when he could prevent it. "If it's so damned important to test this stuff, we can break into university labs. Run the tests for her."

"Her? I'm right here. And for the record, I'm the only one who knows how to operate the equipment and knows what we're looking for." Her eyes tightened with pain like they had when she'd lifted the weights. "I told you on day one, I'm not hiding behind some he-man with an ego the size of the solar system. The day with Echo and the car chase is a prime example. I need to act so I don't panic. I'm doing this with or without you, and right now, without you sounds like a decent option."

"Hold on." Stills pushed between the two, drawing attention to the fact that the argument had shifted to just Debi and Rose. How his anger and focus had shifted was beyond him. They stood toe to toe in the kitchen, surrounded by a large audience.

"This is about the mission. Nothing else." Stills rested a hand on each of their shoulders "She's not yours to boss around."

Those words were an accelerant to the fire burning inside. Stills' smug grin was an easy fucking target. Rose pulled back and decked Stills in the jaw. Stills sprawled into the table, sending a pan of spaghetti clattering to the checkerboard tile in a spray of red. Ryder, Fowler, and Craft pushed Rose across the kitchen, but they couldn't contain him if he didn't want to be contained.

Stills swiped a hand across his busted lip. "That all you got?"

Ryder stabbed a finger at Stills. "Shut it." He turned back to Rose. "We are all of us one bad day from World War III. Go for a run on the treadmill, kick the shit out of the punching bag, or dunk your head in a bag of ice. I don't give a fuck what you do, but do not come back into this kitchen until you have your head on straight."

"Is that an order?"

"Fuck yeah it's an order."

Craft and Fowler pushed him toward the door but he shook them off. Debi's eyes followed his movements. The fear, the way she shrank from his gaze was all he needed right now. The move made it crystal fucking clear why the kiss in the lab could not be repeated. He saw it in her eyes. They were stick-a-fork-in-me done.

No one needed to push him further away. He walked on his own down the hall.

"Sergeant, Rose." Janet's still, calm voice cut through the bullshit in his head. If anyone else in that room had tried to stop him, he would have kept walking, but the touch of her resolute voice stopped Rose cold.

Breath panted out for all he kept bottled inside. Six months he'd compartmentalized the anger and the grief, but the events of the past few weeks had eroded his control. He was a dangerous and volatile substance waiting for the right catalyst. Only Janet's soft voice put a lid back on it.

"I expect you to clean this up when you're done."

The hall in front of him narrowed and fogged. What the fuck was wrong with him? He made it halfway to his room before he called back. "Yes, ma'am."

———

Debi shivered as she watched Rose disappear down the hall. It was the first time she'd seen one of the men lose his temper, except Ryder, but he'd been under the influence of amphetamines and God knew what else at the time. The anger issues as a side effect were academic until she watched Rose face punch one of his best friends.

Janet clapped her hands together and all attention shifted to the petite brunette. "Let's take this out to the great room."

"I'll make coffee," Fowler offered.

"I'll help." Camy's overly cheerful voice didn't fool anyone.

The troops started out to the main room, but Debi stayed back a bit, needing to regain her equilibrium.

Camy picked up the unspoiled tray of spaghetti pie from the table. "I don't want the food to go to waste, because I'm betting it will be a few hours before he gets that much anger out of his system."

"Don't clean up," Fowler insisted.

"Wasn't planning on it. As he is so fond of telling me, he made the mess, he can clean it up." She wrapped aluminum foil on the top of the pan. "That's the first time I've seen my brother lose it." She gave Debi a sympathetic nod. "It's either the woman or the drugs."

Fowler measured coffee into the brewer. "Or a combination of both."

Debi turned back to the main room, no longer wanting to be a fly on the wall. The mood in the other room wasn't much better, but she figured she needed to pull the bandage off the rest of the way. "The equipment I need is in the secure lab. I think I can convince Allyson to let me in. To help me."

"Who is Allyson?" Ryder grabbed a pen and paper, reminding her of Rose.

How to explain? "A friend."

"Barry's sister," Lauren added.

Debi's personal life was bantered around for several minutes before she interrupted. "Her brother is an ass, but Allyson is a good person. The last time I ran into her and Barry, she wanted to talk. Asked me to call her, so I say I give her that call. Set up a meet. In person I know I can convince her to let me use the equipment."

Stills leaned forward, propping his hands on his knees. "Say that's true. How do you get around the brother? Doesn't he run the labs?"

Debi cleared her throat. "One Saturday a month, he has a regular poker game with other faculty members. At my father's house. Barry's a brown noser. He won't miss a night. The labs will be minimally staffed and if Allyson helps me out, we'll have keycard access."

"If you go in with Allyson, you go without backup." Ryder rubbed a hand over Lauren's thigh. "After what happened at the bank, I don't like it."

The ache in her chest marked the beginning of an attack. Debi rubbed a hand over her collarbone. *Deep breath.* She heard Rose's voice in her head counting to eight and back down again. *Deep breath.* "It's a secure area, so I won't be completely exposed." She swallowed. "You guys can stake out the area and make it safe."

"Right now, the plan has holes," Craft said.

Convincing them was paramount. The suspicions she'd had needed to be verified, and for that, she needed the lab equipment. Her heart flexed. "Don't hold back on my account. Tell me how you really feel."

"Fixing holes is what we do." Craft winked. "Which Saturday are we talking?"

"Don't say this Saturday," Stills added.

Her hand twitched with unspent nerves. "This Saturday."

"That doesn't give us much time," Ryder said.

Craft agreed. "But we've planned missions in less time."

They weren't saying no. Debi's vision went spotty around the edges. When she's planned this out in her head, she never thought they'd agree. Lauren hopped out of her seat and grabbed her hand. "I need a word with you." She pulled her into the kitchen.

Camy and Fowler were flirting by the coffee maker.

"The guys were wondering where the coffee is," Lauren told them.

"It's ready." Camy looped several empty cups through her fingers. "Jake, if you'd get the pot."

Neither gave them a second glance on the way to the great room. After they passed, Debi released a breath she hadn't realize she'd held. The fog in her head spread, her heartbeat pounded. She snapped the band on her wrist, felt the sting.

"If they see you have a panic attack, they won't let you go." Lauren pulled her into the pantry. "Tell me why you have to do this."

Debi's mouth opened and flapped closed. Best friend or

not, she couldn't tell Lauren. Not until she knew the truth. "I'm the only one who can."

The next minutes passed with Lauren rubbing her back and helping to normalize her breathing. "I didn't stop to think what would happen after," she finally said. She'd pay good money for a cigarette right now. "I was so caught up in my argument that when they agreed, I panicked."

"I wish I could go with you."

Debi shook her head, her eyes wide. "Not a chance. Echo knows you're the way to get to Ryder. I'll be fine."

"Okay, then let's help them finish the plan."

But by the time they made it to the great room, the men were headed out. Debi snaked out an arm and grabbed Craft on his way past. "What's going on?"

"We're splitting up to gather intel. Meet me in the command post at zero eight hundred. I want to go over the blueprints with you. Mark where you're going and likely paths. Lauren, if you could be there as well to help me go over the campus layout."

"Absolutely. Where's the command post?"

"It's the coolest thing. Have Ryder show you the way. And bring Camy. Time to put you ladies to work.'"

"Does that mean no PT in the morning."

Craft laughed at the hope in Lauren's voice. "There's always time for PT."

Ryder came over to encourage them to get some sleep. He rubbed a thumb over the yellowing bruise on Lauren's face. "You could still use the rest."

"If you guys are working, we're working," Lauren insisted.

"We're not up for much longer. Craft is gathering information for our briefing in the morning."

"Where's Camy?" Debi asked. Rose's sister was tricky.

"She's helping Stills break into the Office of Personnel Management to pull Echo's records. According to Craft, her computer skills are above par. I want pictures and dossiers on every man still alive. Don't tell Rose," he warned Debi.

Rose would go ape if he knew his sister was hacking into government records. "I don't think that's going to be a problem." Since Rose was so mad at her he took it out on Stills. "I think I'm going to hit the sack."

"You need help?" Lauren offered.

The lie came easy. "I'm fine. Physical therapy today helped." If by helped she meant it hurt like hell. "I'll grab an ice pack from the freezer and rest."

The hallway door to the bathroom was wide open. Rose's door was closed. Probably locked. Permanently. She sighed as she stepped into the bathroom to change. She'd come to rely on Rose. He was like a comfortable teddy bear to snuggle up with at night. An incredibly sexy one. With as little movement as possible, she cleaned up and changed into his oversized shirt. As she walked into her room, she rested the ice pack on her shoulder. The relief was instant.

The lamp was on next to her bed. Next to it stood a full bottle of water and her pain pills. A big lump was under the covers. She yanked them back to see that he'd rolled a blanket into a bolster. Tiredness tugged at her eyes. The man still took care of her. Even mad as the devil, he remained a giant sweetheart. She lay down, Rose's scent wafting off the sheets. As an olive branch, the bed setup was killer, but she'd still miss Rose's heat at her back.

———

Two hours of hugging a blanket put Debi in a sour mood. The ice pack had warmed to room temperature. And that wasn't even close to what kept her awake. Going into the university lab was her idea, but going into it without Rose at her back?

She rolled out of bed and turned the lamp on. The light stung her eyes, but she blinked it away. They didn't have time for the silent treatment, so she padded down the hall in bare feet and knocked lightly on his door.

The door opened before she'd had time for a breath. What little breath she had choked in her throat. Rose was wearing boxers and nothing else. Smooth skin covered pecs the size of plates. The corded muscles of his abs made a six pack look like a weak man's game. The defined line down his center called for her tongue. Tonight the boxers were plaid. Navy and green. He braced his hands on his hips. "Little late for a social call."

How was she supposed to think when he exposed so much skin and muscle? She forced her eyes off his seriously hot flesh or she'd never string more than two words together. "If you need a pair of sleep shorts, I have a pair you can borrow."

CHAPTER SIXTEEN

Those dark eyes didn't blink. "Try again."

Debi's heart pounded a sprint in her chest. The easy answer was to claim she couldn't sleep. He was a healer. He'd lose the chip on his shoulder, because he was a caregiver at heart, but that was cheap. What's more, it was beneath her. After two hours of restlessness, she knew what had angered him. She swallowed. "I'm sorry I brought up my plan with the whole group first."

A muscle twitched in his bicep; otherwise he was still. "You don't owe me anything."

"No. But I'd like to."

"What am I supposed to do with that?" He laced his fingers together on the top of his head. His features were impassive, intimidating as hell. "I decked one of my teammates in anger. Rage. Doesn't that concern you?"

"All you did was split his lip." The day before, he'd taken Wade out with one hit. "You pulled your punch."

"Had time to think about it, have you?"

She nodded. The night at Lauren and Ryder's townhouse, Rose had taken out the enemy like a man possessed. One shot, and the man was down. No matter how much guilt Rose carried, he hadn't gone after his friend with the same aggression.

"That should still concern you."

"It's between you and Stills."

"He's got a hard face. He'll live."

"My point exactly. How about you?" Because the guilt hadn't left his eyes the whole time they'd talked.

Shallow breaths moved his chest. "Why are you here?"

The coronary that had threatened since she was a kid was about to be realized. The words stalled in her throat, but if he could expose himself, his anger issues and the concerns behind them, she could speak the truth. Crap. Her heart nearly seized. "I want you to sleep in my bed." She stepped forward and ran a finger down the midline, feeling the muscles twitch. It was quite possible she'd die before he answered. "And I don't want to snuggle."

"Thank fuck." He dove in, his hands tangled in her hair, as he stepped into her. The kiss consumed. What they'd shared in the lab was a chaste kiss between friends compared to the heated exchange in his open door. Lips conquered, his tongue invaded. Desperation rode his hands as he clutched her close. He tilted her head and swept inside, stealing her breath. Touching her soul.

The wait had amplified the desire inside. They knew too much about each other and not enough. She knew the sounds he made in his sleep, had memorized his scent, and fallen asleep on his arm, but she didn't know where to touch that would drive him wild. She planned to find it.

Debi rested the hand of her injured arm on his hip, and let the other roam, wishing she had use of both to explore all his delicious flesh. Muscles jumped under her touch. The defined musculature was enough to send her eyes rolling back. She didn't know nearly enough.

His lips released hers to kiss a trail to her jawline, across her neck, and up to her earlobe. Desire erupted from his touch and flowed through her body to her groin. Her nipples hardened. A few more well placed caresses and she would come apart in his arms, but she wanted to explore more. She memorized his body with every touch, running a hand over the rivers of corded muscle of his arms. "I've wanted to do this from the first."

"I know what you mean." Rose had spent too many sleepless nights imagining her under him. That she came to him now, when he was lost, so fucking alone... It was a gift he wasn't giving back. He'd take this time with her, because it was the only thing warming his soul, the pieces of himself he packed away after Madigan's death. He nibbled the tender spot behind her ear. "I've wanted to do this." His hand slid under the shirt to palm her breast. The points of her nipples through the Army t-shirt had nothing on the weight of her full breasts in his hands. Damn, she was a handful. His thumb teased her nipple and his large fingers kneaded.

The minute his hand touched the bandage, he stilled. Rose breathed in air and breathed out fire. What the hell was wrong with him? She was still recovering.

"Hey." Debi brushed a hand on his jaw, gripped, and forced his gaze. "Don't you dare stop."

"You're—"

"The same woman you forced to do physical therapy today."

"That was for your own good."

She *thunked* her head against his chest and an aborted laugh brushed his skin. "Trust me, this is for my own good as well."

Gently, he tilted her head. Rubbed a thumb across her delicate jawline. Breakable. "I've screwed up enough for one day."

Mischief glimmered in her eyes. "I'm a mistake?"

"Taking advantage of you would be a mistake."

Her hand skimmed over his skin to tease underneath the band of his boxes. "I showed up at your door in the middle of the night wearing nothing but a shirt. Your shirt."

His erection jerked in response to her words. Her touch. "I'm trying to do the right thing here."

"The right thing would be to help me out of this shirt. I might hurt myself doing it one handed."

He'd known she would challenge him. Push him. A part of him had been waiting for that spark of personality to show. "You make it hard to say no."

"Then don't." She reached up on tiptoes to whisper in his ear. "River, take me to bed."

His name on her lips took the choice out of his hands. Sparks shot down the nerves where her whispered words brushed. They'd been barreling to this moment from the first spark. Right or wrong didn't matter. He reached behind her and pushed the door closed.

Her soft sigh of anticipation filled his head along with her scent.

"Don't let me hurt you."

"If it hurts, you're not doing it right," she teased, using his words from earlier in the day. With her good hand, she traced along his jaw. "You don't have it in you to hurt me."

But he did. That's what Debi and those like her would never understand. The experiments had altered him. Tempers flared on the team. Anger was a byproduct none of them could control. Knowing that Madigan hadn't killed his family didn't change anything. They were all a danger to those they cared about, and like it or not—mostly not—he cared about Debi in a way that put her at risk. He'd move heaven and hell to keep her safe.

"You're thinking too much."

"No one has ever accused me of that."

"Then no one knows you very well. All that silence is filled with a very active mind." She rubbed her thumb along his lower lip. "River, you're the best man I've ever met." He opened his mouth to spout a denial, but she pressed a finger to keep him silent. "I'm not backing down now that we're here."

"Good." His heart thumped. Tomorrow he'd deal with the fallout. Tonight. He wanted this one night, whether he deserved it or not. He lifted her and carried her to the bed where he carefully removed the shirt to reveal full breasts and dusky nipples laid out for him like a feast. The temptation was too great. He bent to pull a hard nipple into his mouth. "Been dying to taste you."

"Pretty high on my list too." She twisted fingers into his hair. "Come to bed."

The invitation spiked desire straight to his groin. His dick wanted in on the game. He shucked his boxers and joined her on the rumpled sheets. Silky black hair fanned her face on his pillow. Desire lowered her lids like she was a woman with a thousand secrets and he would give up what he was to discover them. Her lips parted on a sigh filled with need. The sight of her in his bed, on his pillow, would never grow old. A caveman part of him, one he shielded against, roared to the forefront.

Mine. To hell with calling dibs. She was his whether either of them liked it. No other man could touch her as long as he drew breath. The glide of his hand on her bare skin was a dream that slowed everything down and covered them in a fog where the outside world ceased to exist. Not the team, not the enemy, nothing but the woman in his bed. The more he explored, the more intimate the caress, the greater hold she had on his soul.

Hunger bent him over to taste her nipples until they beaded into tight pebbles made for his mouth. "Perfect." The instinct to bury himself and claim her tightened his balls; instead, he trailed kisses down her torso and nipped the taut abdomen that quivered beneath his lips. At her pubic bone he altered course, kissing down her inner thigh.

A moan slid from her mouth. "Fast is good."

He chuckled as his mouth hovered over her mound. "We'll get there." Right now, he needed to hear her scream. He parted her lips and allowed himself a sample. "I love the way you taste." Enjoying himself, he kissed, nipped, licked, alternating until she writhed beneath his mouth. Sweet whimpers encouraged the torment. "You like this." He circled her clit, drawing it into his mouth. Her hips popped off the mattress. "That's it," he murmured. "Show me what you like."

Panting now, she grabbed his hair and the erotic pull spiked an electrical current that went straight to his cock. An orgasm barreled down his spine, threatening to spill before he even got inside her. He fought the urge, concentrating on her pleasure, wanting—needing—to hear her lose control.

Using his fingers, he tested her opening and found her wet. For him. The caveman inside beat his chest. The movement of her hips guided the pace as he set a rhythm of thrusting two fingers inside her wet channel, then circling her clit with his tongue as he withdrew. She met his moves by lifting her hips, drawing his fingers deeper.

Nonsense spilled from her mouth until it sounded like a chant.

He twisted his fingers, pressing against her G-spot.

The chant became words. One word, over and over and over. "Please. Oh, please."

He grabbed her ass in one hand and held her hips at an angle. The rhythm increased and she arched closer. He sucked her clit in his mouth and she exploded, coming on his fingers. Drinking her in, working her, he prolonged the orgasm until she dropped to the mattress, replete. The relaxed satisfaction in her eyes made his cock jerk against her soft leg. Moving slowly, he climbed her body, dropping kisses against her skin, rubbing his hand over sensitive spots that drew shivers from her body.

Finally, he settled over her. They lay groin to groin while he held his weight on his elbows, staring down at her. Vulnerability glistened in her eyes. The expression on her face was no longer shielded, making her look younger and easily broken. He dropped a soft kiss to her lips and then trailed more down her jaw to her delicate neck. He rocked against her, careful to keep the pressure on her pubic bone and not on her tender clit, giving her body time to recover.

She widened her legs to make room for him to settle between her legs. "What you do to me."

"I loved doing that, but sweetheart, that first one was too easy. We're nowhere near done."

Reaching over to the nightstand, he pulled a condom from his wallet. His cock throbbed to the point of pain as he slid the condom on his length, but he wanted her ready again. Kissing her slow and deep, he let their tongues tangle while the tension in her body rebuilt. Until she arched against his lower body.

She slid a hand down his torso to land on his flank, squeezing his ass. It was his control that snapped and he slammed into her in one quick thrust. He stopped, held himself there, buried balls deep. "God, you're tight."

"It's been awhile for me."

The words made him want to pound into her and make the claiming complete. Instead, he pulled back and thrust into her tight channel, stretching her, surrounding him with her wetness.

"Rose, move." Lust coated her words. "I need you to move."

"Say my name."

"I did."

"My first name." He needed to hear it again. To reclaim the man he had once been.

She stilled beneath him. "I thought you didn't want anyone knowing your first name?"

He found he liked his name on her lips. He slid out and back in, torturing them both with the slow tempo. "Say it."

"River." She reached up and nipped his lower lip, sucked it between her teeth. "Finish what you started, River."

The bite knifed straight to his lower back, tightened his balls, making the next moves inevitable. He thrust deep and pulled back, setting a punishing pace until her sex went soft and silky around him. Shifting his body weight, he forced each thrust to grind against her clit until the murmurs turned to a chant. He couldn't hear what she was saying, but the sexy softness, the demand, the complete loss of control came through loud and clear.

Lifting her hips, he punctuated each thrust until she came, screaming his name. An erotic rush fueled his moves and he came deep inside her, and he knew she'd claimed him, body and soul. Her body melted into the mattress beneath him. Her eyes drifted toward sleep.

After taking care of the condom and cleaning up, Rose returned to the bed with his woman. Right or wrong, the connection was a reality. Denying it served neither of them.

He settled around her, draped an arm over her hips, and pulled her close. The rightness tugged at his heart. "Didn't make it to your room. Maybe next time."

"This worked out fine," she mumbled.

"Your bed is bigger." His feet stuck off the bottom of the bed by a good six inches.

"Doesn't matter. We don't use half of it the way you're wrapped around me."

He smiled against her hair. Strawberries and sex. Felt like he'd been wrapped around her for a lifetime. Those nights in the motel where he'd been her bodyguard hadn't stopped his body from wanting. "I like it here with you, but I shouldn't. Ryder called it. We're all one day from World War III and you could get caught in the crossfire." He couldn't be anything but honest. "I didn't lose my temper earlier because you didn't pull me aside and tell me separately. I would have had the same reaction no matter where we were or who was there. People die around us, not all of them bad. Every night I go to sleep, I see Maggie Madigan." The words caught in his throat. "I cannot live with something happening to you. This can go south in countless ways, most of which we will never foresee." He rubbed his thumb over her hipbone, the silence filled with regret. "I don't want to be here without you."

She rubbed her foot up his leg. "Then help plan the mission. Keep me safe."

The knots tied him, but he'd feel them no matter who was going into the brink. "I will," he vowed, but when the dreams came, it wasn't Maggie Madigan's dead eyes haunting him anymore.

———

Morning started before dawn as Rose finished cleaning the mess of spaghetti that had dried onto the kitchen floor. When he was done, he put on a pot of coffee and sat by the fire to watch the rest of the night burn away. One night with Debi had been a mistake, one he couldn't make himself regret, but believing he could have one night without forming a bond was like mixing fuel and a flame and not preparing for the explosion.

What they had wasn't just sex. In the months since Madigan, Rose had cut himself off from everyone. He'd found protectors for his sisters and he'd stayed away. To keep them safe, but to do it, he had to go arctic inside, and Debi found a way to warm that numbness away. He wasn't sure he could go back to the way he was before. He wasn't sure if he wanted to.

The smart mouth remarks and the bravado covered deep-rooted fears, and he wasn't much interested in changing that, but she'd had to bury her heart to protect it and he *did* want to change that. He wanted to be around to help her explore the mysteries hidden inside, but he'd have to live through the coming storm first.

The fire snapped and a body stirred on the couch, sat up, and tossed the blanket aside. "You think too fucking loud," Stills complained.

Rose didn't have Ryder's night vision, but the flickering flames illuminated a face. "Don't you have a bunk somewhere?"

"No point. Finished downloading Echo's personnel files not too long ago. Doesn't matter where I crash. Morning's too damned early." Stills slipped his feet into boots. "Besides, if you were a no-show, I planned to clean up the spaghetti before Janet came down. I'm pretty sure she'd kick your ass for dereliction of duty."

"I'm pretty sure she could kick all our asses, because not a one of us would lay a hand on a female."

"You might want to keep that in mind."

Rose didn't bother denying it. The thought of Debi dying weighed heavy. He didn't think he'd kill her, but if anything happened to her, it would still land on his soul. "It's not fear."

"It sure as hell ain't normal."

"I've seen Echo's tactics evolve. First they went after Mad Dog, killing Maggie to get him to go off the rails. Went after Lauren to draw Ryder into a trap. We're hard to kill, so they're going after our weak points."

"So we shore up the weak points."

"Not sure how to do that now that she's here." Now that they shared a bed.

"Been there, done that, left the girl in Kansas."

"Got any brilliant advice for me."

In the predawn light, Stills' face glowed with unspoken sorrow. "If she were mine, I'd lock her down here at The Manor."

"I was heading that way last night."

"And then my face got in the way." Stills rubbed his jaw.

"You okay?"

"You hit like a pussy."

"Want to go again? I'll give you first shot."

"No. Hate to kick a man when he's down."

Rose sipped black coffee until dawn finally dispelled the gloom.

"I'm too old to sleep on a sofa." Stills stood and stretched his hands over his head. "We worked out a solid plan last night. Come help me find the holes."

Stills briefed him as they walked through the tunnels to the command post. "With his picture all over the Internet and news, Ryder's a hindrance. He's staying back. He can run comms and cameras, keep everyone in the loop and maintain security here at The Manor. Fowler and I are going in midday on Saturday to recon. He'll find himself a sniper's roost and hunker down. I'll maintain surveillance around the science building until showtime."

They climbed the steps from the basement into the barn. Looked more like an indoor used car lot with the finance office looking down from above. "What time is the meet?"

"Debi made contact last night."

She'd called using a VoIP that Craft buried too deep to trace. "She told me."

Stills gave him a look as they climbed the stairs to the command post, but whatever he was thinking, he kept to himself. "She's meeting her friend at a coffee shop off campus at seven. Since you've met the target, your ass stays in the vehicle."

"I don't like that plan."

"I wouldn't either, which is why you can maintain visual contact while listening to audio."

"We're going to have her wired?"

"According to Craft, he's got that covered along with a tracker so you don't lose her when she rides to campus."

Rose crossed his arms. "When she leaves the coffee shop, she rides to campus with me. They can meet back on campus."

"We thought of that, but we don't want Allyson to intentionally or unintentionally broadcast her plans. If Debi stays with her, she keeps her off the phone, but you'll have eyes and ears on your girl the whole time she's in public."

"But once she's in the lab, I lose visibility."

"You'll still have audio." Stills tapped a mouse to wake up the computer equipment. Once everything was awake, he continued. "The last science class ends at six."

"They have class on Saturday?"

"Graduate students mainly. If they follow protocol, campus security clears the building and locks it within the hour."

"We need someone inside the building before they lock it down."

"Already ahead of you. Craft will enter earlier in the day as a student. Evade campus security so he's inside the building when they close it up. Otherwise, the science building should be empty by the time Debi convinces her friend to let her use the lab. Craft downloaded blueprints last night. Let's take a look."

Rose memorized the layout while thinking about holes in the plan. The rest of the team filtered into the command post in groups of two or three. The minute Debi breached the door, Rose knew. He sensed her more than anything. Her hair was up in a silky black ponytail and her face freshly scrubbed and makeup free. She was wearing her own clothes now, jeans and a button-down shirt. Her arm was still up in the sling. "You don't need to wear it now except at night." She needed to regain her strength.

Ryder paused as he walked through. "She'll need to wear it the night of the meet. Build sympathy."

Debi wiggled the fingers sticking out of the sling. "Feeling sympathetic, Rosebud?"

"Not even close." He felt trapped. Something in his gut wanted to lock her down, while his mind acknowledged that she was the only one who could get in the lab and run the tests. "Why don't we use Dr. Branson's lab?"

"He doesn't have the equipment I need, and if he sends it to an outside lab, they won't know what they're looking for."

"Plus an outside lab takes time," Ryder pointed out. "And once the samples leave our possession, we lose control. They could get lost or misdirected."

"Or Echo could intercept."

Which led them right back to the plan that was giving him heartburn.

Craft moved next to Rose with one hand in his pocket and another around a cup of coffee, looking too damned relaxed for a man about to break into a research lab. "There are cameras at every entry point." He pointed to four access points, one on each side of the building. "This half of the building consists of classrooms and staff offices. This half." He pointed to a largely blank area on the blueprints. "This is the research laboratory."

"Labs, plural." Debi crossed the room. "Labs are broken down by type and research project. There are firewalls between the classrooms and the labs. No exterior windows in the lab and no secondary access point. There's a security access point here." She gestured to a spot and Craft made notes on the computer, generating displays as she pointed things out. "It's keycard access here, followed by a keypad here."

"Is there a camera at the access point?" Ryder asked.

"If there is, it doesn't link to campus security," Craft answered.

"Assume there is." Debi shrugged off their incredulous looks. "Research is a highly competitive and cutthroat business. Assume there's security higher than the campus cops."

"Can you make up a keycard?" Rose asked Craft.

"I'm good, brother, but I'm not a miracle worker."

"I might be able to help you out," Camy said from a seat near the door.

"Hell no. Your ass is staying here." One woman in peril was enough. He wasn't letting his sister head into trouble. "And how do you know how to break into a secure access area?"

"At some point, we should probably talk about that," Camy answered. "But do you really want to do this here and now?"

"No." Fuck. They were back to Debi headed into a secure lab without backup.

Craft cleared his throat. "I can try to lift a keycard off a staff member if the opportunity presents itself earlier in the day, but I wouldn't count on it."

"Then how do I get into the lab?" Rose asked.

"You don't."

"You're telling me that once Debi passes through here."

Rose stabbed at the display of the security access point. "That she's on her own?"

"Echo doesn't have a clue we need access to a lab." Debi stepped around to Rose's other side. She rubbed a hand over his arm as if to soothe him. "If they did, they still wouldn't be able to gain access. The security system is designed to keep people out. That includes Echo."

"How many people have keycard access to the labs?"

"I have no idea. Students, researchers, professors."

"That's too many unknowns."

The room fell silent at Rose's proclamation. Ryder nodded his head. "You want to pull the plug?"

The tension building inside released. This was his team. Any one of them could call off a mission with nothing more than gut instinct. If he said he didn't want his woman going in alone, they'd find another way. Whether she liked it or not. "Let me work on it." Getting into impossible spaces was his specialty. "Craft, have you tapped into security cameras yet?"

CHAPTER SEVENTEEN

Debi stared at the wall of photos. Team Echo. The photos looked like mug shots, except the men were in Army service uniforms, and they looked so young with their hair shaved down. Their eyes still had a light to them, or maybe that was fanciful thinking. Several of the men posted on the wall she recognized from the night in the townhouse. Baby Face Joe and his friends had sat at the bar multiple times. Their photos had little red x's in the corner. Dead.

"I wanted to use a little skull and crossbones overlaid on the top, but I was overruled," Camy said. "How are you hanging in there?"

Debi's eyes kept tracking back to the red x's representing men who had kidnapped them, threatened them, and would ultimately have killed them. They were minutes from doing the deed, and yet... "I've never seen anyone die."

"These two." Camy tapped two adjacent photos. "Ryder

recognized these guys from the bluff. This is the one who shot you."

Brown hair, brown eyes, and looking to be Camy's age. Nothing about him screamed killer. The weight of a target settled over her chest, but no panic surfaced. Maybe the constant threat had loosened the potential. "How are you handling this so well?"

"First off, this place is the coolest thing ever, and access to Craft's computers would anesthetize my shock for at least a week, but added to it, I've hacked my way into some dark places."

"I'm afraid to ask."

"Then don't." Camy grinned playfully. "The world isn't all sunshine and rainbows. All this..." She shrugged. "I hoped there were places like this somewhere."

"Yo, Craft," Rose called from the end computer. "I got it."

Debi followed the others to see what the fuss was about.

"This is it. This is where I get in."

The camera showed a metal door embedded in brick. It was an emergency exit. "That's the fire exit from the lab."

"Exactly. Inside the secure area."

"I'm sure there's an alarm on it."

"Watch and learn." Rose rewound the recording several minutes. As the video replayed, three men in white lab coats stepped out. They used a loose brick near the exit to prop the door open before lighting up cigarettes.

Memories of standing there smoking was almost like a vicarious high. She pointed to one of the three men on the video. "That's Dr. Stevens. I don't recognize the others."

"Doesn't matter who they are. It matters where they are.

Craft, can you see if this triggered an alarm and how it was handled?"

Craft pulled a chair to the adjacent computer and started typing. "A silent alert was triggered and overridden remotely."

"Good money says this kind of thing happens all the time," Rose said.

Debi nodded agreement. "During a typical shift, we'd go out maybe four times. No telling how many other people went out at different times. Different shifts."

Rose paused the playback. "Security has gotten used to it. Punches it off. But just in case they bring up the video, can you rig a loop of this for when I get in?"

"How are you getting in?" Debi asked. "There's not even a doorknob."

"I'll get in. Craft?"

"Shouldn't be a problem. Have to darken it to look like night. Otherwise, I can make it happen."

"All right. I'm in." He stood and draped an arm over Debi's shoulders. "Let's go get something to eat."

"You're mighty cheerful all the sudden." It looked good on him, plus his arm around her in front of the others didn't suck.

"You're not going in alone."

"You were worried."

"It's like a puzzle. How to get you what you want—inside to run tests—and still maintain security."

"So you weren't worried?"

"Maybe a little." He dropped a kiss to her head.

"I have another puzzle for you."

"What's that?"

"Something I need. As long as I have access, I need to see

if Ryder has any residual toxins in his blood from when he was dosed."

"I'd be more than happy to draw Ryder's blood."

"Oh, I got it earlier."

"Than what do you need from me?"

"Blood."

They'd been moving toward the door, but Rose stopped. "Why?" He'd had a lifetime of people poking and prodding him and he was done.

"I need a control. Someone from the team who was dosed originally, but not since."

"There are plenty of other suckers we can tie down and draw blood from."

"But I'm not sleeping with them."

"That implies past and future."

"Why quit something we're both so obviously good at."

"You make it hard to say no."

She reached up and kissed the underside of his jaw. "I try."

Rose eased her toward the door. "Craft, you coming?"

"Can't. Now I have to alter a video and lay the groundwork for sneaking into the surveillance footage."

"I'll stick around," Camy offered.

"You." Rose stopped in the doorway and pointed to Camy in that bossy way of his. "We're having a come-to-Jesus meeting as soon as I get back. I want to know what you've been up to, because your skill set does not match the nursing degree I was told you were earning."

Camy's shoulders slumped and she cast a look at Debi. "One day. Is it too much to ask?"

Friday night, Debi tracked Rose down to his room. He was at his desk, making notes in his ever-present notebook. With finesse, she wrapped the latex tourniquet around his bicep before he looked up. He tossed the pen to the pad. "You're supposed to ask."

"I did."

"I didn't say yes."

"Quit being a wuss." Fowler leaned against the doorframe.

His eyebrows lifted. She'd surprised him. "You brought backup."

"I warned you not to bet against me."

"Fowler can bleed just as well as I can," he insisted.

"The day I got shot, you shoved him up against the wall."

"Stills?"

"You punched him."

"I haven't laid a hand on Craft."

"That I know of. We're building good will here, so it's your turn to take one for the team." Debi unrolled her supplies on the desk. "Fowler can draw blood if you don't want me to. He trained on goats, so I'm sure he's good." Although the last guy Fowler collected blood from was now dead. No way was Fowler getting anywhere near her with a needle. "The choice is yours. Fowler or me?"

"I trained Fowler."

She pulled her hands away from the supplies. "Fair enough."

Rose shook Fowler off. "Go ahead, sweetheart. This dumbass would enjoy drawing blood a little too much."

Not giving him time to change his mind, Debi swabbed the area and slid the needle into a vein and watched the blood spurt into the vial. Somehow once it filled a collection tube, blood no longer turned her stomach. Now it was just an interesting liquid to study.

"Didn't feel a thing."

"You weren't supposed to."

She slipped the tourniquet off as she slid the needle free. "Fowler, do you mind putting this with the rest."

"I live to serve." He took her used supplies and the blood collection tube. "Let me know if you need more blood. I'd be happy to tie him down on that torture device downstairs."

"You'll be the first to know."

The door clicked closed as Fowler left.

"You're a good stick," he said, a compliment to her skills.

"So are you."

"I've never drawn your blood."

"Wasn't talking about needles." Debi leaned back against the door, but her smile turned sad. "You've been avoiding me. Worried about tomorrow?"

"No. We all know our jobs."

The assessment in his gaze strengthened her pulse. Not for the first time, Debi wished for a dose of his fearlessness. She'd lived with panic for too long. "Then why are you edgy?"

"You know I don't have a future."

The way he said it, accepted it, knew it to the soul, added more layers. He was warning her off. One more way to protect. She pushed off the door. "Silly man." His whiskers bristled against the tip of her finger. Unshaven he looked a little less military, a little less civilized. "I'm not looking for a future." But he was. She saw it in his eyes, in the need cascading off him. He was the kind of man who planned to settle down with one woman. The Army interfered with the life he'd planned from the moment he'd slept with his first girlfriend. She knew his type. "We're both caught in the same messy trap. Let's take it one day at a time."

"Is that what you want?"

Debi had tried not to think about what she wanted since the day she'd gotten kicked out of the lab, but where she'd once hungered for vengeance, she now longed for peace. Getting shot had cured her uncertainty, the dissatisfaction with her life. She didn't want mindless sex and forgetfulness. She wanted Rose. "I'm no prize." It seemed only fair to warn him. "I don't want you to put me on a shelf for some mystical future. We have right now." She braced a hand on the back of his chair and straddled his lap.

He widened her thighs so she sank against his growing erection. "As it happens, I have time right now."

"What did you have in mind?"

He leaned forward to drop kisses along her collarbone, nipping and licking and long wet kisses before biting down on her neck. Not enough to leave a mark, but enough to zip desire straight to her sex.

"Keep that up and we're not making it to the bed."

"Right here is good." Releasing the clasp on her bra, he bowed her back over his large hands and leaned in to feast on her breasts through the soft cotton of her shirt. With deliberate care, he teased around her nipples until they were so hard they hurt, and then he wet the material around them and blew. The cool breath tingled over her chest and neck.

Her hands grasped his broad shoulders and her hair brushed the desk. The position forced the juncture of her thighs against his groin. Delicious, slow torture. He settled in like he enjoyed working one breast and then the other, alternating until she grew damp and needy. She tilted her hips to increase the friction of fabric between her legs.

"Does this hurt your shoulder?" he asked around her nipple.

"What shoulder?" Flames engulfed her body wherever he touched and places he had yet to touch.

"Good." He righted her briefly to pull the shirt and bra off, and then he leaned her back, this time his lips against bare flesh. "I can never get enough."

Truth echoed in his words. There was no room for awkwardness of insecurity when he so sincerely loved giving her pleasure, but she wanted the same, wanted her hands on all those delicious muscles. Wanted to see and taste and touch. "Your turn. Take off the shirt."

He reached back with one hand and stripped it over his head. Flames erupted in the air around them, or maybe that was her libido.

"That was sexy as hell." As was his toned flesh. Where the other night they'd been in a hurry, tonight she wanted a chance to explore. She ran her hands along his shoulders, appreciating the definition and strength hidden behind muscles bulky enough to make her mouth water. Salty. He tasted like salt and man. Her caress continued down his arms while her mouth wandered his neck and chest. His pec jumped under her kiss, so she explored what appeared to be a sensitive body part. She gave in to temptation and drew his nipple into her mouth.

His entire body flexed. Without warning, he lifted her, yanking her jeans and panties off. He set her on her feet while he pulled off the remainder of his clothes and dropped them to the floor. He grabbed a condom and slid it on before sitting into the chair and pulling her back on his lap. "Only one condom left after this."

"That's a shame." She gave in to her inner temptress and gyrated her hips, causing her thighs to rub the top of his. With a low laugh, she pulled her hair over her head, drawing her boobs higher, along with his heated gaze. "You should hit a drug store when we're in town tomorrow."

"Count on it. Do that again."

"What?"

He clamped his hands on her hips and swiveled her in a dance that brushed her most intimate flesh against his groin, teasing, softly moving in a slow grind.

"I'm not sure that's what I was doing." Decadent tremors washed over her skin as he pulled the strings moving her against his erection.

"Is that a complaint?"

"Definitely not." She gave herself over to his control until her wetness slicked the spot where their bodies met. When her arm tired, she dropped it to his shoulder and used it to balance. With her toes touching the floor, she was able to get a good balance. Using it, she adjusted the rhythm and glide, sliding her wetness back and forth along his thick erection.

He groaned. "Sweetheart, I'm not going to last long if you keep doing that."

"That's the plan." The last time, he'd been in control, using his body to drive hers wild. Now, she wanted to take him to the point where his control snapped. Where he drove into her because it was either that or die. "I need you inside me."

"Not yet."

"Now." Still straddling him, she lifted enough to maneuver

him to her entrance. Slowly, she slid onto him until she was fully seated.

The tendons in his neck flexed. His shoulders bunched under her hands like he was holding himself in check, but he let her set the pace. She slid slowly until he was barely inside her, then back down, making him slick, then she changed the moves to a back and forth grind, pressing her clit against the base of his shaft.

He grabbed the back of her head and pulled her close. He controlled the kiss, his tongue invading and mastering hers. He thrust in time to her moves until she was mindless with the need to chase the orgasm that tingled under her skin. Her thighs trembled.

Rose clamped both hands around her ass and used his arms to push and pull her through each stroke. His cock stroked nerves and pulsed against tender flesh. He thrust up each time her grind hit the top, putting pressure on her clit. She gave up trying to control and rode out the sensations coursing through her veins. The strength of his thrusts increased. Faster. More. Still more until she shattered. He followed her with a low groan.

Panting, they sat on the chair while they recovered, then, still embedded in her, he lifted to his feet and strode for the bed. "That was an appetizer." He took her to bed, where he showed her true stamina.

Arms settled around Debi and she wiggled into position next to him like it was an assigned parking spot. A blanket of possessiveness settled over Rose. What they had might be temporary, had to be, but he cared for her. Too damned much for either of their well-being. If they were out in the real world, he could walk away, leave her whole and safe and free, but that was not the way the cards played out. They were both targets, needing refuge at The Manor, and he couldn't safely send her away. He didn't have it in him to sleep next door instead of in her bed, so for now, she belonged to him, and he took care of what was his. Protected. No matter what happened Saturday, she made it out. He wouldn't live with any other result.

CHAPTER EIGHTEEN

"Allyson." Debi gave her a one-armed hug. "Wow, you look great. Did you get a new haircut?"

"I did, thanks." She fluffed the new style away from her face as if it were more distracting than anything. "What happened to you?"

Debi grimaced and played up the sling. She probably looked like hell. That's what happened when a team of science experiments chased after you. Bruises, scrapes, bullet holes. "Car accident." The lie came easy. She should feel guilty, but in two years, Allyson had never called or checked on her. Not after what her brother had done. "Happened right after I saw you the other day."

"Wow, so sorry." Allyson removed her coat and draped it over the chair. "I'm going to get a coffee. Want something?"

"No." She lifted her cup. "I'm good."

Debi tapped her feet and tried not to think too much. Rose had told her to keep the conversation normal. Don't seem too anxious. Don't lead with the need to use the lab. The drive into town had been one long oral exam. She'd memorized every picture of every member of Team Echo. She was wired with a transmitter and had an earpiece with Rose's voice on the other end. If things went south, she was supposed to use the code word. Slipper, because Rose thought her Goofy slippers were hilarious.

Right now, nothing was funny. She had a dozen scenarios in her head of how things could go wrong, planted by Rose and the rest of the team. It was a miracle her blood pressure was anywhere near normal. She glanced around the coffee shop. It was a small, off-campus place that stayed open late for students. Coffee flowed freely, but on a Saturday night, it was slow. A guy with headphones sat on the opposite side of the coffee bar, and for a minute, Debi's heart rate increased, but as she looked closer, he was built too small to be a part of Team Echo. Aside from headset guy, the place was empty.

Allyson came back with a to-go cup. "Thanks for calling me. I wasn't sure you would after the altercation the other day."

"It wasn't just the other day." It was two years of abandonment and lost friends. Debi toyed with her cup, but didn't drink. After the GHB incident, the days of drinking coffee someone else made were over. She twisted the cup in her hands. "I don't blame you for Barry."

"I should have warned you."

"What? That he was a dirtbag?"

"I don't think... I mean, I didn't. He's clearly focused on his career."

"Right." The word stretched, the tip of her sarcastic iceberg. "He's a backstabbing, research stealing—"

"Slow down," Rose said into her earpiece. "Remember, no confrontation."

"He's a brilliant scientist," Allyson said, sitting primly in her chair. "But I think you may be right."

Debi *thunked* back into her seat. "Which part?"

"If I believe one, I guess I believe it all. After we ran into you, I looked at his research grant. It's your work. DV1028. He renamed it of course. Tweaked the formula, but at the core of it, it's your work."

God no. Debi's head started to spin.

"Breathe deep, sweetheart. You're doing fine."

Then why was her breath stuck in her throat?

Allyson tapped her fingers on the lid of her cup. "I know how he thinks. He wanted to make your formula stronger. Better. He gets a bit overzealous when it comes to scientific discovery—"

"Quit making excuses. What he wants is recognition. He stole my work, and now you're the one working late hours in the lab and the one checking and rechecking data and calculations. He's there to steal your accolades."

"I don't really want accolades." Allyson rubbed a hand over her arms like she was cold. "Mark quit six months ago."

"Wow." That had to hurt. Debi always figured Allyson and Mark had a thing, a secret work affair.

"Mark's replacement is a complete waste, but Barry won't fire him. Probably because he has a penis."

"Oh. Hmm." Debi had never seen Allyson like this. Likely as not, Allyson had never used the word penis out loud, let alone in public. "That's an interesting theory."

"You know how it is. The men have this freaking bond that

has nothing to do with skills or actual scientific talent. Robert is already working on stuff for the research grant, but Hannah and I are stuck with undergraduate level work. Hannah's ready to walk."

"Really." The lab assistant lived for science. "Has she been applying to other universities?"

"I don't think so. She's got some new boyfriend. I think she's hoping he'll sweep her off her feet."

"What are the odds?"

"Right? I mean, if he leaves, she's going to be hurt. And still stuck in the lab." The words sounded autobiographical. Allyson knotted her hands together. "I like the lab. I don't mind if Barry uses my work, so long as…"

The anger was still there, hidden. Some wounds healed, and some festered. Her time with Barry was a puss-filled lesion. "What? As long as he lets you keep your job? You're as talented as he is. Smarter, probably."

"Don't alienate her. You need her help."

Debi wanted to toss the ear bud into her untouched coffee cup. Maybe Ryder should have been the voice in her ear. "Look, Allyson, I don't want to fight." She reached across and grabbed the other woman's hand, and it was frigid to the touch. "Let's talk about something else."

The guy with the headset left the coffee shop, leaving the two of them and the late-night barista.

Allyson smiled shyly. "Tell me about the man you were with the other day."

"No names," Rose practically shouted.

"No kidding," Debi snapped. She coughed to try to cover her mistake. "I mean, that's a three-margarita story."

"Sounds promising. Was he with you when you crashed?"

There was her opening. "Yes, actually, and I'm starting to

wonder... The crash was such a fluke. You wouldn't believe me if I told you. Total drama. But when it was over, I started to wonder. Maybe he was on drugs and that's why we crashed."

Allyson gasped.

"Don't oversell it," Rose warned.

"If you even think that's possible, you should leave him."

Poor Allyson. The world as she knew it was black and white.

"You're right, I know, but the thing is, he's, uh, well, you saw him. He's built like Thor. And after Barry, there's really no comparison."

"Careful," Rose warned.

Not being able to snap back at him was getting on her last nerve. She lived on cigarettes, sarcasm, and bravado. She'd quit smoking, she couldn't be sarcastic because they needed something from Allyson, and her bravado was slipping. She needed a boost and took it out on Rose. "Plus, he's a rock star in bed, and a girl would have to be crazy to give that all up without proof."

Rose went radio silent. The rest of the team had access to audio. She just bet they were razzing him right about now. Served him right.

"Maybe we should go get those margaritas now," Allyson teased.

Debi barked out a laugh. "Girl, you surprise me." That was the God's honest truth. Something about Allyson had changed in the last couple years. She didn't dress as plainly. She'd cut her hair, Debi realized. Maybe she had a man. Or wanted a man. "But I was actually hoping you could help me figure out if he was on drugs when we crashed."

Allyson stared at her. That was the look, Debi thought.

The look that coined the phrase there was a sucker born every minute. "How can I help?"

Debi pulled the end of a vial to let it peek from her pocket. "Let me into the lab to test this."

"How did you get his blood?"

"Girl, you do not want to know."

————

The woman had a way about her. Rose listened as Debi and Allyson walked across campus. Fowler had a visual through his riflescope on the top of the administration building. Stills was stationed near the back entrance to the building. Craft was hidden inside the science building but outside the labs, hoping to capture Allyson's passcode when they entered the lab.

No sign of anyone from Team Echo, but Rose's gut screamed. No mission went this easy.

CHAPTER NINETEEN

Debi didn't see a soul as she entered the science building, which did nothing for the level of tension buzzing under her skin. Knowing Team Fear was out there, watching her back, should have made her feel safe, but instead made her question the illusion of safety she'd walked around with her entire life. Four men had her in their sights, and the only reason she knew was because she'd helped plan the mission. No hidden instinct protected her. The bad guys could be out there, and she'd be clueless. All those years of panic attacks? She hadn't had a clue the dangers that existed in the world that she *should* fear.

Allyson swiped her keycard to get into the first round of security. A loud *buzz* released the bolt and allowed them through the first set of doors. The determined *clunk* of the door closing behind them was decidedly more intimidating. Trapped between the two layers of security, Debi's heart raced. The white space between two doors, well lit, had always made her feel claustrophobic, but Allyson quickly punched in the code. 1492. Craft had asked her to memorize it, just in case. In case what, she hadn't asked, but as they stepped into the open lab, the oversight seemed important.

Glass and lights dominated the open space. The glass ceiling wasn't a metaphor, not here where the worker bees toiled on the lower level with long rows of florescent lights and no windows to the outside. The higher the office, the more glass along the wall. No woman had ever moved her office to the top floor where cigars were smoked, budgets planned, salaries hiked to ridiculous levels that those in the lower levels would never see.

The cool wash of fluorescents should have been cheery yet the aura of menace covered her. She wasn't the prodigal son returning to his birthright, but a thief in the night. The last time in this space had not ended well, and the memory of it sucked the air from her lungs. Once upon a time, she'd been a trusted, valued researcher and this had been her domain. The austere surroundings were foreign now, and she noted for the first time the odd scent that wasn't quite antiseptic. Neither was it wholesome.

It was cold, she realized, as she briskly followed Allyson across the pristine tiles. The lab had sucked her in once upon a time and turned her frigid. Slowly, so slowly she hadn't known until just this moment, feeling the icy grip of intellectual temptation surround her. The time she had spent with Rose banished the distance and solitude that had defined so many lonely years. She'd never met a man who understood her—all women maybe—the way he did, or one less likely to put up with her evasions. He made her feel present and fully alive, so she'd really rather not die trapped in an ice cave.

The left wall was a series of glass panels peeking into separate labs that required additional clearance. To the right were rows of open lab space. Beyond the offices in the back, behind multiple layers of security was an NMR machine. The MRI for molecules took more clout than the president to gain access.

"Come on." Allyson wove through the maze with a path born of familiarity. And maybe additional speed as the guilt started to weigh on her. Allyson was a rule follower. "Let's do this and then get that margarita." She flipped on machines and the task lights in her area.

Behind them, a mechanical whirring shattered the silence. Debi jumped, and Allyson laughed. "You didn't used to be so jumpy. I think it's just someone in one of the secure labs."

Just? The pulse racing in her head wanted her to run. Hand shaking, she pulled out a blood vial. "I didn't think being here would freak me out."

Once the machine was ready, Allyson inserted the first sample. The noise of the machine echoed in the empty lab. Allyson used her hand like a thumping rabbit's foot pounding against her chest. "Feels good to break the rules."

"God, what have I started? Next thing you know, you'll bring a biker to the faculty mixer." Debi laughed, but it sounded like a braying horse. She was a complete jackass for suggesting this trip to the lab. She wasn't some superspy. "Do you mind going to see who's here? It's stupid, but I really don't want to run into—"

"Right now, me either. We'd have a devil of a time explaining this to your father." Allyson glanced at the machine. "I'll be right back."

The second Allyson stepped around the corner, Debi slipped the extra vials from her sling. She worked fast to run the extra reports, so she could hide the evidence before Allyson returned. The need for speed fed the shakes in her hands and arms. Her legs were like overcooked spaghetti. The voice in her head that sounded like Rose told her to take a deep breath, but the real Rose hadn't piped in through her ear piece since they'd walked into the lab. Maybe the signal cut out when they went through security. Maybe all the equipment messed with the signal. Whatever the problem, she was working solo.

Debi leaned away from the machine half in shock at the sudden realization. Solo was normal for her, or it had been, but since this started, she'd come to depend on the team. Worse, she felt a part of them, a part of something. Being in the lab wasn't simply an attempt to find what had been done to Team Fear. It was about the camaraderie and friendship and the trust. Guilt weighed on her, because they trusted her, and no one knew the truth, or what she suspected was the truth. She hadn't told an outright lie either, but that was an excuse her conscience didn't buy.

Allyson's shoes squeaked on the tile as she approached, and Debi tucked the reports into her sling. "No worries. It was Robert."

"Don't you mean Dick?"

"I think that's Richard... Oh, you mean because he has one and is instantly in the club?"

Something about being with Allyson always made Debi smile. "Right. Or because he is a dick."

"Did you just call me a dick?" A tall man in a white lab coat stepped around the corner with a smarmy grin on his face. And it was a good-looking face hidden behind thick glasses and a goatee.

"Oh my god, I am so sorry." Debi wanted to bury herself in the nearest lab manual. "Open mouth, insert foot."

He shook his head sheepishly. "All's fair in love and science. If you hate me, I must be doing something right."

"Robert, I am so sorry you had to hear those words out of her very, very big mouth." Allyson glared at her.

"But it's a very pretty mouth." His eyes had the look of a predator ready to pounce.

"And you're charming." Debi shook her head. A lab guy who knew how to work women was a rare thing indeed. "On that note, I think I'll be going before I say something else completely horrifying." Plus, something about the man put her nerves on edge. Freedom was two secure doors away.

"Actually, if you don't mind, I needed Ally to check something for me real quick. Something about this formula doesn't look right."

Ally? *Please.* Now the guy was being an idiot, acting all buddy-buddy when Allyson had made it clear the guy was not a team player. Still, Allyson followed him around the corner. He peeked his head back around the credenza when she didn't follow. "Coming?"

The shoulder up view shocked a memory loose. In the picture she had memorized, he was younger, with no facial hair or glasses, and he wore a military uniform. He was on the Team Echo wall of shame.

Debi's fight or flight neurons kicked into gear, slamming her with adrenaline. The smile on her face felt synthetic. "In a sec. Let me clean up my mess here."

Their voices moved down the lab, but not fast or far. As if he was waiting for her. If what she suspected was true, he was Echo, and he was toying with her. Either he expected her to run or the move with Allyson was meant to draw her deeper into the lab and farther from help, not that she'd make it through both levels of security before he caught her, and she couldn't leave Allyson. Did he know about the men stationed outside?

Desperate, Debi scanned the lab looking for a weapon. Anything she could use to brain him was too heavy for her to use one handed. The fire extinguishers were stationed on the opposite wall and he'd see her. The bottles and vials on the closest shelves wouldn't slow him down. The slicing and dicing tools were down in the dissection lab.

Think.

Debi glanced up, her vision already swimmy, when her gaze landed on a bottle that might do the trick.

"Are you coming?" The tone hinted at impatience.

Bile twisted in her gut. "Slippers," she whispered, hoping at least the outgoing bug worked. No response from Rose, which had her head spinning.

"Debra?" The tone escalated, held a bite that went beyond irritation.

She stepped into the open passageway. "You know, I always wanted to bring a pair of slippers in here and do a slip and slide down the hall."

Allyson smiled from halfway down. "I did it in stocking feet. Once, after they buffed the floors. Don't tell Barry."

"I'm not really worried about him." She was more worried about the psychopath locked inside with them. It had not occurred to her that Team Echo would have access to the labs. Debi wished there was a way to get Allyson free. "Maybe you should go before Barry shows up. I don't want you to get in trouble. Robert can show me out."

Allyson's features tightened at the tension in Debi's tone. "Do you two know each other? You called her Debra."

"Just like Barry." Which confirmed Debi's worst fears.

"That's right," Robert confirmed. "We have some mutual friends."

The rapid beat of her heart bruised her chest cavity. Fear pulsed in every beat. She was in a very big trap. "Allyson..."

"She's not going anywhere." Robert wrapped a beefy hand around Allyson's bicep clamping down hard enough to bruise. And suddenly, the white lab coat failed to hide his bulk. In height and width, he resembled the members of Team Fear. Tall and broad like the others, but if Allyson's assessment was correct, more muscle than brain.

"Hey." Allyson tried to yank, but he clamped his hand down harder.

"Debra, come here. We're going to go sit in my office and wait for reinforcements."

"You have an office?" The hurt in Allyson's tone was unmistakable.

"That's not going to work for me," Debi answered Robert's command. No way was she going to go deeper into the maze where Rose and company wouldn't find her. She had to believe they heard her code word. That they were even now working to get inside.

Robert pulled a gun and pointed it at Allyson. "Does it work for you now?"

"No." But Debi stepped forward to avoid the danger he posed to her friend. She hadn't given the team the key code for the second level security access, so even if Craft had acquired a keycard, he wouldn't be able to get past the second layer of security. The knowledge had her temperature rising, but she couldn't afford a panic attack. Not now.

Allyson stilled. "What's this about, Robert?"

"Do you want to tell her or should I?"

"No." Debi angled closer, trying for a position that kept Allyson out of the line of fire.

"Let me go." Allyson twisted her hand and yanked, successfully freeing her hand.

Robert retaliated with a backhand that sent her reeling to the floor.

Debi raced to step between Robert and Allyson. "She doesn't need to know. Let her go. I don't think Barry would want his sister hurt." Although she couldn't say definitively. Barry was an egomaniac.

"I don't give a shit what Barry wants. He's not in charge."

"You might want to tell him that." Debi would love to be privy to that conversation. Her heart threatened to beat out of her chest as she asked the inevitable question. "Who is in charge?"

"You'll find out soon enough." He motioned with the gun. "Move." He shoved Allyson into the back hallway. With his hand now free, he grabbed Debi's sore elbow to tug her faster.

"Ow, asswipe." Struggling against his hold kept his attention off her good hand. She tucked it into the opening of the sling and gripped the vial she'd grabbed from lab. Carefully, she pried the stopper free. When the tile floor gave way to carpet, she tripped, freeing her arm from his grip.

"Watch it—"

His gun hand rose, but she was already in motion. She aimed for center body but failed. The acid splashed his gun hand and the white lab coat covering his arm.

"Fuck." He dropped the gun, screaming as he raced for the eye wash station.

Allyson turned to run back to the security entry, but Debi stopped her. "We'll never make it. The fire exit." Debi hauled ass on a serpentine path through the offices, praying that one of the men from Team Fear was waiting on the other side. Even the campus police were something, although Debi was the one trespassing and she had no doubt Echo could incapacitate anyone but another member of their twisted experiment. Bile rose. "I'm gonna throw up."

"Later," Allyson pushed from behind her to keep going.

They rounded a corner and ran smack into a wall of muscle. Tall, blond, and silent, he wrapped an arm around her, stopping her from bouncing back from the impact.

"Echo," Debi panted. She grabbed Rose's hand and tried to pull him to the exit. "Need to go."

Rose metamorphosed in front of her. Taller and wider, even his muscles appeared to grow in the dark back hall. She felt like Alice, shrinking in size while the world around her stayed the same. Rose's eyes darkened to near black and not a drop of empathy lived in his cold features. No longer a healer, this Rose was the machine they'd created in the lab. The one designed to kill without remorse.

Bulletproof? Maybe. Fearless, definitely.

He was bigger and stronger and more terrifying than any soldier on the planet. "Echo is here? Excellent." He turned toward the lab.

"Wait." Debi put her hand over her mouth, but he heard and turned.

The dominant expression on his face threatened violence. "What?"

"You can't go alone."

"How many are there?"

"One." Which to her was too many.

Rose's smile could only be called feral. The easygoing medic had gone bye-bye. This Rose wasn't turning back.

"He has a gun. And..." The impatience in Rose's stance halted her words, but she swallowed the panic. "Wait for backup. Please." She was afraid for herself, but more afraid for Rose, who looked on the edge of something dark that shimmered through him like a ghost.

"He's not getting away. Period." The roughness in his tone dropped an octave, as deep as he was wide. He gave her a gentle nudge toward the exit. Gentle, the contrast reminding her of the man who wrapped around her at night. The man she was starting to believe she couldn't live without.

Echo had killed two men on Team Fear. Debi couldn't lose Rose to the psychopaths the government had created. "I'm not leaving without you."

"Yes. You are." He turned, pushing into her space until he had her backed against the wall. "That wasn't a request. Move out."

Terror trembled in her legs, and she didn't know if it was fear of Rose and the heated intensity of his demeanor, or the encounter with Echo. "What if. There are more. Outside?" The hyperventilating meant she'd soon be incapable of coherent thought or movement.

"Suck it up, right now." The unbending authority acted like a bucket of ice water. "You will not have a panic attack. Do you understand?"

Holy crap. He scared the voice right out of her, so she

nodded her agreement, because to do less would piss off an already angry soldier.

"You will be safe. Not fine. Safe. Craft is on his way around the building as my backup. Stills is on the back of the building waiting for you. Go straight to the drug mobile parked directly behind this building. I cannot work with you in the line of danger. Move out."

Allyson gripped Debi's hand. "Maybe we should listen to your friend. We can contact campus security. I don't know—"

"No security," Rose ordered. "Straight out." He turned, a man accustomed to having his ordered followed. The path down the hall was dark and monsters filled the shadows. Debi swallowed as her vision narrowed and the hall seemed to waver like a fun house mirror.

"Come on." Allyson pulled her along. "I didn't know you still had panic attacks."

The hiccups started the instant Rose disappeared. "Only when people. Try. To kill me." Debi attempted to count each breath in her head, slow it down, but with Rose headed into an inevitable war with Echo, her breath wouldn't cooperate. They made it to the fire exit and a shadow separated from the wall.

CHAPTER TWENTY

I n the silhouette of the exterior emergency light, the shadow was faceless, but was definitely a male that stood nearly the height of the door. Almost as wide. Debi's hiccup echoed against the cement cage around the fire exit.

Allyson stopped mid stride. Debi stumbled right into her. Together, they inched backwards.

The shadow stepped with them in a wicked dance that brought him closer as his stride was longer. More certain. As he moved away from the blinding emergency light, his features came into focus.

"Craft," Debi choked. She squeezed Allyson's hand. "He's one of the good guys."

"That's debatable," he countered.

"Shouldn't you reassure us," Allyson said.

"Why? This is a volatile situation and you're more than a thousand feet to a secure location."

Debi had an image from *Jurassic Park* where the woman had to run from the raptors. Yeah, same odds. Acid rose up her throat with each hiccup. "Maybe we should hide." Great plan. Hide in one of the offices until the team took care of Robert.

"And if reinforcements from Echo arrive? Not a chance. I'll escort you ladies to Stills. He'll drive you to a secure location away from the scene."

"New plan." Stills entered through the fire exit. He wore a ballistics vest loaded with enough supplies to start a war. "Fowler repositioned overhead. He can pick off any threat. You have a clear path to the car." He tossed keys at Craft. "I'm on backup—"

"Bullshit." Craft slammed into Stills hard enough to crack a rib. "We all have an axe to grind, but we don't change mid-mission. Stick with the plan. I'm backup."

"You're needed on the computer, dumbass, if we're going to keep this off campus security video."

"Fuck." Craft stalked off, anger vibrating off his massive chest. "You have a point—"

A feral bellow sounded through the tunnel-like hall that lead back to the lab. Rose. Was he okay? The sound echoing down the hall was not okay.

"Saddle up, ladies. We need to roll," Craft ordered.

"Debi stays," Stills said.

"What?" She and Craft spoke at the same time.

Stills stood in the hall leading to the dark. "You saw what happened to Ryder. Rose is just as likely to take off my head as listen to me. If we need someone to talk him down, you're it."

"You want me to walk back into the burning building?" Sounded insane when she said it out loud.

"The building isn't burning," Allyson said.

Even Allyson's literal interpretation did nothing to ease the tension.

Stills stared straight into Debi's soul. "Do you care about him?"

Debi froze. The darkness of the back hall was like a dark cave, but that didn't keep her locked into place. It was the sound of Rose's scream. What had Robert done to him that elicited such pain and rage? She wasn't one of the few and the proud, but she couldn't walk away when the man she loved...

Loved? The thought of him dying left her cold and achy inside. Not three-margarita achy, but never leave the house again pain that threatened to drop her to her knees. Crap, there hadn't been enough time, but the emotions she wanted to deny were real. Love was the only thing that could explain why she wanted to follow Stills. Why she needed to follow the sound of Rose's pain. "I can't leave him."

"Move out." Stills ran into the fray, one of the few brave souls who ran into situations the rest of the world ran from.

"There's nothing you can do." Allyson grabbed her by the arm.

Yet her gut said she needed to go. That Rose needed her, and for him, she'd face her greatest fears. A gunshot sounded from deep in the lab. Debi yanked her good arm from Allyson's grip. "Go without me. My choice."

Craft handed her a Glock. "Do not engage," he ordered. "You are there only to deescalate the situation if Rose goes off the deep end. Understand?"

"Absolutely." Yeah, that was more bravado than truth, but she didn't have time for cold logic. It was time to follow her instincts and not her education. Checking to make sure a round was chambered and the safety off, she shook like a teen at her first dance, but her moves didn't give her away.

Craft grabbed Allyson and disappeared into the night.

Debi swallowed a breath that didn't stop the trembling. She twisted and jogged back down the hall anyway.

At the intersection to the well-lit lab, Debi's bravado faltered. Once again, her mouth had taken her where her body didn't want to follow. Her feet stuck to the carpet as she peeked around the corner and took in the scene. Robert stood in the open expanse staring down one of the narrow spaces hidden behind bookshelves and credenzas. A blood trail smeared down the otherwise polished floor.

"Rose." She whispered his name, hoping to somehow summon him, whole and complete. Robert stalked forward like the predator the government had created, ready to kill. Debi couldn't let it happen. She lifted the gun, but her arm shook too much to get a decent shot. She needed a brace. She ran forward, crossing the threshold of tile and lab, her hated tennis shoes squeaking. She made it ten feet into the open before Robert turned. He'd lost the glasses. Something inhuman swam through his eyes. He blinked, and then he smiled like a demented clown. Exaggerated and scary as hell.

Debi wanted to turn tail and run, but he'd be on her like a coyote on an injured deer. She'd come this far. Widening her stance, she faced him. No way would she shoot straight. Too much adrenaline ran through her system, making her quaky and her moves uncertain, but if she brought him close enough. Maybe she had a chance. The words she wanted to use stuck in her craw. For once, her mouth wasn't running away with her. She used her body instead. She lifted the weapon and aimed at center mass. Her injured arm shook from the exertion, but she thought back to her physical therapy. If she could lift weights, and they burned her shoulder like a hot brand, then she could hold the gun long enough to shoot.

As it happened, she didn't have long to wait. Robert stepped toward her with a definite swagger. Dead certainty that she wouldn't, couldn't hurt him, added to his ego as he walked calm as preacher on a Sunday stroll. "Have you embraced the fear yet?" he yelled. He smiled at her as he took another step. "Not you, baby. I smell your fear."

Oh. Hell.

The slow pace was more threatening than a fast assault. Heat rose through her body in waves of pure terror. Her feet took a step back without talking to her mind. He took another step, his stride longer. Nothing could stop the backward glide of her feet across the tile. For every step she took, he took a larger one, moving him closer.

Panting a breath out, she slid her finger around the trigger. "I will shoot you." Even her voice quivered.

He tilted his head to the side like he was looking over a used car. Assessing. "Baby, I'm invincible."

Wow, this guy had nothing on the criminally insane. Maybe they should strap his ass down on the torture device in the basement at The Manor. "What's your plan here?"

"They join us or die. Simple as." He held a syringe out like a psycho stabbing a knife. "Direct injection works much faster. Your rescuer has more chemicals flowing through his system right now than a napalm factory."

Debi wanted to close her eyes, say a prayer that Rose was okay, but she didn't dare take her eyes off Robert. Glass rattled in the direction of the blood trail. Debi raised her voice so Robert wouldn't follow the sound. "He won't turn. None of these guys will. You can't turn a sane man crazy."

"He doesn't have to be crazy. He needs to do what the government created him to do. Kill."

"He's not like you." But God only knew what was happening in Rose's head right now. Ryder talked about hallucinations and fear.

"We're the elite. If he doesn't want to kill with impunity, he will die. By my hand. Tonight. As for you..."

She didn't want to know. "What?"

"The plan is simple. Fuck you until you can't move, and then I'll eviscerate you. The Company wants you dead."

Ok. More than criminally insane. Sweat dripped down her forehead from the fear, from the weight of the gun in her hand. The brand stabbing pain through her shoulder turned to a hot poker burrowing under her skin, but letting go of the gun was certain death. She stepped back until a countertop gouged her back.

"Well, will you look at that. Nowhere for you to run."

"Come get me, then." She needed to shoot him before her arm gave out. Joy lit his face as he increased his speed. She pulled the trigger, hitting him center mass, but he kept coming.

A shot rang out, echoing in the glass and steel lab. Blood spurted from Robert's thigh. He dropped to one knee.

"Run," Stills shouted at her from within the bowels of the lab, but she couldn't see where he stood.

Paralyzed, Debi couldn't be certain which way to run. The way out, through the fire exit, was unguarded. Anyone could come in that way, including more of Team Echo. Craft was gone by now. The only safe place was with Rose. No matter what they'd injected him with, he'd protect her. Running a wide circle around Robert, she followed the blood trail.

At the corner, an arm snaked out and pulled her behind the protection of the equipment. "Rose." Thank God. Her body sagged against him, but it was like hugging a wall of granite. She looked up and her breath caught. Any resemblance to the man she knew was superficial.

Sweat coated his skin and shirt. His pupils were dilated and his breathing ragged. Rage lit his eyes like a red glow stick. "I told you to go."

"I told you I don't take orders."

"Feeling brave, woman?" He pressed his hard body into hers, and it wasn't sexy.

Debi stepped back until her heels hit the bottom of a cabinet.

"Leave this spot and I will spank your ass so hard you won't walk for a week."

The threat sparked her anger button. Maybe it was better than fear. Maybe it was reckless. "Try it, you overgrown Neanderthal—"

"Do. Not. Move." The heat of his breath brushed her cheek.

Debi bit her tongue to keep her overactive mouth shut. She was using it to fight the fear, but now was not the time. This was not gentle, pliable Rose. He was dosed.

"Stills," Rose called, his voice tight. Controlled.

Stills dropped down from the row of shelves separating the different lab spaces, a rifle slung over his left shoulder. He moved swiftly, silently, suddenly looking more like a killer than Robert.

"If anything happens to her, I will haunt your ass." Rose disappeared around the corner. Moments later, a splat sounded like someone dropping a raw turkey followed by a groaned *oomph*.

Fury invaded where fear dare not. The thirst for revenge still burned his throat and coated his tongue. The last few days, he'd been a complete ass, visiting violence on his brothers because he could, because they would take it, because, in the end, they were the same. Monsters all.

Just like Echo. The man had stabbed Rose, not with a knife but a downward slash of a full syringe. The fluid burned as it was forced under the skin of his thigh. The pumping of his heart pushed blood and poison through his system. It was only a matter of time before the poison won.

Enough of this shit. The man in front of him was one monster he could put in the ground without remorse.

The side effects. In his head, he heard Ryder's warning and gave him the mental finger. The anger felt fucking fantastic as it burned away the cold and the numb of the past six months. Awareness was like stepping into the sun after cowering in a cave. He felt everything. Grief at what happened to Mad Dog, the loss of his family, the loss of a future he no longer had. All these added fuel to the fire he didn't want to control. He wanted to blow something up, not defuse it.

"Help him."

Stills shook his head. "He's got this."

"He said he'd haunt you. As if he's planning to die." True panic dripped down her tight throat. "How can you..." Violence. Flesh on flesh. Fists. Curses. The stuff of nightmares.

"I know why you stepped into the open, but it wasn't necessary. We were drawing him into the kill box."

"Kill box?" Oh, she really wished her mouth didn't bypass her filters.

Stills drew a rectangle in the air, motioning from one end of the lab area to the other. "We were trying to take him alive. I was up there." He pointed to the top of the shelves. "Rose was down here looking like a drugged-out meat sack to draw him close enough to contain."

"Oh." One more mistake in a line of too many shoved off the panic and the grief that had gripped her since her father disowned her. She'd screwed up because she'd thought with her heart and not her head. "And then I came out."

"Rose nearly had a coronary when he heard your voice. Trying to draw Echo off was brave but stupid. I get why you did it. Can even respect you for it, but Rose isn't that evolved."

"Not right now. But normally."

Stills snorted. "Not ever. Not when it comes to protecting women."

Six sisters. Sadly, Stills made a solid point. The noises Stills tried to distract her from got louder. Kicks, maybe. Cracks. Broken bones? She slipped past Stills to peek around the corner.

Robert lay on his side, slithering across the slick tile like a snake. He gripped his leg trying to staunch the flow of blood. Rose pulled back a large work boot and slammed it into Robert's ribs.

Snap.

Debi swallowed. As she watched, Rose tore into Robert.

Robert laughed, a wet, gurgling sound. "You're just like me."

Rose pulled back his fist to pummel, to visit death on the bleeding man. In profile, Rose was terrifying to behold. His jaw was hard, his eyes empty, and his body soulless. A bulge of muscle and anger throbbed in his throat. An animalistic growl emerged as if Echo's words were the catalyst to unleash the beast within. The background blurred, turned to fog, with her focus on the rage in Rose's normally calm demeanor. There was no humanity left in either man.

Guilt beat a constant mantra in her heart. This is what she'd done. "Stop him."

Stills rubbed a hand over his jaw. "He already clocked me once. I'm not getting between him and his prey."

"What if he kills him?"

"Sweetheart, Echo was a dead man the second he turned on you."

Debi closed her eyes against the death match. Robert no longer fought. He took hits and kicks. Grunts and groans. Squishy sounds like a sponge. Her stomach turned and she threw up across the counter she leaned on. With a final *snap-crunch*, the sounds silenced.

She opened her eyes to see Rose standing over a bloody, swollen mass of flesh barely covered in the clothes Robert had worn. The white lab coat soaked up blood. More trailed along the floor reminding her of the night she'd broken her nose in her father's pristine condo. Now the blood covered her father's lab, and she was afraid for a whole new reason.

His back to her, Rose's shoulders slumped like a man under a yoke. Defeated despite the dubious win. His knuckles were bruised and coated in blood. Flesh. He turned. Faced her, his eyes empty like Frankenstein's monster suddenly confronted with his own strength. His own inhumanity. Cuts scraped his face. Blood dripped from a wound in his forearm, but it was the desolation that cut her heart out. Here he was, the Frankenstein monster created from her thoughtlessness. Her ego. She was the reason he'd beaten a man to death with two hands.

The recognition, the knowledge of what he'd done, shimmered in his eyes. She stepped forward with the need to save him from the hopelessness, but before she could reach him, he dropped like a massive boulder hitting the highway, out cold.

No thought, no fear could keep her away. She raced across the tile, her shoes squishing through the still wet blood trail. Rose's skin went pasty white. While she watched, his chest stopped moving.

CHAPTER TWENTY-ONE

Debi dropped to her knees at Rose's side. His chest started again, panting out breath like she did in the middle of a panic attack. His pulse raced. Too damned fast. Cardiac arrest fast. "Beta blockers. The stuff he gave Ryder after they dosed him. Tell me you have some."

Stills dug through his vest. "We all do. After what happened with Ryder."

Ryder had nearly gone crazy, took risks, acted in random and illogical ways, and then spent three days recovering, but what they'd done to Rose looked worse. Robert had delivered the drug subcutaneously, making the reaction stronger and faster. Rose was strong but human, and the side effects were getting worse not better. His heart could flat give out while she watched. God, she couldn't lose him. The hand she held out trembled. "I'll administer."

"No offense, but you're shaky as fuck. I wouldn't want you anywhere near my veins." He slipped off the lid and stuck Rose. Inserted the medicine.

Seeing Rose fall had happened in slow motion. The big man was supposed to be invincible. Tears dropped down her cheeks. Stills' reaction was clinical, much the way she had been working in this lab. "Do you have to be so calm?"

"Actually, I do." His eyes went cold. "We all do. Isn't that the problem?"

"No. Damnit, the look in your eyes is the problem. This isn't a death sentence." Although Rose looked half dead on the floor surrounded by blood she prayed wasn't his. "Was he shot?"

"Flesh wound. Enough to draw Echo into the box."

She had panicked. Not only had she failed at the mission Stills gave her, but she'd failed to protect Rose from himself. It was her fault he was on the ground. The reason Robert was dead. The weight of knowing he could be the dead man floored her. She dropped to Rose's chest to feel the movement of his breath under her cheek. To know he lived. Tears wet his shirt, but not enough to wash away the blood.

"Careful. He might wake up swinging."

Debi didn't acknowledge Stills as he stepped away to mutter on the radio. It was quite possible she was having a nervous breakdown. Every muscle in her body twitched. Her nerves backfired, her pulse raced, and the longer Rose stayed unconscious the more fear twisted her in its cruel grip. "Fight, damnit," she hissed at his still frame. Words settled on her tongue with the need to express the emotion inside, but it was too new. Raw, and the once sterile room was too ugly. "You want to protect me? Protect your sisters? Then fight."

The clock in her head stopped ticking until the moment his eyes blinked open. "River?"

He hugged her close, and that moment of sweet connection filled the hollow ache inside. Tangling a hand in her hair, he levered her back so he could see her face.

"Jesus, you have blood all over you. What the fuck did I do?" He crawled back, trying to scoot away, but she was wrapped around him. "Where's Stills?"

"That's the first thing you have to say?"

"I asked a question." Patience was not his virtue.

"He's calling backup."

"Good." Rose untwined her fingers. "Get off me."

Okay, so he was still the asshole Rose. He was on drugs. No one knew the half-life of the garbage running through his veins.

"You've got blood all over you." His lips twisted in disgust. He climbed to his feet and stepped away from her. "Stills. Where the fuck are you?"

"Yes, master?" Stills came limping in, hunched over like Igor, Frankenstein's assistant.

"Knock it off. We have work. We need to clean up the mess. Get rid of the body. And figure out how to turn these damn lights down."

"You thinking straight?"

"Straight enough." But he slurred the words.

Debi sat three feet from a dead body in a pool of blood, watching the two men make plans, and she wasn't sure Rose was okay. Not really. A few more minutes and she might have had to administer CPR. "Maybe we should go see Dr. Branson."

Rose looked down at her, his eyes glazed. "Stills, get her the fuck away from me."

————

The ugly words wore a groove through her brain. The shoulder wound burned, but it would heal. The stabbing pain in her heart might break her wide open. The deal with Barry had injured her pride. Compounded with getting kicked out of the program, it had festered and filled with angry puss, but one that stayed on her skin. It didn't wind as deep as the words straight from Rose's mouth.

There was no good way to take what he'd said. He hadn't even spoken directly to her, as if he couldn't stand looking at her. Talking to her. She followed Stills to join the rest of the team as they discussed what needed to be done.

Craft and Stills huddled at a table in the opposite corner of the restaurant. Fowler had stayed behind to take care of Rose. Rose had stayed to take care of the body. Debi wasn't sure she wanted to know what that entailed. The rest of the team argued about the plan. They called it a strategy session. They were on and off the phone with Ryder while hovering over plates of bacon and eggs. She and Allyson sat across the restaurant, and they may as well have been invisible for all the men looked at them.

"I hate this," Allyson said. "It's the good old boy program all over again."

Okay, if Allyson was the voice of women's independence, Debi had fallen way far down the rabbit hole. "You're right. Apparently to be in the club you have to have a penis."

"You're never going to let me live that one down, are you?"

"Not in this lifetime." Debi smiled. It was faint, and didn't reach her heart, but it was real enough. "I wasn't sure you knew the word."

"I know the word. I'm not as socially awkward as you think. I just don't like people."

"Last I checked, I was a person. Should I be offended?"

"No. I mean, I like individuals, just not people." She gestured around the diner with its teal booths and neon signs. "Groups of people get me worked up. That's why I was always happy to let Barry take the praise. I don't need it. The one thing I knew from the age of eight was that I'm smarter than the average bear. I don't need praise." She coughed into her coffee cup as she realized the implication of what she'd said. "I mean, praise isn't bad if that's what you want..."

Allyson was talking about Debi's convoluted relationship with her father. Debi had another moment she could misconstrue the statement or she could acknowledge what Allyson was trying to say, even if she was doing a piss-poor job of it. "I didn't want praise. Not the way you mean. I wanted my father to see me, really see me and what I was capable of."

"With or without a dick."

Debi snorted. "Exactly. But he's buried so deep in his own ego that I never had a chance. The only reason Barry has his attention is because of the money Barry brings into the university. Barry makes dear old Dad look good."

"They're a lot alike," Allyson mused.

"Truer words." Debi rested her elbow against the table to take the pressure off her arm. The sling only helped so much.

"I still think I should call campus security."

On the drive over, they had convinced Allyson that Robert was a corporate spy. Stealing research was a big money business, not so unusual considering the grants Barry had brought into the program. "Robert got through the background check, which means he had inside help. These guys need to investigate, and they can't do that if this goes public. The insider will walk away clean."

Allyson scrubbed a hand over her forehead. "All of this is outside of my comfort zone. I just want to do the job I'm good at."

"Then go back to work and pretend it never happened. The two of you weren't friends or even friendly, really. No one will know you were there tonight."

Lines creased around Allyson's tired eyes. "I wish I hadn't been there."

"Me too." Although, knowing that a member of Team Echo was on the staff at the university research center opened up their investigation. She owed the guys to distract Allyson from all the questions she surely had. "What did you want to talk to me about the day we passed each other outside the admin building?"

"After the night we've had, it seems juvenile."

Debi jerked her head toward the men in the back. "We've got time for juvenile."

"It's girly." Allyson whispered the words like it was a sin. She ran a finger over the tabletop design.

"Sounds even better." Allyson hadn't had much room for juvenile and girly, two things every woman had a God-given right to experience. Middle school cured you of it, or should, but Allyson hadn't had a chance for normal middle school. She'd been to prep schools and had graduated high school at fourteen. Debi rested her back against the wall and stretched her legs along the vinyl bench seat of their booth. "Is it about Mark?"

"How did you—"

"There are no secrets in the lab especially when you take every chance you can to rub elbows with the only male who isn't your brother. So tell me all about it."

"Mark and I started hooking up about a year ago." Her face turned a splotchy red, which spread to her neck and chest.

"I thought sooner the way he looked at you. Watched the way you walked." The budding academic hadn't done much to hide his infatuation.

"Took me awhile to recognize the signs Took even longer to act on it, but once we did, we were all in. We planned to run away, which is stupid. I'm a grown-ass woman, I can date who I want to date. Or hook up. Or anything I want. I don't know if I loved Mark. What does love feel like?"

Hell if Debi knew. The fairy tales had it all wrong. It wasn't a song in your heart. More like a knife. "If it's supposed to be easy, everyone I know is doing it wrong." Debi had seen Lauren flattened by Ryder's disappearance. Lauren's mother had died of grief. Debi's own heart resembled chopped beef.

"I think I mostly wanted a secret adventure. Something all my own with someone who wanted me enough to sneak away. It felt romantic in a Shakespearean way. Then Mark disappeared, which felt tragic. Also like Shakespeare. One night, we were planning our getaway, the next he had packed up his apartment and moved back to Ohio. It doesn't matter." Her eyes watered. "Barry would never have let me go."

"You're integral to his success." Which sucked six ways to Sunday.

"I'd feel better about that if he acknowledged it, but if you asked him, the work is his and he's showing me a kindness by letting me keep my job. When I saw his notes—proof that he'd stolen from you—I realized the depth of his narcissism." Allyson's throat flexed. "Being ambitious isn't a sin."

Ambition was all kinds of wrong when you pushed it to the levels Barry did. "But?"

"When I confronted him—"

"You actually told him you knew?"

"He didn't deny it. He bragged about how easy it was. It was like..." She blew out a breath to ruffle her bangs. "He deserved it. It wasn't a question of right or wrong, but of his right to take whatever he wanted. He deserved it, he kept saying. He was too smart to get caught. Even the old man, that's what he called your father, even the old man didn't catch on. It was like watching a stranger."

Nerves fluttered to life under Debi's skin. Once Barry exposed his true self to Allyson, he'd turn on her. Sister or not. Debi leaned forward. "I don't like that he's aware. Maybe you should consider coming back with us."

"Where?"

"A safe house. Stay until we figure out what Barry's involved in and if you're in danger."

Allyson stared across the coffee counter to the clock that was nearing midnight. "He wouldn't hurt me."

"I'm not so sure." Barry might not get physical, but Echo was definitely watching the lab. They wouldn't hesitate to kill Allyson. "Robert said Barry wasn't in charge."

"Robert was insane."

"Obviously, but..." Oh, hell, in for a penny. If what Debi suspected was true, Allyson deserved to know the risks. And Debi needed to tell someone before her head exploded. "The changes Barry made to my formula? I think the Army used it for an experimental program."

"It hasn't gone through human trials yet."

"Oh, yes it has, but not the kind you can put in a report." Debi faltered. She didn't mind warning Allyson, but she wouldn't expose the team. "Robert and men like him *are* the human trials."

The implications were stamped on Allyson's shocked face. "Was Robert crazy before they tested it on him?"

"That's what I'm trying to figure out, because it started as my formula even if Barry perverted it." At least that's what Debi suspected. She hadn't had time to look at the results from the blood tests. "I really wish you'd come with us before one of the test subjects decides to go after you."

"Barry might be an ass, but he wouldn't let anyone hurt me."

Debi gnawed on her bottom lip. "Going back probably isn't smart."

"I wanted to run away with Mark, but I chickened out. The week I delayed sent Mark away and I can't live with myself knowing I'm doing it again. Failing to live up to the person I want to be. I'm not chickening out. Maybe I can find something out for you."

Voices raised across the room, drawing all eyes to the men in the corner. If they were trying for covert, they failed miserably. Their size drew attention naturally. Their anger drew everyone's eyes.

Sounded like strategy had the men divided. Debi avoided their stark gazes. No way would they approve of what she was about to do, but they weren't exactly sharing their plans. And Rose had sent her away, pushed her away if she were honest, and it made the divide between her and the team greater. If they wanted to work together, great, but as long as they kept everything segregated, the women were on their own. Careful to avoid the needle, Debi pulled a used syringe from her sling. "You can start with this."

"What is it?"

The syringe Robert had stabbed into Rose. "My formula plus whatever Frankenstein-level stuff Barry added. I need you to reverse engineer it. Figure out exactly what they're using."

"You think Barry's completely off the reservation."

"I think he's playing God."

A chair scraped across the room. Craft stood, agitation stamped on his hard jaw, which was unusual for the normally low-key soldier. "No fucking way."

Allyson tucked the syringe deep in the pocket of her jacket. "I have an appointment next week for the NMR machine. I'll run my regular tests, and then I'll run this."

"I'm going to see what the big bad he-men have decided." Debi dropped money on the table to cover their breakfast. "If you don't want to go with us, I suggest you disappear while I distract them." Debi sauntered over to the table where Craft still stood, his face blazing red. "Gentlemen, there are only two of you. Can't you get along for an hour or two?"

Stills shook his head. "You don't have to like it, man, but it's operational security."

"Like what?"

Craft pulled Debi down to sit in a chair beside him. "He wants to give Allyson GHB."

Debi turned to where Allyson still sipped coffee from a yellow mug. "Craft's right. No fucking way."

"Jesus." Stills ran a nervous hand over the back of his neck. "Put it in context. She knows too much, so we help her to forget tonight. Can't be the best memory anyway. Knock her out, put her in her own bed. We've all been there. She loses time, but is no worse off. She wakes up with no memory of the night."

After her own experience, Debi wouldn't sanction it. No way, no how. "First of all, there's no guarantee she would forget. And that's assuming you get the dosing right, you ignoramus. Second of all, forgetting everything that happened could endanger her more. She'd be an easy target."

"Then we bring her with us."

"Oh, hell no." Craft was equally emphatic, his voice growing agitated. "You can't kidnap a woman. An innocent."

"We don't know she's an innocent. She's working at the lab."

The guys might be big, but they weren't stupid. They'd added the numbers of why a member of Team Echo was working at the lab. This wasn't a coincidence. Robert had been at the lab for a long-term surveillance operation. Debi needed to convince Stills, because she wouldn't let him give a drug to Allyson. "The lab has something to do with the experiments. Why else would Robert be there? He wasn't waiting for me. I was a target of opportunity. He said that Barry wasn't in charge, which implies Barry is involved." That much they could figure out on their own. She lowered her voice. "We can go into details when we're all together." She wanted to discuss this back at The Manor. "Allyson's presence does not equate to guilt. I know her. I know her dickhead brother. He's a control freak. Trust me, he did not share this project with her."

Stills leaned back until the chair propped up on hind legs. He crossed his massive arms over his chest. "Not worth the liability to the team."

"Not your call." Debi would go over his head if she had to. Maybe Lauren could reason with Ryder. "What's more, I think Allyson can help us. She has access to more of Barry's records than I ever would."

Stills dropped the chair down to all four legs. Oh, she had his attention now.

"What's wrong with you," Craft hissed. "That's like leading a lamb to the slaughterhouse."

"She doesn't want to come with us. I offered. Outside of forcing her, and I'm against that on principle, what choice do we have?"

Craft glanced over his shoulder and cursed. "None now. She bolted."

The waitress had already cleared the table and set up for the next customer. Allyson was long gone.

A slight smile gave her away. Stills shook his head. "You helped her."

Debi neither confirmed nor denied. "What's the rest of the plan?"

CHAPTER TWENTY-TWO

S weat dripped down the wrist restraints to pool on the plastic-covered mattress. The image of Debi replaced Maggie Madigan in his dreams that were no longer dreams. The images—memory or fear—played repeatedly in Rose's brain until he roared with the need to get free. To protect her. To protect his sisters. His heart raced like a greyhound pounding toward the winner's gate or death, and either seemed preferable to the light stabbing behind his eyes. If he closed his eyes, he saw the images of Debi's death. If he opened them, the light stabbed like an ice pick in the brain.

"You need to sleep," Fowler told him in a pitch designed to drive him insane.

"Jesus, do you have to scream?" Rose croaked.

"I'm going to give you something to make you rest."

Rose yanked on the restraints of the rusty gurney, but they held firm. "Don't touch me."

The needle pricked the skin stretched taut over his bones.

"What the hell did you pump into my blood?" He cursed

his teammate until his mouth ran dry. Sleep called, but Rose resisted. He needed to get up and protect her. He couldn't live through her death one more time, and he wasn't sure if the *her* in his nightmares was Maggie or Debi or Camy.

———

A feral scream punctured the silent night. Debi shivered on the stairs but forced herself toward the scream that broke her heart. At the bottom of the stairs leading to the basement clinic, Ryder sat on a bench tucked into an alcove. His head rested against tile and he looked deceptively calm. Almost sleeping. Debi tiptoed, hoping this time to make it past the night guard.

Then she hit the bottom step. Ryder sat up and stretched his legs. "I'd bet every dollar in my bank account that Rose doesn't want you seeing him like this."

"I'd bet every dollar I have that he does."

The smile on his face had a knowing quality. Sadness and pain. "Guess we'll have to wait until he wakes up to ask him."

"I don't care what he looks like. How he acts. I need to see him." The fear beating in her chest wasn't the panic attack variety. What Robert injected into Rose had lasting consequences. She needed to see Rose to assure herself he was okay. DV1028 had cost her everything. Her career. Her father. Her friends. She couldn't live with the drug taking away the man she loved. "Please." She hadn't even had a chance to tell Rose how she felt.

Ryder shook his head. "He's fine."

A knot formed in her throat. "Fine means a lot of things, but okay isn't one of them."

"Rose will be okay. We've all been through the detox."

Another scream echoed. "Sounds worse than it is," Ryder assured her.

"He shouldn't be alone." No one in that much pain should suffer alone.

"Fowler is with him."

"But Fowler trained on goats." Even she heard the whine in her voice.

"Fowler's a trained medic, no matter what story Rose told you. He's in good hands."

Debi turned and climbed two steps. She turned back. "I need my research notebook. It's in the lab. The last exam room."

"Nice try."

"I really do need my notes." She needed to confirm the chemical makeup, in the off chance she was wrong. "I'll wait right here."

The smile on his face almost looked real. "I'll bring it to you. After you're gone."

"You're really not going to let me see him?"

"I'm really not."

She made it three steps this time. "Ryder, he means something to me."

"You mean something to him, too. That's how I know he wouldn't want you to see him. I wouldn't ever want Lauren to see me like this."

"Promise you'll come get me if anything changes."

"You'll be the first to know."

She shuffled up the rest of the steps, her head hung low. If anything happened to Rose, she'd never forgive herself.

The straps on his wrists were slack, but still buckled. Rose's hand shook as he lifted it off the mattress. "You think you can give me another inch of wiggle room? I can't sleep like this."

Fowler opened his eyes to slits. "I give you another inch and you'll be out of those restraints and on my ass in under ten seconds."

"Damn straight. I'd kick your ass."

"I don't want to fight another brother."

Rose glanced around his surroundings. The lights were dimmed, but still showed enough to make out the exam rooms at The Manor. He didn't remember the return trip. "She saw me beat a man to death with my bare hands."

Fowler was crashed on a sleeping bag on the floor. "So I heard."

The logical course would have been to keep the man alive. Interrogate him, but anger had bubbled up like lava blowing the top off his control. "I couldn't stop it. The rage." And beyond where the Army quacks had hidden fear, a niggle of worry broke free. Just because Mad Dog was exonerated didn't mean they were harmless. Any one of them could lose it. "What if I had turned on her?"

Fowler didn't give him comfortable lies. "Was that a possibility?"

"Hell if I know." Rose wet his cracked lips. "Can I get a drink?"

"You're hooked up to an IV. I'm not getting close enough for you to kick my ass."

"Smart man." Rose didn't even know what he'd do if he could get free. He couldn't trust himself around Debi, but he craved her like water. Like she was life, but he still didn't know if she was safe. What if he was the worst thing chasing her?

————

Three days passed before Fowler declared Rose drug free and ready to leave the torture device they'd strapped him to downstairs. The detox was killer according to all involved, and the sound of his moans had sent Debi scurrying away when she'd normally have pushed. She'd caused him this pain.

When he returned to the land of the living, Rose sat half a table away, leaving her crammed between Craft and Fowler feeling like a Barbie doll in the midst of GI Joes. She'd refused to discuss the findings from the lab until they were all together. Considering what she had to say, she didn't want Rose to hear things secondhand. Now she didn't know how to begin. Dinner—Ryder and Lauren this time—went down like sand. Debi couldn't get enough water. When Rose wouldn't meet her gaze, she turned to Craft. "Have you heard anything on the dummy email account?"

"No." He had setup a dummy account for Allyson to contact her. It was untraceable according to their resident computer expert. "After the way she left, you still think she'll help?"

"She didn't go to the cops." They'd monitored police blotters and 911 calls. "It's the first thing I would have done."

"She doesn't know Echo is dead."

True. Allyson had hightailed it out when she'd had the chance. Lucky her. "There was a lot that went down that night that was abnormal. Robert hasn't shown up back to work, and he did attack her. Plus breaking and entering."

"Which she participated in."

"You really don't like her."

"I don't know her. I know we're in a world of hurt. Friends are few and far between. Her staying away from the cops doesn't look good. Means she could be working with Echo and they now know too much."

"You're paranoid."

"That I am." He didn't sound ashamed of it.

"Yet you didn't want to give her GHB."

"Hell no. I didn't join the Army to take the war stateside. I'm not drugging civilians. We'll leave that to Echo. Whatever they're up to, it's wrong and we may be the only ones in a position to stop them. Until we know more about the lab, I'll stay paranoid."

Paranoia was a side effect. It wouldn't go away, at least not that they knew.

"I may be able to help with the lab." She swiped her sweaty palms on the front of her jeans. They had threatened on multiple occasions to destroy the monsters responsible for creating the experimental drug that changed them. Inside, the fear lived like a bright fire, but she couldn't live a lie no matter what she risked by telling the truth. "I have a few answers and more questions."

"You've been awful quiet since that night."

She'd been thinking about Rose. Thinking that you couldn't control who you loved, and wasn't that a shame. "Had stuff to think about."

"Done thinking?"

"That never really happens. The human brain... Oh, you don't care." And she was too nervous to put more words together. She should use Camy's excuse. Girl stuff. Shut men up every time. She pointed discreetly at Rose, who had his face buried in his food. "I wanted him to be awake before we talked about all this."

"Ready now?"

Not even close. "I love jumping into fires."

Craft whistled to draw everyone's attention. "Debi has information."

"You and Rose took the same class in subtle," she mumbled.

He grinned. "Worked, didn't it?" Every eye in the place focused on her. Except Rose. He focused on the clock behind her head.

"Why don't we take this to the great room," Janet suggested. "Jake and I can make coffee."

The delay spiked Debi's nerves, but people were already moving. Jake pulled his mother aside. "Janet, I'd rather you stayed out of this."

"Suck it," Janet answered.

Jake pulled back in surprise. "Excuse me?"

"You heard."

Debi tried to follow the conversation as she moved with the crowd. The two had an interesting parent-child dynamic.

Janet added water to the coffee maker while Fowler added the grounds. Voices stayed level as Janet continued. "I appreciate you trying to shield me, but I never wanted that. Big Jake never tried, which is how I ended up with you. The fact is, you're my son. You signed up to let the government poison your system. I was involved the moment they hurt you."

Lauren bumped into Debi on the way out of the kitchen. "I'd love to see Janet lose her temper."

"The guys are all a little terrified of her. She'd be magnificent."

Lauren squeezed Debi's elbow and whispered as they walked. "You okay doing a briefing?"

"I may throw up."

"I think that's normal public speaking, not panic attack stuff."

"It's firing squad stuff."

"They're not going to shoot the messenger."

"I'm not just the messenger." Debi didn't have time to explain as the men went out of the way to draw her up front and center. Like a firing squad. Should she sit or stand? Stand, she decided, and wished desperately for her boots and that extra four inches. Her heart pounded.

Janet leaned against the door to the kitchen, waiting on the coffee with Fowler at her side.

Debi twisted her fingers together. She wanted to ease into it, but her brain focused on the bad stuff first. "You guys know I have panic attacks."

"Not exactly a secret," Ryder responded. She'd had a major attack the day Echo shot her.

Debi took a deep breath. Talking to this group was like walking into an AA meeting and sharing your story for the first time.

"You'll do fine, honey." Janet's warm smile brightened the room, but did nothing to ease the nerves.

"That's the thing. The attacks aren't solely relegated to moments like this. The attacks started when I was a kid. No one ever explained why. Mom couldn't afford much in the way of doctors, so we accepted them as normal, but they got so severe I had to quit sports and academic clubs. The older I got, the more I needed to understand what was happening to me. Inside me. I studied fear, the rational and irrational kind, but understanding why didn't stop the attacks." She popped her knuckles and the crackles were the only sound except the coffee brewer in the other room. "After a good run at the university for my undergrad, I took a research position in the university lab. Trust me, if I wasn't a good chemist, my father never would have hired me."

Why did she feel the need to justify her position? Her intelligence? Because she needed them to understand what motivated her to go down this dark road. "The lab became my second home. I worked sixty or more hours a week studying any and every chemical combination that would unlock the fear that paralyzed me, that made my father hate me."

"Dr. McMahon shamed you for it," Lauren piped in from her seat on the sofa next to Ryder. "We all saw it. It's like he knew your triggers and when things didn't go his way, he'd push you into an attack to take the pressure off."

Debi stepped back, flattened by Lauren's words. "I never realized..." But the more she thought about it, the more she saw the truth. "I thought if I could stop the attacks..." Tears filled her eyes as she reached out for Rose's gaze. "Without the attacks, maybe he would..." Love her. "Be proud of me, so when I hit on a promising compound that did wonders in animal testing, I used myself as a guinea pig."

Lauren's eyes brimmed with sympathy. "That's why you broke protocol." Lauren had never asked, which made her the best friend on the planet.

"The compound worked like magic. The first week, I felt..." Fearless. "Amazing. I did a presentation at the staff meeting without a single hiccup."

"Which is probably how Barry figured it out," Lauren said.

"He went to my father that day. Turned me in for failure to follow protocol. For a breach in ethics. You name it, he added it to the complaint. My father kicked me out immediately. There was no hearing in front of the ethics committee. They didn't have physical proof. I was just out. My biological promised to destroy the formal complaint if I walked away. Gave me the bar—the place Lauren and I used to party as undergrads—as a token if I never spoke to him again." Being paid to avoid her own father hurt worse than losing her job.

Some wounds festered and others scarred. Barry had done both. The damage to her career was a scar, and she'd be damned if she'd slow down because an asshole used her, but the wound to her confidence festered like a pus-filled limb that needed an amputation.

The bruised walls of her chest tightened like a band under her ribs, but once the words started she couldn't stop them. They spilled out in a fast stream of nonsense. "The letdown was severe. Not emotionally, but going from a position of emotional strength to having panic attacks again, sometimes two or three a day. The rebound effect lasted for weeks. I might have locked myself on the ranch and never come out, but Lauren hounded me to get my life back on track."

She'd never be able to repay Lauren for all she had done. It's why she had made sure Lauren had a safe place to land when Ryder took a walk. "The day we searched Lauren's office, I ran into Barry. He made tenure." Lousy SOB. "He brought in a big research grant, and that's like winning the academic lottery. I have no proof, but I bet—"

"He sold your idea to the Army," Ryder finished.

The men all stared at her like she was a three-headed goat

at the county fair. Rose wouldn't meet her gaze. Camy gave her a big thumbs up with a perky smile. Janet came in, passed coffee around, getting the men moving, getting their eyes off Debi.

"What do you know for sure?" Ryder finally asked.

The rest came easier. Was less personal. "Echo's blood tested positive for amphetamines, which means he was actively dosing since the detection window in blood is twelve hours. He could be on a time-released dose, which means a daily pill. The water bottle Echo used to dose Ryder had high doses of amphetamines and steroids, which you knew. It also contained elements similar to DV1028, the compound I developed."

Rose sat up and broke his silence. "So you knew? All along, you were the answer we were looking for?"

She was the evil scientist they were looking for. The quack they had threatened to destroy. Debi clasped her hands together, squeezing tightly to hold back the shakes. "I suspected."

Red crawled up his neck and burned in his cheeks. "You *knew* and you still..."

Slept with him. Fell in love with him.

Camy smacked him in the bicep.

Debi brought her entwined fingers to her chin as if praying for him to understand. "I wanted to be wrong."

Rose shook his head, disgust in every move. "I'm going for a run." Without another word, another glance, he disappeared.

CHAPTER TWENTY-THREE

Confession might be good for the soul, but it was a stab to the heart. A giant flaming blade dead center, and Debi didn't have time to repair the damage. They were nowhere near finished. "I took the syringe used to dose Rose from the scene and gave it to Allyson to test. Using more sophisticated equipment than I have access to, she's going to reverse engineer it so we can compare. Once I hear from her, we'll know for sure."

"You gave our only physical evidence to someone who works in the same lab that created the little green pills?" Craft stood, his arms swinging like he wanted to deck someone and needed a target.

"You don't like Allyson, do you?"

"I don't like any of this. I don't like that you started the ball rolling—and don't get all defensive—I know you had your reasons. Doesn't make it any more palatable. You've been at the center of this from the beginning. Those men trying to break into the ranch weren't after Lauren or Ryder. They were after you. The prick who took a shot from the bluff wasn't after Rose, he was after you."

Heat washed her skin. She hadn't thought of that. Once again, she'd been the target, and had been completely unaware. She hadn't known to be afraid. "When I left the lab, my research was trashed. I assumed it died. I didn't know otherwise until I ran into Barry at the university."

"That's another thing." Craft was wound up. Jittery and moving with slight tics and twitches. "I don't like that the drug came out of a civilian lab in a university. That takes this beyond a government conspiracy. Aren't you doctors supposed to take an oath? Do no harm?"

"I'm not a doctor." But she had wanted to be a PhD.

"That little experiment of yours was playing God."

"Hold on." Camy jumped up and took a position at Debi's side. The little pixie stood in front of Debi like a mama bear guarding her cubs. Fierce. "This sounds a lot like blame, and I didn't hear anything that makes Debi responsible. She didn't actively engage with the scientists who did. So what's her sin? Echo followed me to the bar, so does that make me complicit? For that matter, they followed Lauren to trap Ryder."

Ryder stirred on the couch, looking uncomfortable with the direction of the conversation, but Camy wasn't done.

"You get to be as paranoid as you want in the privacy of your own mind. That's one of the side effects or so I understand, but have a little respect for the person giving you answers."

Janet came up, handed Debi a cup of coffee for her frigid fingers. She winked as she flanked the other side. "My house, my rules. You gentlemen can't keep a civil tongue, there's the door."

Fowler raised his eyebrows, but didn't do a thing to contradict his mother.

Ryder squeezed Lauren's thigh. "We know more now than we did two weeks ago. Every piece of information helps us get to the bottom of the problem. Plus we have a chemist on board who can help decipher this faster than we could on our own. Sounds to me like the research didn't take a turn for the worst until after you left the program." He nodded at Debi. "You have more?"

"I do." But she was weary to her bones.

Fowler took a long sip of black coffee. "Makes sense why they moved us to Fort Bliss. The lab is local, which means the doctors poking and prodding us are in El Paso, or were when the trials started."

"Which lends more evidence to the idea that Captain Johnson was on campus," Ryder added.

"There's more good news in all this," Lauren said.

"What's that, baby?"

"Easier to break into a research lab at the university than some military think tank." Lauren's feet swung gleefully against the bottom of the sofa.

"I like the way you think." Craft blessed her with a wink and a smile before turning to Debi. "Sorry. Let my mouth get ahead of my brain."

Debi linked her good arm through Janet's. "Do it again and my posse will take you out."

Fowler chuckled. "You have no idea. Janet's a better shot than me, and I've seen her take down a man three times her size in hand-to-hand."

"Girl, will you train me?" Debi asked, only half joking. If she'd learned nothing else, it was the need for survival skills.

"Girl." Janet squeezed her arm tight. "I was waiting for you to ask."

Not a single man complained, but there was some uncomfortable shifting in the seats.

Janet pulled a wing chair around for Debi, and then directed the men to rearrange the furniture until they had an informal circle. Harder for the firing squad to hit her that way. In the less stressful environment, Debi finished her briefing.

"From here on out, it's a lot of supposition based on what I know of the initial compound and what we found in Ryder's dose."

Rose came back and listened from the kitchen door. Didn't look like he'd gone running after all, but he had changed into workout gear. Not a single light softened his dark gaze, so Debi turned her attention to those in the circle. For now, he was outside.

"Without seeing your medical files I can't say for sure, but best guess is that steroids were a part of the regular dosage for the reasons we discussed before. Higher aggression, more risk taking, increased strength and performance."

"I disagree," Fowler said. "Steroids were not, are not part of our strength."

"We should start a pool, you know, like offices do for football scores." Camy grinned up at Fowler who stood behind her chair. "Points given for drugs you are or are not given. Another set for side effects."

"Put me down for five bucks on no steroid usage," Fowler insisted. "I'm good for it."

Camy grabbed the notebook Rose had left behind and started taking notes.

"You boys haven't seen yourselves side by side," Janet said. "Put me down for steroid use in the regular cocktail."

"I'll put five on no." Lauren squeezed her husband's hand. "No change in Ryder from regular dosage to after. I think if he were enhanced, you'd see a decline in physical condition afterwards."

"You make a good point, my friend," Debi said. "But I'm still betting on steroids. Put me down for five."

The men all voted no on steroids, except Rose who stood on the sidelines. Their bets might be more wish than fact, but you had to give the team credit for hope after what the Army had done.

"I'll get online and enter everything into an online pool," Camy said. "Make it more official."

Fowler was shaking his head before she finished talking. "Wait—"

"With codes so no one knows what we're betting on." Camy cast a sideways glance to her brother. "I may or may not have run a sports betting pool on campus."

Stills reached across and gave her a fist bump. "You have layers."

"You have no idea, and won't as long as my brother is in the area."

"Can we get back to work?" Rose complained.

"Point of clarification." Debi faced Ryder with her question. "Did your pills or delivery method change when you were stateside versus overseas?"

He leaned back, crossed a leg over his knee to give him time to catch the gaze of the men. They nodded, with the exception of Rose. Finally, Ryder met Debi's gaze with a direct stare. "They did. The first four weeks or so, they delivered the dosage intramuscularly. Daily injections. Some days, we'd wig the fuck out—pardon me, ma'am," he said to Janet.

"I know the word. Have been known to use it as an adjective," she offered. "And the name is Janet."

"Yes..." Ryder caught himself short. "I hear you."

Debi cleared her throat. "That first four weeks, they were adjusting your dosage based on height, weight, metabolism. When they switched to pills—"

"Week five," Craft offered.

"Were the pills universal or individual?"

"Individual," Ryder answered. "Is that important?"

"Could be. Camy, hand me the notebook."

"I can take notes."

Debi nodded to Camy. It wasn't like anyone else could read her writing anyway, and apparently note taking was a Rose family trait. "When you guys wigged out, as you put it, I think they were testing the amphetamines to get the dosages right." She concentrated on the circle. Rose was still outside. "Amphetamine usage isn't unprecedented. They used it with pilots during the Gulf War."

Lauren tucked herself under Ryder's arm. "I vote no on amphetamines."

Camy made the notation in the notebook.

"Is that wishful thinking?" Debi asked.

"I just..." Lauren's eyes watered. "Do you know the side effects?"

Ok. Lauren needed a little hope, and despite all the joking, this was serious shit. The more serious the consequences, the more they joked. "Anxiety, insomnia, involuntary tics or twitches." She'd witnessed all of that and more in the members of Team Fear. "Usage can lead to kidney or liver problems.

Heart attacks, especially in someone with undocumented heart abnormalities." Debi didn't want to go on, but they deserved to know. "Stills, you mentioned someone on one of the other teams having a heart attack at thirty-one. That could well be the amphetamines, at least in what Echo is trying to dose you with. In an overdose situation, you would have a rapid pulse, panic attacks, hallucinations, increased aggression, and extreme paranoia."

"That nails every side effect I had when they dosed me, but not during normal missions."

Fowler finished his coffee. "I bet no on amphetamines in our regular dosage. The shit Echo is dosing with, yes, but not us."

Camy scribbled as the men all voted against amphetamines in their regular dosages.

Debi wished she could agree. "Amphetamines are a stimulant. Benefits are increased focus, energy, and mental awareness. High energy. Less need for sleep. Exactly what the Army would want in fearless soldiers."

Rose took an aborted step forward, but remained silent.

If he could warn her about the realities of Echo chasing them, she could warn the rest of them about the drugs that had been used against them. "Did they give you a different set of pills when you were deployed?"

Ryder nodded.

To Debi, that sealed the deal. "You'd feel a rush, not unlike going into battle."

"Fuck." Craft glanced at Janet, but didn't apologize for his words. "Change mine to yes on amphetamines."

"Ditto," Stills said.

"There's more. Here's the one that concerns me." Debi

glanced around at the team. The group had grown beyond Team Fear to include the people in this room, part of something bigger than they were alone. And they all deserved better than being hunted and exterminated by Team Echo. "Psychosis is a long-term side effect, and no, I'm not worried about Team Fear, but here's the thing." She stared at Lauren, because she didn't know how to tell these men who had already risked so much. "Amphetamines are a hazard for anyone with psychotic symptoms such as schizophrenia, bipolar disorder, or any other brain disorder associated with psychotic illnesses."

"Fuck me." Ryder dropped his head back to stare at the ceiling. "You're saying if someone started out crazy—"

"Mentally ill," Janet insisted.

"Then they're more likely to be affected by the use of amphetamines," Ryder finished.

"So if the Army targeted different groups for different results..." Debi let the idea hang.

Fowler picked up her train of thought. "We were picked for our loyalty to team and country."

"And Echo was chosen for their psychotic imbalance," Craft finished.

CHAPTER TWENTY-FOUR

Craft paced, his camo pants standing out against the cozy interior. "Any doctor or clinician in the research arena would know these side effects?"

Debi nodded.

"So Echo wasn't an accident?"

"No." At least Debi didn't believe so. "Not if it affected all twelve men. For you guys, fearlessness promoted good results. Maybe better than good if you're looking at traditional warfare, but for a man prone to psychosis..."

"No fear. No restraint. And the government set them free. Stateside." Ryder dropped back against the sofa. "They're a ticking fucking time bomb."

Stills dropped his head between his knees. "Betting aside, how sure are you on all this shit?"

Debi chewed the nail on her middle finger. "The side effects are a fact. My original formula is a fact, but until I reverse engineer the mixture from the syringe, the combined formula that includes steroids and amphetamines is an educated guess."

A fist slammed the wall, shaking plaster loose. Rose struck again, ramming straight through the lathing strips. "Of every meat sack in this room, who do you think Echo wants to silence most?"

Seconds ticked down on the clock, but before the hand struck twelve, every man's eye turned to her. Well, hell. She knew the original research as good or better than anyone. She knew the players and had accessed the lab. Made her the perfect whistleblower, or a target, depending on how you looked at it. Debi shivered, and her mouth ran ahead of her brain. "Guess we know how to draw Echo into the open."

"The first man to suggest it forfeits his life." Rose stalked from the room in a trail of testosterone and rage.

Janet didn't bother telling him to clean up the broken plaster. Even a badass like Fowler's mom knew when *not* to push.

———

The rage flowing through his veins hadn't cooled when Debi tracked him down to the workout room. He needed space. He'd wanted revenge on the men who did this to him, and Debi's admission had stolen that from him. "Now's not the time, sweetheart." The endearment couldn't hide the venom in his tone. The more he listened upstairs, the greater the anger. She had put herself at risk, both in the lab and again, now, by being alone with him. She had watched him beat a man to death. The sight of blood had started her panic attacks as a kid. She hated blood, yet she'd ended up covered in it. The panic attacks were sure to get worse. Because of him. There was no way to heal the damage he'd caused.

She peered around the room, avoiding his gaze. "I have a way to gain access to the team's medical files, or at least get access to the drug information."

"No." He kicked the treadmill up a notch.

"When Allyson and I were at the café, I hadn't put two and two together about Barry's involvement. Now that I have, we can have her skip the testing and go straight for Barry's records."

"And how would that work?" He needed to know she wasn't walking into danger again, because even as anger flowed through him, he needed her safe. He kept his gaze on the wall in front of the treadmill.

"I know where he keeps his research records."

She wanted to go in? "I said no." All he wanted with the time he had left on this planet was to protect his sisters. Protect Debi, and she made that damn hard when she put herself in the line of fire. Temper disrupted his run and he spewed it on her. He hopped off the treadmill and got so close he smelled her fear.

Her spine stiffened and he could see her digging in. "Why won't you even discuss it?" she asked.

There were two options facing him, and they both sucked big hairy donkey balls. Either he would hurt her when his anger cut loose and he wasn't able to contain it, or he'd fail to protect her. He couldn't live with either. "We're done. Do you hear me? Done."

She flinched as his words struck home. Tears glistened in her eyes, but she batted them back before walking away.

Morning came with a giant headache pounding in Rose's skull. Camy plopped a scoop of oatmeal into a bowl and headed for him, but Rose shooed her away. He didn't have time for his baby sister when the shit barreling down on them was about to land. He needed her the fuck away. He needed her and Debi a million miles from where they were right now. Debi sat catty-corner from him, and when he shook Camy off, she moved to sit next to Debi.

Great, his sister teaming up with his almost girlfriend. Rose scooped a heaping pile of eggs on his plate and shoved the serving bowl at Craft. Hard.

"What crawled up your ass?"

Across the table, Debi and Camy glanced up.

"Watch your mouth." Rose didn't want to deal with Craft's shit today.

"What did I miss?" Stills grabbed a biscuit and cut it open on his plate. Steam rose.

"Something has Rose pissy this morning," Craft answered. His gaze tracked between Rose and Debi sitting on opposite sides of the table.

"I'm pretty sure it crawled up his ass last night and stayed there." Fowler dug into biscuits and gravy like it was food of the gods.

This was why Rose kept his mouth shut. No one needed to know his business. He was angry as hell at Debi, and not for the reason she believed. Echo wanted to get rid of the men of Team Fear because they were walking evidence, but Debi had the background to blow the experiment wide open if she went to the press. She was a target and he wanted to lock her up, but it didn't matter what he thought, because every member of the team had rallied around her last night, because he'd lost his shit. And he never lost it. He kept it tightly contained.

And the hell of it was, he hadn't slept a god-damned wink because his bed was fucking cold and his feet stuck out the bottom of his small fucking bed. He couldn't look at Debi without wanting to roll her in bubble wrap and move her to Alaska, which she wouldn't allow because he was being a he-man in her estimation. And damnit all to hell, when had his life revolved around an entire fucking team when he wanted five minutes alone to set his woman straight? So he spooned eggs into his mouth and wished them all away.

The sound of forks hitting plates was the only sound for long minutes until Lauren and Ryder walked through holding hands. "Hey, morning, everyone." Lauren fairly glowed despite the bruises still marking her pretty face.

Ryder held a chair for her and then went to get them coffee. The cocky swagger was enough to send Rose's blood pressure up several notches. Asshole didn't need to flaunt the fact that he was getting regular sex.

Across from him, Camy smacked his hand to nudge him out of his thoughts. "Pass the gravy."

He passed the bowl, helping himself to more biscuits and gravy in the process. If he couldn't have regular sex, at least he had regular meals. Lauren smiled at him like he hadn't been a complete ass the night before, one more reason he liked and respected Ryder's wife.

Across from him, Debi stood and took her plate to the dishwasher. The tension in the room was like the air minutes before Hiroshima.

"So, last night we decided." Lauren cleared her throat. "Next time it's our turn to cook, Ryder and I are having a barbecue. The whole deal. Potato salad, pasta salad, baked beans, grilled meat." She glanced at Fowler. "Grocery wise, do you have what we need or do we need to go shopping?"

"Probably have most of it," Fowler answered. "We can make it happen."

"Good." She smiled at the men. "We didn't do this when you guys were active duty, but we should have. *I* should have, so we're making it right. We're a team, all of us now, so we should start acting like it."

Her sweetness made staying morose and angry near impossible. "Burgers and brats? I'm there."

"How about beer?" Debi asked.

"Not for the team," Ryder answered. He set a cup of coffee in front of Lauren and took a seat. "That's been on the forbidden list from day one."

"Echo drinks alcohol. They were at the bar all the time."

"And they're mental. No alcohol," Rose insisted.

Debi ran hands over her thighs. "I've been thinking about it, and I believe the restriction was because of the amphetamines they may have used. Now that you're not on the drug protocol, there shouldn't be any reason you can't have beer with dinner."

"I said no." His tone brooked no argument. The rest of the room went silent.

Debi released a slow breath like she was counting under her breath. "No need for you to do my physical therapy today. I'm training with Janet."

"Says who?" Rose asked.

"Says me." Janet stepped in from the pantry wearing digicamo and combat boots. If she looked like a civilian the last few days, it was because his eyes were jacked. There was no doubt the woman was a soldier. The clothes fit her small frame like they were custom made, but they weren't shiny new. They had that comfortable, worn-in feel. There were no tears or fraying threads. A tan t-shirt peeked through the collar of her shirt. She pulled a clipboard off the dingy wall. "Schedule is up here every morning, and I've let you boys off easy. The girls want to train, so they train. KP is in addition to the daily training and we rotate. Last night's cooking was on Lauren and Ryder. Tonight it's Camy and Dean. Otherwise the daily training includes weapons, hand-to-hand, explosives, and escape and evasion."

Rose's gaze cut to Debi. The bruises on her face were barely starting to fade. The damn bullet hole was barely sealed. She looked fragile. Training with her in hand-to-hand knotted up something inside. "Hell no."

"Hell yes," Janet answered. "You got a problem with women in combat, soldier?"

His gaze cut to Fowler who forked in a heavy bite. Rose couldn't be the only one wanting to keep the women out of special training, but the others were too busy forking in chow and avoiding his gaze.

Stills made eye contact with a heavy grin. "You dug that hole all on your own, son."

He turned back to Janet. A spark lit her eyes like she enjoyed this exchange, but Rose would rather chew glass. He had no doubt Janet could cut him open and filet him for dinner, because he wouldn't move a single muscle against her. She was female, fragile, and deserving of protection. It wasn't the women's job to fight, but telling Janet so would likely end up getting him KP for the rest of his life, no matter how short that time might be.

So he switched tactics. Looking at Debi, he slowly shook his head. "You're still injured and on light duty for the foreseeable future. Physical therapy, yes. Training, no."

"Really?" She braced her one good arm on her hip. "You're pulling the medic card?"

He finished his last bite and pushed his plate back. "That's right."

"Good to know. As it happens, that's fine by me. I'd love thirty minutes alone with you." Her tone implied she'd use the time to kick his ass. "Plus, if you're running my physical therapy you won't be around to rain on Camy's parade."

He glanced across at Camy, sensing a trap, but Camy ignored the exchange as she passed a bowl of scrambled eggs down the table. "How's that?"

"Everybody trains." Debi's eyes glinted. "Even your sister."

"Oh, I wasn't planning to ask his permission." Camy stood, wearing yoga pants and a tight black t-shirt. "This should be fun."

Fun? As far as Rose was concerned, he had landed in hell.

———

Training with Janet made every muscle in Debi's body ache, but she couldn't complain because she'd asked for it. Hell, she'd demanded it. And Janet had encouraged her, which should have been a warning. Debi had ignored it. Fool that she was. Rose had given her permission—damn but that burned—

to train in kicks, but no hand-to-hand, after which he turned her physical therapy over to Fowler who was as cruel and unfeeling as his mother.

Debi paused during a kicking lesson and leaned heavily against Camy. "The men are up to something. Do you have any idea what the plan is?"

"No." Her chest heaved with the extreme effort of keeping up with Janet Fowler. "They're doing a good job of keeping us otherwise occupied today."

Somehow they'd used training to keep the women out of the loop. "Any word from Allyson?"

"No." Camy kicked the punching bag, hitting higher on the bag than she had a week ago. When she wasn't training, she worked in the command post doing computer stuff Debi didn't understand. "My brother still being an asshole?"

Rose hadn't spoken to Debi since the breakfast showdown. "Is he still breathing?"

"As far as I know."

"Then he's still an asshole."

"On a positive note." Camy bent at the waist trying to get a solid breath. "He hasn't asked me a question about school since I got here."

"Lucky you."

"Kick higher," Janet ordered.

Debi panted out a breath. "I take back every nice thing I ever said about you, Janet."

"Thank you. Now, move your ass."

They finished the lesson in silence because there wasn't enough oxygen to talk and train. Janet didn't take it easy on them because they were female. If anything, she expected more of them.

When the lesson was over, Debi plopped onto the mat. She wasn't sleeping much at night in her big cold bed, and that made her as frustrated as a cat in a cage. Rose had shut her down, not wanting her to take any risks, and the rest of the men had followed his lead. They wanted to fold the women in bubble wrap and keep them on a shelf, but they needed her access to get the information they sought. She didn't see any option but around Rose and his stubborn wall of silence.

"I need to get a message to Allyson." But she didn't want to endanger the team by trying to bypass security on her own. She did not have the skills. Camy did. "You asked me to help you get time away from your brother and I delivered," she told Camy. Even if she wasn't distracting Rose so much as pissing him off. Debi dropped onto her back. "Now you need to do me a solid."

"What did you have in mind?"

"Contact Allyson without the guys knowing."

"Craft has safeguards in place and Fowler is paranoid as hell."

"You're good. You can do it. Just don't get caught."

"Nice. A challenge and a warning at the same time. You've been taking lessons from the men."

"If they're not going to work with us, then we work separately by default." She'd rather work together. She'd come to rely on the team, think of them as her own. But ever since she'd watched Rose go after Robert in the lab, her nerves had been in tatters. She was about ready to resort to pyrotechnics. "Can you do it?"

"Girl." Camy mimicked Debi's tone. "I hacked into the student loan records database."

"Really?" Debi wished she could do the same. "How much do you owe?"

"Not a damn thing."

Wow. "You're hired." Debi frowned as they walked back upstairs. She'd just asked the world's peppiest hacker to help. What could possibly go wrong?

CHAPTER TWENTY-FIVE

With her shoes in one hand and keys in the other, Debi stepped into the hall outside her room. Sneaking past Rose's room was simple as he'd locked her out of it. His words from the other night still haunted her.

We're done.

The memory squeezed her heart dry. Trying to cure her panic attacks had cost her everything. Her father had washed his hands of her after Barry ratted her out. DV1028 had cost her friends from the lab and a sense of security she hadn't regained until she'd settled in with the team here at The Manor. She couldn't lose Rose. It was time to stop letting everyone else take care of her.

The information in Barry's computer could save them and she had it within her power to get it. Rose couldn't stop her from doing what was right for the team.

In her stocking feet, she made her way to the kitchen. Camy and Dean had cleaned up and were the last to go to bed.

A single light over the oven lit the way to the pantry. Debi sat on the stairs leading to the tunnel to put on her shoes before heading to the barn. The lights in the tunnel were horror-movie scary and the walls echoed with the memory of Rose's screams when he'd been in recovery.

A shiver chilled her skin, but she forced herself to walk—not run—to the other end of the creepy tunnel. Footsteps followed her, or they were echoes of her steps, or she was crazy. She ran up the stairs to the barn and headed straight for her car.

"Where do you think you're going?" The deep male voice stopped and restarted her heart.

"Crap." She stumbled back and hit the side of Fowler's pickup. She twisted toward the voice.

Stills stood between the cars with his arms crossed over his massive chest. "Going somewhere?"

The keys in her hand were pretty damning. "Uh, looking for something in my car."

"Tell me, do I look stupid?"

"That's one of those no-win questions." The hand holding her keys trembled, so she stuffed it in her front pocket.

Camy peeked around Stills. "Sorry. He busted me when I came over to check the email."

Debi closed her eyes for a split second, her thoughts going fast, but not fast enough to make up a lie big enough to cover her tracks. "You can't keep me here if I don't want to stay."

"Actually, I can."

Ugh. The men all had an annoying ability to stay reasonable and calm when she wanted to scream. "Okay so you're bigger and meaner and could physically restrain me. Is that the kind of man you want to be?"

He chuckled, but only a fool would think he was amused.

The silence stretched, and it was one of the moments like when you were in school and got busted breaking into the science lab. The teacher merely sat there waiting until you couldn't take the silence and had to fill it. And damn, but Debi's breath was ragged. Panic threatened. "Fine. What do you plan to do?"

"That depends."

"On?"

"What's your plan with Allyson?"

"Well." Debi scratched the back of her skull. She wasn't exactly expecting him to be... open to discussion. "The plan is to meet Allyson and steal a copy of Barry's records while he's asleep. I thought I'd make it back for breakfast and no one would be the wiser."

"How do you plan to get past Fowler's security system?"

Debi's heart pulsed with hope. He'd used the present tense.

Camy raised her hand like a student in class. "Getting past security here at The Manor is my job. I plan to bypass it and reset it in five minutes once we're clear of the gate."

"Wait, there's no we." On this, Debi was emphatic. "Rose would destroy me if anything happened to you."

"You think he wouldn't kill me for helping you escape and then letting something happen to you?" Camy asked.

"Not even. Right now, he's mad enough to kill me himself."

"Let's table that discussion for a moment." Stills interrupted. "How are you getting into the lab? Or are the records somewhere else?"

"I think the records are at the lab in Barry's office. And I'm getting through security with Allyson like I did last time."

"What happens if Echo shows?"

"On that point, I was hoping for a little good luck. We're due."

"That's about stupid. Luck has nothing to do with it. One of their men disappeared from the lab. Of course they have it under surveillance."

"You're a killjoy." For her, going was worth the risk. Her heart hurt with the separation from Rose. Maybe getting the records would help to redeem her in his eyes. It certainly couldn't hurt.

"What you need is a bodyguard." Stills stared at her, his gaze void of emotion.

"As in... You?" Her voice rose hopefully.

"Possibly. Let me see Allyson's email."

Camy handed him a computer printout. He glanced over it before looking up. "Will Allyson let me through with you?"

"Doubtful." After the attack last time, it was a miracle she'd agreed to let Debi in. "I told her I wanted evidence to prove Barry had stolen my research. She doesn't know about you guys, and I don't think she should."

"Then Camy needs to come along to help me get into the lab."

Camy drew her hand into a fist and pumped in celebration. "Yes!"

"No way." Rose hated Debi enough already.

"It's the only way it works. You're not going into the lab without backup. Camy, can you get me past security?"

She rolled her eyes. "Piece of cake."

"Things like this are seldom easy. Put ego aside. Can you do it?"

"Of course. I'll need to borrow some of Craft's equipment."

"Run get it."

Camy spun on her heel and raced to the command post. Debi waited until she disappeared before speaking. "How did you know something was up?"

"I've come up with some particularly dumbass plans, which is how I recognized yours."

An ache started in her stomach. Camy was bubbly and sweet, and every single time they faced someone from Echo, people got hurt. "We should leave right now, before she comes back."

"We need her to get off property and to get me into the lab."

"If anything happens to her, he'll kill us."

"If anything happens to either one of you, he'll kill me."

"Then why do it?"

"Fastest way to the desired result. We've sat on this information for too long, and sooner or later, the Company will eliminate your friend Barry and probably Allyson and the rest of the people in the lab. While we sit around fighting or negotiating or planning or whatever the hell we're doing, we're letting Echo take the lead."

"You're quite the strategist." Or fearlessness made him reckless.

"I'm flying by the seat of my pants here, and it will probably come back to bite me."

Debi had the same feeling, but she needed to do something, because waiting for Rose to change his mind hurt too much.

"I think we have more than the cone of silence going on.

Believe me, I've been there," Camy said with a shake of her head.

"The cone of silence is real," Stills insisted. They debated Rose's cold-shoulder treatment on the drive into El Paso. "The most consecutive days on record is twenty days. We don't even know what caused it. Rose simply tuned everyone out. No words for twenty days."

Camy weighed her thoughts. "That makes it seem like he was in a protracted bad mood, but my brother doesn't have a temper."

"The brother you knew before joining the team."

"He doesn't have a temper," Camy insisted.

"Girl, you did not see him beat a man to death."

Stills shook his head. "That wasn't him."

"The drugs may have pushed Rose over the edge to kill Robert, but it wasn't drugs that made Rose want me to get the fuck away from him. The way he said it was more than temper."

"That's what I was trying to tell you before Dean so rudely interrupted," Camy said. "Sounds like the zone of protection."

"Is this some weird sci-fi thing?" Debi asked. She was never quite sure what was going on in Camy's head.

"He's protecting you."

Right. As he carved her heart out with a spoon.

Stills nodded slowly. "Zone of protection, huh? Sounds like him. Hell, sounds like all of us. I ditched the girl back home. Told her I found another girl. A woman. Made sure she wanted nothing to do with me. Ever. Didn't want her trying to look me up the way Camy went after her brother."

"That's you. And, by the way, that makes you an ass. You could try honesty."

"Sure." Stills watched the scenery drift by in the headlights of the car. "Let's see, how does that conversation go. Hey, baby, I'm a walking experiment. No longer human. No fear. No emotional ties. And if you stick with me, you'll probably end up dead. By my hand."

"Are all of you guys so melodramatic?" Camy asked.

"This isn't melodrama. Look around. Debi, how many dead bodies have you seen since you and Lauren got kidnapped?

"Baby Face Joe and his team at the townhouse. The two guys from the meth house. Robert."

"Seven. Does that sound like melodrama to you?" Stills asked.

"Sounds like a nightmare." Debi wanted to feel something, but sadness oozed from her pores and negativity spewed from her mouth. "Did you love her? The girl back home?"

"It's not past tense." Stills pounded a soundless tune on the steering wheel. "But I wasn't going to see her gutted in front of me. After Mad Dog, I figured we were marked. Maybe we are, maybe we aren't, but I'm not going to bring her into this. We made our choices. Signed on the dotted line."

"It wasn't informed consent," Debi contradicted.

"We agreed. We deal with the consequences. And wanting to keep the woman I love out of harm's way is not an asshole move. It's the right choice."

"Which is what I've been trying to tell you." Camy peeked up between the bucket seats. "River is trying to protect Debi, the same way Stills is protecting his girl back home."

"I'm hardly an innocent. Rose knows I was the one who developed the drug."

"You didn't use it on him or anyone."

"I used it on myself." She'd been desperate to get rid of the panic attacks. To make her father proud. "God, I make myself sick. I don't want to be near me. Can't say I blame him for the distance."

"I do," Camy answered. "That's why I'm here with you now. Plus, The Manor is starting to creep me out."

"Same." Debi laughed, but it sounded hollow in her ears. Sleeping by herself, she jerked awake at every old house noise, imagining ghosts or monsters or Rose moving even farther away. "Do you think Janet sees dead people?"

Stills laughed. "I think she orders them around like her own private army."

"Somehow that's comforting," Camy answered. "I mean, if she can see dead people that's creepy, but if she can order them to protect us, that's the coolest thing since the Internet."

They rode in silence the rest of the drive into El Paso. The closer they got, the more nerves twisted her thoughts. When the lights flickered and grew closer, she pulled out the printout of the email. "Allyson said to meet her at an all-night café a block from the bar. I know the place. It's where Ryder took Lauren the first night they met." And Debi tried not to be jealous of the love they shared.

———

Camy watched Allyson and Debi slip through the first line of security. "How long before we sneak in behind them?"

"As soon as backup arrives."

"Backup?"

As if the word conjured them, Ryder, Craft, and Fowler gathered with them in the shadow of the science building.

"You traitor." Every bit of fun she'd had faded into reality. "I thought you were on our side."

Stills shrugged. "There's only one side. Team Fear."

"Hooah," the soldiers agreed.

She had considered Dean a friend because he'd been with her longer. He'd hitched a ride. He'd let her come along on the mission.

"I may be fearless, but I'm not crazy. At least not yet. We need backup. This forced the team here sooner rather than later. They got the alert ten minutes after we left. With the time we had to meet Allyson, I figured they'd beat us here."

"Ran into a complication." An earring glinted in Craft's ear, and with his wicked grin, he looked like a marauding pirate.

Camy turned her back on Stills, her *former* friend. "Where's my brother?"

"He's the complication," Craft answered.

Fowler grinned like he was thoroughly enjoying himself. "We had to tie him up a few miles back." He gestured at Stills. "Won't take him long to get free. You might want to avoid him for the next couple days."

These men were not right in the head.

Ryder stepped up and started giving orders like he was born to it. "Craft. Recon. Fifty feet around the perimeter. If there's a squirrel in a tree, I want to know it." Craft disappeared into the night as Ryder continued. "Fowler, find a perch. Craft and I will find the asset. Does Debi have her phone on her?"

"Of course." Stills pulled out his phone and showed a red blip where she worked her way through the lab.

"Excellent. Stills, find a place to stash Camy."

"Hey." That did not sound like a good time.

"Just until your brother shows. He'll need access to the lab, so you get to show off your skills again."

"Oh, I'm sure River will love that." Sometime soon they needed to talk about her new life plan.

Stills rubbed his jaw. "You do not want to position me with Camy when Rose shows up. Not if you want both of us in top shape."

Ryder gave a swift nod. "New plan. Craft—"

"Was the one who tied Rose up in the first place," Fowler said.

Ryder cursed. "Fowler, trade places with Stills."

"I'm a better shot."

"True, and as much of an asshole as Stills can be..."

Stills flipped him off.

"I'd like the whole team to survive tonight's fight."

Fowler handed off the sniper's rifle and Stills disappeared into the night.

Craft reappeared like a ghost flickering back into view. "No one on the ground or in the air."

Fowler shrugged the muscles in his shoulders like he was stretching awake. "I don't like that one damn bit. Either they've got eyes all over this ground—"

"Or they're inside," Ryder finished. "Craft, let's roll."

"Wait," Camy called, but nearly swallowed her tongue when they turned. They were all fierce warriors with hard jaws and cold eyes. "The inner code is 1492."

They disappeared in silence, leaving Camy alone with the gorgeous and completely intimidating Jake Fowler. "So." She cleared her throat. "How come you call your mom Janet?"

CHAPTER TWENTY-SIX

The lights in the lab were on power-saving mode, so only one in ten was lit, leaving shadows in corners and around shelves. Debi peered over her shoulder. She couldn't shake the feeling someone was watching. Probably Stills, although she hadn't felt this nervous last time when four of the team members were watching over her. Maybe it was from having too little backup. Great. Now was the perfect time for that epiphany. What she wouldn't give to have Rose's pissy voice in her ear.

In front of her, Allyson walked briskly to the back, her pencil skirt swishing. The only sound in the place. The fans were off, the equipment was off, and so were all the researchers.

An easy in and out. Debi forced a breath. She'd been kidnapped by drug dealers and shot at by enhanced soldiers. Nothing in the lab was as scary as that. Even if she ran into Barry, what the hell? She could let him have it. Lay every complaint she'd ever had at his feet. A nervous giggle escaped.

Allyson put a finger over her lips. Yeah. Quiet. The whole covert thing was testing her warrior skills. Really, after one day training with Janet she felt like a badass. Until she walked through the secure doors and felt more insecure than ever. Her arm hurt because she didn't wear her sling today, her legs hurt because Janet *was* a badass and trained like one, and all Debi really wanted was to drop to the ground and have a good cry. Instead, she was breaking into a lab and stealing government secrets. That was probably a felony. Or treason. Did they still give you the electric chair for that?

Deep breath. She heard Rose's voice in her head. After everything she'd done in the past few weeks, this was the easiest. She followed Allyson down the hall to the offices. Barry's was in the back. Corner office one floor down from her father's. The lights came to life when they walked through the door. Allyson went to the computer and booted it up. As Barry's assistant, she knew his passwords even if she didn't know his secrets.

"Which files?" Allyson whispered.

Debi moved around the desk and plugged in the drive that Camy had given her. She wasted precious time flipping through the directories looking for the right folders.

"These." Allyson tapped the screen. "I've never seen these before."

"Are you sure?"

"Start moving the files. We can verify while they're copying."

They opened the first one as the door clicked open.

———

Rose jogged through the shadows until he spied his sister and Fowler. He approached on foot and unarmed. Fowler turned at the last second, but Rose was on him with a solid hit to the jaw. Fowler crashed against the brick wall. Camy jumped in front of him. "What's wrong with you?"

Fowler wiped blood from the corner of his mouth. "I wasn't the one who tied you up."

"It was your turn." The anger was tucked away. He'd jogged three damned miles thanks to Craft and his dumbass stunt. "Where's Debi?"

"Inside."

"With?"

"Allyson."

"Who's running this operation?" Rose pointed at Camy. Okay, maybe some residual anger still flowed through his veins. "If I have to lock you in a basement cell, you're not leaving The Manor until this is finished. You got me?"

She stuck her tongue at him. "First you need me to get you inside."

"How do you plan to do that, little sister?"

She pulled a slim electronic gadget from the bag she wore across her body. "Follow me."

———

Barry gloated in the doorway. "Debra. I knew you'd be back."

He didn't ask why she was here, which meant he had a pretty good guess, but Debi wasn't giving in easy. She leaned over, panting like she was having a hard time breathing. "I'm looking for evidence that you stole my research, you arrogant prick."

"I think we're long past that kind of lie. After Robert disappeared, I knew you'd be back, but finding you with my sister. That's a surprise." He frowned at Allyson. "I'll deal with you later."

Allyson's face went white.

"I figured you'd bring one or two of our science experiments. Make it easy on everyone."

Debi didn't have to fake the gag. God, she hoped Stills and Camy were hidden.

"Still having panic attacks? You should have kept some of your illicit supply."

If she'd had enough time, she would have, but depending on the drugs to eliminate the fear wasn't a cure. It was a weakness, one that she was finally facing. The Army wanted to use the pills to create a fearless fighting team. Maybe that had been a noble purpose once, just as hers had been. Or so she wanted to believe. "What did you do to my program?"

"Improved it."

"Improved my ass. You perverted it. It had legitimate uses and you turned it into a money maker to fuel your ego."

"You do realize that's our job."

"Our job is to help people." Bent over like she would during a panic attack, Debi tried to focus her thoughts to prevent an actual attack. Losing it now would cost her her life.

"You can't really be that naïve. Our job is to bring money into the university. Our job is to find paying sponsors." Barry pulled out a cell phone and dialed. "She's in my office. She appears to have come alone, but search the lab."

Please, please, please let Camy and Stills be somewhere *not* in the lab.

Allyson dropped back in the chair like she'd been slapped. "Barry, what are you involved in?"

"We'll discuss that after my new friends take Debra away."

Allyson picked up the phone off his desk. "I think we should let the police sort this out."

Barry pulled out a handgun. The fussy scientist carried a weapon? "Put the phone down."

"You're working with Echo," Debi guessed.

"You mean Team Echo."

"Are you their creator?" He really was a mad scientist.

"They're magnificent, aren't they?"

"You're as crazy as they are if you believe that." How many were left? Six? No, that was before Robert, so five left. Great. She had no skills and was bent over like an old woman. Best-case scenario was to get out the fire exit before Echo arrived. Coughing, she stumbled as she might during an attack, moving closer to Barry.

Allyson stood, the sound of her skirt swishing closer. "Debi, are you okay?"

"No." She rasped the words like she struggled to breathe. She stumbled, brushing the desk. At the last minute, she altered trajectory and rammed her head into Barry's midsection. They tumbled into the hall.

Her shoulder hit the wall and his gun went flying. She didn't have to fake the pain that dropped her to the ground next to Barry.

"Well, well." Strong hands picked her up by her hair.

"Ouch, you prick." Hair in her eyes, she couldn't see the attacker. She kicked out and he backhanded her into the wall. She dropped back down by Barry who had struggled to his knees. Allyson flew at the man with claws out and aimed for his eyes. She must have hit something, because he used his fist to knock her back. She landed on the opposite side of the hall, out for the count.

"Hey, leave my sister out of this. I need her to compile our results."

"There will be no compiling." There was no warning. One minute Barry was spouting orders and the next brain matter spattered the wall. "Once the smoke clears, it will look like you killed your ex-boyfriend."

Debi struggled to her feet and pushed her hair out of her eyes. She stopped cold. "Wade?"

———

Rose slipped into the lab after ordering Fowler to get Camy the hell back to The Manor. He went in hot, no time for finesse. Where the lab ended and gave way to offices, Ryder yanked him to the side. "Who trained you?" he asked in a low whisper. "You can't come marching in like a fucking cowboy unless you want to get shot."

"Where is she?"

"Last ping was from right here."

"No cell service," Craft explained. "We have to find her the old-fashioned way."

A gunshot sounded around the corner and down the hall. Rose lurched forward, but Ryder slammed him into a cement wall. "I will tie you up again if you don't pull your head out of your ass. You're no good to her dead."

Rose nodded tightly. Every muscle in his body strained to move out, to find her before it was too late, but Ryder was right. He needed to pack that shit up. "No fear."

"Now you're talking, brother."

————

"If it isn't my favorite bartender." Wade gave Debi his best shit-eating cowboy grin. "You didn't really think that I sat on that damn barstool night after night just to grab your ass?"

"No." She thought he was a decent guy who drank too much. He'd been coming to the bar from the beginning. Erratically at first, but more often recently. Nearly every day. The implications chilled her to the bones. Wade was involved even before they started training the teams. He'd been keeping an eye on her because it was her formula. Why hadn't they killed her like they did Barry? Debi gagged and spit the bile on the floor next to the body she couldn't look at. "Who's in charge?"

"Right now, I am." He nodded to a soldier who had taken up a position behind him. "Grab the girl on the floor. Lock them in the server room."

The other soldier dead lifted Allyson onto his shoulder.

Debi swallowed. "If you let us go now, I'll forgive your bar tab."

Wade dropped a hand over her shoulder and pressed into the wound. "You can come hard or come easy, but you're going into the closet."

Debi followed the soldier, frantically trying to find a way out, and not finding a way past Wade and the soldier she recognized from the Echo wall of shame. Another soldier dressed in black cargo pants and t-shirt approached from the opposite direction. "Team Fear is in the building."

"How long until they find the women?"

"They have to do a room-by-room sweep. Best estimate is seven minutes."

"Set the charges for six and then bug out." Wade shoved Debi into the server room and slammed the door closed.

"What? No goodbye?" she muttered. She tried the door, but it was locked from the outside, which was backwards. Obviously they'd planned this ahead of time. Debi yanked the cell phone out of her pocket and checked the time. They had six minutes to get everyone clear of the building. She dialed, but there was no cell service.

CHAPTER TWENTY-SEVEN

Debi pulled a server from the racks nearest her and slammed it down on the doorknob with all her strength. The doorknob didn't even bend. Okay, so she had no upper body strength, especially in her dominant arm. She wasn't going down easy. Echo was evacuating the building, which meant there was no one to attack Stills and Camy if they made it into the building. She had to let Stills know where she was.

Banging on the door tired her arm quickly, so she switched to kicking. What she wouldn't give for a loud pair of boots to smack against the door. That would make some serious noise. She clicked the power button on her phone, illuminating the time. Two minutes had passed. Her heart raced, but she didn't have time to give in to the panic. She sat down on the floor and started kicking like a toddler with a temper tantrum.

The door swung in. "Ryder." She jumped up and hugged him. "There's a bomb in the building set to go off in three minutes."

"Where?"

"If I knew that I might not be so freaked out."

"Craft, grab Allyson."

Craft stepped through and hoisted Allyson over his shoulder.

"Fire exit is closest." She pushed through to lead the way and ran smack into Rose. "Crap."

A muscle twitched in his jaw and then he picked her up and swung her over his shoulder like Craft had Allyson. "Wait." She lifted her head up to find Ryder, the voice of reason, or so she hoped. "There's a USB drive in Barry's office. We copied files."

"Where?"

"Next to the dead body."

Ryder nodded. "We passed it." He turned to go but Debi kicked out. "Wait. Don't go alone." The idea of him getting shot terrified her. Lauren wouldn't survive if anything happened to her husband. "Please. Take backup."

Craft set Allyson back on the ground and followed Ryder.

"You can put me down now," she told Rose. "All the blood rushing to my head probably isn't good for me."

"Not another word." He ground the words into dust.

Crap, he was pissed.

———

The woman over his shoulder stopped struggling a block or two back. Rose cinched a hand behind her knees to stabilize her position. They rendezvoused back at the cars. Fowler and Camy had already taken off. Stills met up with them carrying a rifle on his shoulder and whistling a tune.

"Team Echo did not egress out of any known exits," Stills insisted. "There has to be another way in or out."

A half a mile back, an explosion sent plumes of fire and smoke into the sky. Windows rattled, car alarms blared.

"Time to bail."

Rose stopped Stills with a hand to his upper chest. "Give me your keys."

"I'm not letting you drive my drug mobile. I stole it fair and square."

His teeth ground together. "You took two women into battle without backup."

"I sent you guys the information, so we had backup."

As if that made it right. "Give me the keys or you will bleed."

Stills pulled the keys out. "Don't scratch it."

Keys in hand, Rose plowed a fist into Stills' smug face.

Stills shook it out. "I probably deserved that."

"You deserve more, but my hands are full right now." Rose went around to the passenger side, opened the door, and dropped Debi to the seat. He strapped her in with a warning. "Do not try to leave this car."

Her eyebrow lifted in a sign of rebellion, but she didn't reply. Good, he needed time to cool down. He started the car and headed out of town, watching for a tail that never showed.

No doubt he'd been a belligerent asshole by refusing to talk to Debi the past few days, to hear her plan and make it happen, but he'd been too set on protecting her. Which wasn't what she needed. The life they lived wasn't a safe one, and he needed to accept that he couldn't always protect her. If it came down to it, she needed to stay busy to ward off the fears that had ridden her all these years. He'd risked what they had because he'd tried to force her into the mold he had shoved his sisters into.

Innocents.

Soft didn't make you weak, something his sisters had tried to tell him, but he'd never listened. It was his job to protect. It had been since he was thirteen years old and it was too late for him to change, but he could accept Debi for who she was. She was soft, she was a body full of contradictions, and she'd been alone too long to accept help easily. And he hadn't even tried to help. He'd hindered who she was at her core. When he found out where she'd gone, he went ballistic, because all he could imagine was her dying before he had a chance to make those things right.

She was asleep by the time he found a motel that took cash. He carried her in and laid her on top of the bedspread. He wanted to wake her and get this over with; he wanted to let her sleep.

He stood at the end of the bed and watched her before pulling off his boots and lining them up by the door. When he pulled off her shoes, she woke and slid toward the headboard. Away from him.

The anger had faded, leaving him oddly calm. From the time Madigan had died, Rose had walked around defeated. Numb by what he carried in his blood. They were angry, all of them, and even without the garbage Echo tried to dose them with, they were still volatile, but at his worst, when he'd beaten that man—and Echo had deserved to die—Rose hadn't posed a serious threat to a teammate. He'd never lifted a hand against a woman, although he'd threatened to. He smiled at the thought of giving her the spanking she deserved.

"Whatever caused that smile, get it right out of your head."

"Right now, you don't want to order me around. You willfully put yourself in danger. You snuck off like a thief." And his heart had nearly split in two. He pulled off his socks and dropped them by his boots. "Since I left the Army my first priority is to protect what's mine."

"Is that why you left your sisters alone?"

The verbal shot was sound, but off target. He removed his flak vest and all weapons from his person. Set his Glock on the nightstand. "I have friends there to protect my sisters. Not for one minute are they unsafe. It's not my sisters I'm worried about right now. It's a hardheaded chemist who runs headfirst into danger."

"I'm not yours."

"If you think that, you haven't been paying attention."

"You said you were done with me."

He reached behind and grabbed a fistful of shirt, yanking it over his head. "No, I said I was done. *For the night.*"

"It was more than a night."

"I can't talk to you when I'm angry. I can't talk to anyone when I'm angry."

"Why not? That's when I find my best words."

"Have you been paying attention? I beat a man to death. In anger. If my number one job is to protect, sometimes that means protecting those I care about *from me*. From the crazy man the government created."

"You were angry, I'll give you that, but you didn't really hurt any of your friends, even Stills, and I know he annoys the hell out of you."

"What if I hurt you? I won't endanger those I love."

Her chin jerked up. "Say that again."

He shook his head. "Stop trying to distract me."

"It's not a distraction. It's the most important thing you've said all night. Maybe ever."

He unzipped his jeans and let them drop to the ground.

"Talk about distractions." She gestured with her left hand.

"What is?"

"You're finally wearing the blue and green paisley." She scooted to the edge of the bed and removed her socks. Dropped them on the floor. "You haven't been speaking to me and now you're wearing my favorite underwear. Is that a sign of anything?"

He sat on the edge of the bed. "I don't know what to do with you."

"I have some really creative ideas."

Damn, but she pulled a smile out of him even in the middle of a rant.

"Sergeant Rose, are you afraid of me?"

"Of course not."

She pulled off her shirt. The top of her breasts pushed from the cups of her bra creating the kind of cleavage he wanted to lose himself inside.

"You are a very dangerous woman."

"Remember that the next time you threaten to spank me."

"Oh, sweetheart, that wasn't a threat." He tucked a finger into the waistband of her jeans and pulled her close.

A low, sexy laugh bubbled from deep inside her. "You wouldn't hurt a woman."

"Who said anything about pain?" He unzipped her jeans and together them slid them off her body. "If it hurts, I'm doing it wrong."

Her ample chest lifted. "You wouldn't dare."

"Now's not the time to challenge me." He lifted her and shifted so she landed on her hands and knees in the center of the bed. He stood behind her and tried to stay on topic despite the tempting vision in front of him. "You were reckless, put yourself in danger by going alone instead of with the team. I about had a panic attack, and I don't feel fear." His voice rose with the memory, but his hand was gentle as he caressed the soft globes of her bare ass. Not in a million years would he mar one inch of her sexy flesh.

She shivered. "You locked me out. Wouldn't talk."

As her father had done. "I'm sorry," he said. For failing to understand who she was until it was almost too late. "You need to be part of the solution."

"The silence gave me too much time to think."

He caressed down the cleft of her fine ass until his fingers found her opening. Wet already. He teased a finger along the edge. "You don't want to think?"

"I want to feel." Her hips pressed back into his touch, moving his fingers deeper. "You. I need to feel you."

He wanted to memorize the look of her on her knees, open to him, begging him to grab her ass and go. Fast. He wanted to take her so hard that his body shook with restraint.

She widened her stance, opening more fully so his hand settled easily between her legs. Wet coated his fingers as she used him to get off. Her body milked his fingers. Her ass arched in the air and she started to move. Shit, the way she moved. Need, desire, emotion too deep for words propelled him to the inevitable conclusion. He needed to feel her from the inside out. He pulled his fingers free to yank his boxers off, and she moaned at the loss.

She peered over her injured shoulder at him. "River, don't make me wait."

"Never." Never again would he leave her in silence and cold. With one hand, he guided his cock to her entrance and slid inside like a wet dream. The position put him so deep he could lose himself and die a happy man. He had to stop moving or come before he took another breath.

Her breath caught and her core clenched around him. She leaned forward before slamming back, and his body answered. He gripped her hips and let himself go. The movements were frantic, out of control, the kind of raw sex they'd been barreling to from the moment they'd met. He reached around to rub her clit. So wet he nearly lost it. He continued the punishing pace, his fingers working her until mindless words and sighs spilled from her mouth. Still he moved, hips flying, pounding deeper, harder. He couldn't get enough.

A cry sounded as she went slick around him, as she milked him so good, but it wasn't enough to burn away the fear that she had run from him and into danger. So he pounded through her orgasm. She dropped onto her elbows, deepening the angle, giving him the best view of her sweet ass and the gentle glide of her back.

His balls tightened as they slapped against her bare skin.

"Yes. Yes." She moaned, caught up, at his mercy.

He pressed closer, widening her completely. On her knees with her head down on her arms was the most beautiful sight he'd ever seen. The angle rubbed his cock against her G-spot and she gasped, too trapped between him and the mattress and the wide open legs to do anything but take what he gave her.

So he gave her everything. He crawled over her, around her,

and took her all the way to the bed. She bore down on him as she came again with a cry of ecstasy. When the pleasure like pain stabbed his lower back, he let himself go. He lost himself and found himself in her.

In the anger and passion, he'd forgotten a condom, but he couldn't make himself regret it. She wasn't going to be with another man ever again. Not as long as he lived.

———

Much later, when the lights were off and their bodies slick, he pulled Debi into his side. "You know I don't have a future."

She ran a tentative hand over his chest. "You do if you fight for one."

"I'd die for every man on the team. I planned on it." He twisted his hand in her silky hair. "But I'll fight for you."

"Do me a favor? Turn on the light."

The light pushed the darkness back a few feet, but she pressed him into it and asked him to turn around. "What's going on?"

"There's something I need to see."

He turned his back to her. That was trust. She was a tricky woman. But she didn't run or even try, but rather ran a gentle finger in a circle around his back.

"Are these runes?"

Ah, his tattoo. "It's a Viking Compass."

She traced the symbols. "It's beautiful. What does it mean?"

"It helps to see the way through a storm, even in the unknown."

"It guides you?"

He nodded unable to speak as she continued her exploration.

"The compass helped you raise your sisters."

It had helped him raise himself, to craft an image of the man he wanted to be outside of his father and those who had come before him.

"Tattoos are incredibly sexy." Her lips ghosted across his skin. "I swore I wouldn't be the first to say it, but I can't help myself. I love you, River Rose. I love that you're a protector and a healer and a warrior. I love that you tell the truth even when you don't want to, and God help me, I even love your silence."

The words thawed pieces of him that had been numb since he'd joined the team.

"Okay, I'm not loving this silence."

He smiled into the cool night air. "I love you."

"Look at me when you say that."

He turned, lay on his back and pulled her close, made eye contact. "I love you."

Her brown eyes softened like velvet. She ran a finger up his midline. "What do you love most?"

"Definitely not the sarcasm or fearlessness," he teased.

"I'm not fearless."

"Darling, you walked into the belly of the beast to get the information we needed, which is possibly the least intelligent thing you've ever done, and the most brave." He couldn't keep a woman like her locked up. The isolation would kill her inside. He had to accept the potential for each of them to get hurt in this mess, even if it went counter to his instincts.

"I am so glad you don't see me as I really am," she said.

He flipped to trap her between his body and the mattress.

"Sweetheart, I see you exactly as you are. Loyal, intelligent, brave, beautiful."

Beneath him, she went as still as death. He sensed tears he couldn't see. And he knew the scar of her father's desertion tore her up inside.

"I will fight for you," he vowed. "I will move mountains to earn your love and respect."

A deep sigh whispered in the night. "You don't have to move mountains. You already have my love and respect."

Then he had everything. For the first time since Madigan's funeral, Rose let hope seep into his bones. A future began to unfold that didn't include his inevitable death. For the rest of his life, Maggie Madigan would visit his nightmares. He would regret Mad Dog's suicide. Time did not heal all wounds, but his love for Debi healed what he thought would be forever broken. His soul. "We will win this thing."

"Never doubted it for a minute, but you know you can't lock me up at The Manor for safekeeping."

"I could." The act would tear them apart. "But I won't. I get who you are. The risks you take, all the way back to using yourself as a guinea pig. You have to be involved."

"You won't stop me from playing a part in this?"

"No. But I will walk in front of you."

"Asking me to walk three steps behind?" she teased.

"No." Tension halted his heartbeat then sped it back up. He could learn to work with her, fight with her, but he couldn't be the man he'd created unless he protected. "I'm asking you to let me be your shield."

A smile lit her eyes and lifted her full lips. "You already are."

———

For sneak peeks at upcoming books, excerpts, and contests, signup for Cindy's newsletter at www.CSkaggs.com

TEASER: SURVIVE BY THE TEAM

12 MONTHS AGO

The *thwack-thwack-thwack* of the rotors vibrated the seats and echoed through the interior of the Chinook helicopter. The team lined up along one side of the bulkhead with their gear stacked on the floor in front of them. Dust permeated every pore and coated his beard. A dull throb that had no beginning and no end pounded through his skull despite the wrap-around sunglasses that blocked most of the light.

Stills gripped his rifle between his legs and dropped his head back. Since they'd been cut loose to do what the Army designed them to do, the missions had rolled one on top of another until they bled into one disgustingly dirty deployment. The interior of the helo reeked of man funk. He hadn't shaved in weeks; hadn't showered in nearly that long. The ache in his lower back spread around his hips and down his thighs. He was getting too fucking old to sleep on the ground in the middle of BFE where they'd been holed up the last two weeks.

He was tired to the bone, sore, and too annoyed to take part in the chatter of the crew and his team. He'd give half his signing bonus for a soft bed and a warm woman. Instead, he tuned out the noise and closed his eyes to catch some rack time because they'd likely spend the next month hunkered down in the Afghan mountains.

A kick to his boot woke him with a jolt. He gripped his rifle as he straightened. Next to him, Gault gave his boot a harder kick.

"What?"

Gault answered by nodding at Captain Johnson pacing the aisle and kicking their gear out of his path. A black comm cord followed like a snake as he spoke into a boom mic that swung down from his headset. A muscle along his jaw tightened as he nodded at whatever was being said on the other end. His eyes narrowed before he said something Stills couldn't hear over the ambient noise.

"Something's going down," Gault said.

"No shit," Stills muttered. In the months they'd worked for Captain Johnson, the officer had maintained an even keel. With everything they'd gone through during the initial protocol, Johnson had never once lost his temper, and they'd done some seriously stupid shit. Johnson didn't smile much either. If the Army made them fearless, then Uncle Sam had made Johnson emotionless. Right now he was a firestorm blazing a trail of anger as his hands jerked in agitation.

At the end of the row, Ryder removed his helmet like he was trying to hear the conversation. Stills did the same.

Johnson whipped the comm cord behind him as he paced

toward the front of the craft. "No, sir. What you are suggesting is ill-advised. We need more information before we —" The lines around his eyes tightened as he listened. "Sir, after everything we've invested in these men—" He yanked the headset from his head and slammed it against the bulkhead. "Fuck."

The boom mic broke free and bounced under Rose's boot. No one said a word. Johnson glared at the twelve-man team, his gaze sweeping down the line at each man in turn. He cursed before heading to the cockpit to talk to the pilots.

Stills shifted his gaze to Ryder, the second in command. Ryder shrugged as he unbuckled and followed Johnson. The helo dipped and made a sharp turn. Moments later the craft tilted forward and headed for the dirt. They rode low and fast over the desert as the door gunner set up a machine gun in the crew door on the starboard side.

"Must be going somewhere hot," Gault said. "About time."

Stills nodded. They needed a briefing if they were deploying to a hot zone, but Ryder and Johnson didn't come back from the cockpit. Fifteen minutes of high turbulence passed before gray smoke muddied the horizon. The helicopter headed for the smoke, maneuvering to come out upwind of the scene.

The acrid odor of a chemical burn hit moments before a village shimmered through the gray and white vapor. Soot, ash, and smoke scraped his throat like sand paper. Stills unbuckled and stepped over his rucksack to peer out the crew door behind the gunner. The buildings at the edge of the village were rubble with masses of rock, metal, and bits of fabric poking through. As they made a sweeping pass over the village, they flew over more demolished houses. The closer they got to the center, the more smoke interfered with visibility and stung his watery eyes.

The pilot swung around the other side where smoke rose from holes in the walls of cement buildings. When Stills caught sight of people, they were too distant to make out the details. "Fowler." He motioned their sniper close. The man had the eyes of a hawk. "What can you see?"

Fowler pulled his rifle up and peered through the scope. "Where?"

"Three o'clock. Near the line of black smoke."

Fowler adjusted his scope as he focused on the scene. "Two men down. Locals. Female in a black hijab about ten yards behind them. Kid right next to her. Smallish. Can't be more than five."

More men stepped across the aisle at Fowler's words. Stills' gut ached. Wherever they were, they'd gotten there too late. The sickly sweet smell of death hovered over the village. Details jumped out as they drew closer. The bodies were bloody as fuck. Additional bodies littered the dirt road that ran through the center of the village. "That's a helluva lot of bodies down there. Anyone know what happened?"

Responding to something on the headset, the gunner motioned everyone back and slammed the door closed. Stills couldn't get the image of the family from his head. The way they were laid out, they'd been running and someone had gunned them down from behind. The woman and kid first. Who the hell did that shit? The helicopter banked hard right and lifted like a fat bird. Stills gripped a seat back until they leveled off.

Captain Johnson stepped back from the cockpit and

leveled Stills with a hard glare. The past half hour had aged the officer. Circles rimmed hard eyes. "You didn't see that."

"Sir?"

"You never saw that village. We were never here." Johnson did an about-face before anyone could question his order.

Moments later, Ryder came through carrying a Ziploc bag. "Take a seat."

Stills did as he was told, settling between Gault and Craft.

"They're pulling us in," Ryder said without inflection.

"We're not going after the assholes that did this?"

"The assholes that did this are on our side," Ryder answered.

Stills dropped back against the bulkhead as the implications hit him. What happened in that village happened with American soldiers.

"Drones?" Fowler asked.

"Couldn't be drones," Gault argued. "A drone isn't perfect, but it's more precise than taking out the entire village. This was up close and personal."

Stills gripped his rifle. "All the more reason to send us in to bag and tag the fuckers."

"Shut it," Ryder ordered. "You heard the captain. We were never here. Now pull out your meds and put 'em in this bag." He handed the Ziploc to Bennett on the end closest to the cockpit.

Stills reached into a pocket on his vest and pulled out what amounted to a million dollars in research. Inside those innocuous pills was artificial courage. They were down to one pill a day after months of titrating the right dosages to induce fearless. Honest to God killing machines with no fear and no regrets. Like an addict, he gripped the bottle in a fist; noticed the men down the line doing the same. Giving up the meds felt like a death sentence. Beside him, Gault continued to dig through his backpack. He pulled out a secondary pair of boots and lifted the insole. He dropped three white pills into the heel before covering it with the black flap.

"I didn't see that," Stills said in low voice.

"We were never here and this shit didn't happen," Gault answered.

True. They'd blocked more than their share of operational bullshit, so it wouldn't take much to forget one small breach in protocol. Stills wished he hadn't seen Gault's dumbass move, though. He damn sure wasn't going to talk about it, especially since the company decided to pull them in after something they weren't supposed to see.

"Tell me your gut isn't screaming," Gault said.

On the other side, Craft handed him the bag nearly full of prescription bottles. "Yeah, it's screaming like a girl at a Bieber concert." Stills dropped his meds into the clear plastic. "Not a damn thing I can do about it."

"You've got that wrong." Gault dropped the prescription bottle into the bag and held it out for Ryder. When Ryder stepped out of earshot, Gault leaned close. "I've got my ace in the hole against those dodgy bastards."

The ride smoothed out as they lifted in altitude for a fast trip across the desert. Next to him, Craft drifted to sleep, but Stills was too spun up. Gault was right. Shit was about to hit the fan. On the other side, Gault patted his pocket before pulling out a picture of a petite brunette with eyes as bright as the sky behind her. She stood in front of an old Victorian wearing a green and gold cap and gown.

"Girl back home?" Stills asked. They all had one, that

dream they clung to when the job cut too close to the bone.

Gault shook his head no. "Sister." He swapped it out with another picture, giving Stills one with the girl and another graduate.

The girl looked nothing like Gault, except the color of her hair. She was petite standing next to a giant of a man with dark skin contrasting to her pale freckled complexion. "Her boyfriend?"

Gault laughed. "Not even. She's not his type."

That wasn't possible. The woman was petite, curvy, and had a smile on her face that could burn away the cold threatening to destroy him. Everything about the woman in the picture was sunshine and light. "She's every man's type."

Gault started to laugh like a jackass. "Dude, you're more his type."

"Oh." Stills kept staring at the picture. At her smile, at the way she hugged the big black man. "His loss." Stills handed the photo back, but Gault shook him off.

"Keep it." He ran a hand along the edge of the first photograph as if he needed that connection. "Anything happens to me, I want you to watch out for her and—"

"Fuck you. Nothing is going to happen to you."

"Odds aren't good. And she'll be alone if I don't make it home. If..." Gault cleared his throat. "Anyone you want me to contact, if?"

Stills tried to bring up a memory of Shelley, his phantom girl back home, but his mind blanked. Somewhere in his ruck was a picture she'd sent, and a few printouts from her recent emails, but the longer he stayed in the desert, the less he remembered. The less he wanted to remember. He'd tucked her away to be pulled out if and when they survived their tour.

Did he want Gault to contact her... if? "Leave her in peace." No final message, no letter, no need to prolong the grief. The girl back home deserved a life free of this shithole.

Ryder returned empty-handed. He'd turned in their medicine, and with it, their reason for existing as far as the Army was concerned. "Rest up," he ordered. Not one for words, he took his seat, leaned back, and closed his eyes. Less than a hundred miles later, they descended to land at a forward operating base. The team stretched and reached for their packs.

"Hot shower here I come," Santiago said with a grin. His dark mustache had turned to a full beard in the desert.

Ryder's lips thinned into a frown as he blocked their path. "This is a fuel stop. They're pulling us all the way back to Germany."

"Fuck me." Stills zipped up his pack, the sound vibrating against his skin much like the now silent rotors. One by one, the men reclaimed their seats. Stills shook his head to clear his thoughts. The girl back home no longer mattered. "They're cutting us loose."

ALSO BY CINDY SKAGGS

UNTOUCHABLES SERIES (ENTANGLED IGNITE):

Untouchable (Untouchables 1)

An Untouchable Christmas (Untouchables 1.5)

Unforgettable (Untouchables 2)

Unstoppable (Untouchables 3)

TEAM FEAR SERIES:

Live By The Team (Team Fear 1)

Fight By The Team (Team Fear 2)

Survive By The Team (Team Fear 3)

ACKNOWLEDGMENTS

Many thanks to the awesome people who made this book possible, especially Hannah Schrank for being the science behind my writer mind. Any errors are my own. You tried to teach me the ways of organic chemistry, but I am a Humanities major. There was only so much you could do.

To my writing friends Beth Rhodes and Jennie Marts, you ladies made this book possible through your friendship and your persistence. To Jessa Slade, the talented editor whose work forced me to be a better writer. To L.J. Anderson, for giving me such an amazing cover design. To Karen Gault Skelly for letting me use her last name for my DB and for being my first reader for this project. To the fabulous people at the Pikes Peak Library District, especially Christine Dyar for never blinking an eye at my weird writer questions.

And, as always, a lifetime of thanks to my children, Brianna and Noah, who support my dreams and give me the time and space to write. I am blessed and honored to be your mom.

ABOUT THE AUTHOR

Cindy Skaggs grew up on stories of mob bosses, horse thieves, cold-blooded killers, and the last honest man. Those mostly true stories gave her a lifelong love of storytelling that enables her writing addiction. She is the author of *The Untouchables* trilogy and a novella for Entangled Publishing and the *Team Fear* series. Her nonfiction essays have appeared in Progenitor Art & Literary Review, Soundings, Wanderlust Journal, and the Fredericksburg Literary Art Review.

She holds an MFA in Creative Writing, three jobs, two kids, and more pets than she can possibly handle. She also plays the flute, makes crazy-good sculptures out of tortilla dough, and can wrangle the neurotic dog without getting mauled.

And she loves to hear from readers like you.

www.CSkaggs.com
Cindy@CSkaggs.com

Made in the USA
Columbia, SC
03 October 2021